FOBOLOUS

Finding love on the other side of the world

Rainne Mendoza

Second Edition

2018

Publisher's Note: This is a work of fiction. Names, characters, places, and incidents are a product of the author's imagination. Locales and public names are sometimes used for atmospheric purposes. Any resemblance to actual people, living or dead, or to businesses, companies, events, institutions, or locales is completely coincidental.

For Dennis, Ethan, Emma, Mochi and Appa

Cultures clash. Cultures blend. Love survives

Prologue

Ever wondered what life is like in America?
I asked myself that question once, seventeen years ago to be exact.

***

I was on the patio of a trendy restaurant in Manila one humid Friday night, watching cars go by across the busy street.

Sitting at a table reserved for six, I marveled at the usual scene from the scrapbook of my life, enjoying the sights and sounds of urban living. I listened to people chatter while plates and glassware were set meticulously by servers in their handsome black and white ensemble, patiently waiting for my friends to come join me for another round of catching up over wine and coffee and our payday favorites, *adobo* flakes on rice and buttery *bibingka*.

It was our self-indulgent ritual.

A quiet dinner, followed by an hour or two of gossiping and comparing notes, careful not to spill our trade secrets among each other, and when there was absolutely nothing else to talk about, there would be poignant musing about our lives that none of us would trade for the universe, anyway.

We were the toast of our version of Madison Avenue—young, brilliant minds that powered the thriving, cutthroat, enticingly competitive, fun and frivolous advertising industry—each of us representing an ad agency entrenched in the most prominent financial hubs in the Philippines, our corporate headquarters located in high profile cities in Europe and the United States. I had no doubt any white-

1

collar professional newbie fond of business duels and corporate ladders would love to join our troupe.

And then it hit me.

What would life be like if I chose to give up everything I had—my career, lifestyle, ambitions, friends, family, and freedom—to start a brand-new life in an unfamiliar place? What would happen if I turned my back on everything I had, forgot about my dreams, and moved far away?

Ridiculous, I told myself as I savored the cold water from my glass.

After all, I was only twenty-five, single, flourishing, sprawled in my bed of roses, the whole world at my feet. In two years I'd be promoted at my job, the youngest assistant vice president of our account management team, set to win my dream account—the fastest-growing telecommunications company in the country.

I would then move out of my parents' house and be able to rent my own apartment in the more upscale area in the city. Instead of parking on our street every night after coming home from work, praying no one would scribble their initials or run their key across my newly bought silver Honda Civic, I'd have my own designated parking space in my new apartment with free twenty-four-hour security. I knew we weren't rich, but I grew up with maids—because maids are affordable in the Philippines—and I planned to employ one of my parents' household help to take care of housekeeping, cooking, and laundry for me.

The princess-cut diamond set in my gold engagement ring suddenly caught a ray of light, blazing momentarily like a torch, as if blinding me on purpose. I stared at my hand absentmindedly as I watched my slim fingers play with the bread crumbs on the tiny plate in front of me, pushing them back and forth ever so slowly.

And then I remembered.

I was sitting on a time bomb.

My heart tingled in bittersweet anticipation as the handsome face of my fiancé flashed in my mind.

I could feel my heart beating faster, my knees getting weaker. I quickly finished the glass of cold water in my trembling hand. It was like my feet were dangling over the edge of a cliff. A part of me wanted to turn around and run back to safety in the comforts of my normal everyday reality, yet another part of me wanted to close my eyes and jump off without a care in the world.

I loved Anthony, and because of that, I wanted to hold onto my belief that once I jumped off the cliff, I would land on soft grass, unscathed and safe, just as he had promised. I looked around anxiously. I knew I had to make a decision soon.

Ridiculous, I repeated silently to myself.

My friends started streaming into the restaurant one by one, smiling from ear to ear, laughing their hearts out as usual, genuinely thrilled to be in one another's company, yet absolutely clueless as to what was going on inside me.

Two days later I bought a round-trip ticket for my leap-of-faith adventure in the fabulous and much romanticized "Land of Opportunity."

"America, here I come," I whispered nervously.

My name is Janelle.

This is my story.

Chapter 1

April 2, 2000.

I fell asleep on the plane while reading *The Chamber of Secrets*, the thick hardbound *Harry Potter* book my dear older sister had given me as my going-away gift.

And boy, did I go away.

We were probably cruising at thirty-two thousand feet from God knew what was down there at the bottom of nowhere, as I curled up in one of the plane's seats by the window. It was pretty comfortable if you asked me, except when the ride got really bumpy due to some crazy, mind-twisting air pockets. Contrary to what others had been complaining about traveling cheap, the coach class of a humongous American commercial jet wasn't so bad, even for the dragging and mentally stressful fourteen-hour non-stop flight I was on board for.

I guessed for a ninety-pound, five-foot-tall Filipina like me, anything was spacious enough to accommodate my deceivingly undernourished body.

Speaking of nourishment, I was getting hungry. My last meal consisted of fried rice, eggs, and bacon—the quick breakfast our maid had cooked for me before my parents took me to the airport that morning.

In a hurry, by the way.

Ironically, my parents, who were traditional and conservative post-war babies, did not believe in Filipino Time—read: fashionably late by almost an hour to infinity and beyond—whereas the modern Filipina in me was a chronic abuser, if there was such a term, of that backward cultural habit of ours.

In the Philippines, where I worked as a senior accounts executive for a sophisticated global advertising agency, I had to dress up in trendy, tailored business clothes every day of the week. Consequently, since it was my first time to fly to the United States, I thought I should also dress appropriately.

I wore my chic-looking tan chinos and a most flattering black, body-hugging turtleneck sweater that my sister had bought for me in Japan. The turtleneck sweater could very well be a medium for physical torture if worn in tropical Philippines any time of the year, but it would be great for the currently freezing—by my standards—weather in Houston, where I was headed. I also wore my newly bought black ankle boots to match my outfit, and my soft taupe trouser socks to keep my feet warm and toasty.

So imagine my shock when I mingled with my fellow passengers at the airport who were wearing sweats and sneakers. To my monumental chagrin, I found myself sticking out like a sore thumb in a crowd of underdressed backpackers as I headed to the gate prior to departure.

***

I noticed the Asian-looking flight attendant rolling the lunch cart in the aisle, two feet away from my seat. She missed our row and started serving dinner for the passengers seated behind me. Before she could roll the cart two steps farther, an older-looking Caucasian lady sitting next to me, who was probably in her sixties, called the attention of the flight attendant with apparent distaste.

"You didn't serve this young lady's dinner," the older lady told the flight attendant, referring to me. The seemingly clueless flight attendant answered back, "I beg your pardon?"

"You didn't give my little friend here her dinner," the older lady reiterated.

The snobbish flight attendant raised her thick eyebrows, then frowned and looked at me like she wanted to put a sizable portion of *wasabi* in my mouth. With her perfect, mindboggling Southern accent, she told the older lady, "Well, I thought she was asleep when I was serving y'alls dinner."

The older lady looked at the flight attendant as if squinting from blinding sunlight. Apparently irritated yet resigned, she told the flight attendant that I was awake now, and could she please give me my dinner already.

To make the long story short, the flight attendant obliged and handed me my tray of airplane delicacies. I noticed her eyebrows were raised, forming quite a freakish straight line on her creased forehead.

For an outspoken advertising executive, I was speechless. *Did I just get snubbed by my own kind and was rescued by another person of a different race? Talk about shattering cultural myths on my first day away from home,* I thought.

"The captain has advised that everyone go back to their seats. Please fasten your seatbelts as we may experience turbulence. Thank you," the flight attendant announced on the intercom.

"Here we go again," I muttered to myself as I braced for yet another dose of heart-stopping plane jiggles, postponing my much-needed trip to the claustrophobia-triggering restroom. I shook off the jitters as I started doing my countdown.

Five more hours to go and I'd get out of that big metal bird and breathe the much-talked-about air of everyone's dreamland.

Chapter 2

It was early spring in Houston, Texas.

The arrival area of the George Bush Intercontinental Airport was surprisingly empty, a stark contrast to the arrival area of the smaller airport in the Philippines that I was familiar with.

In comparison, the Ninoy Aquino International Airport in Manila bustled with life, even in the wee hours of the morning as cars got stuck in traffic and hundreds of people—some bearing leis made of *sampaguita* flowers to welcome arriving passengers—waited outside.

I looked at the few passengers around me who were waiting patiently for their rides to arrive. They looked tired; quiet, as if deep in thought. I picked a spot by the glass doors and waited along with them.

I stared at the frigid cup of coffee in my hand. After collecting my luggage from the baggage carousel half an hour ago, I'd absentmindedly headed to a Starbucks inside the airport and ordered a large Mocha Frappuccino, *sans* the whipped cream, out of habit. But then, as soon as I'd managed to get out of the building to wait for my aunt to pick me up, the cold wind hit my face. It felt like a thousand ice daggers had landed on my cheeks. The iced coffee numbed my hands. I wanted to quickly toss the plastic cup, but my fingers refused to obey my bidding.

It was extremely cold and windy in Houston. I had heard the city was at the tail end of a rare cold front, and I was lucky enough to catch it. My black turtleneck sweater kept me warm, but it wasn't enough to ward off the chills running through my travel-worn and incredibly shocked system.

I recalled a scene when our plane landed, more than five hours ago at the Detroit Metro Airport, my point of entry to the United States.

As soon as our plane had been attached to the jetway, I was suddenly filled with a mixed set of emotions. Excitement was interspersed with panic as I walked out of the terminal gate.

The Detroit airport was huge and intimidating, like a modern cornfield maze with all sorts of signs pointing in different directions. I felt like a lost child on my first day in kindergarten, yet excited at what was about to happen.

As I stood, frozen in the middle of nowhere it seemed, I tried to still the voice of panic inside me.

Let the fun begin, I thought.

I quickly fumbled for the itinerary hidden in my purse and studied my connecting flight information.

"Dito tayo sa may escalator. *Kukuhanin yung mga bagahe."*

I thought someone had pinched me. I looked around carefully, wondering where the voice was coming from.

"Head towards the escalator. They're taking the luggage." That's what the mystery voice seemed to say.

I almost jumped when I saw an elderly woman staring at me from behind her gold-rimmed glasses. Judging from the words coming out of her mouth, I gathered she was also Filipino like me. Her accent sounded familiar.

"Pinay ka din, hija?" The old lady spoke to me again in Tagalog, one of our main local languages in the Philippines.

She wanted to know if I was Filipino like her.

I said *"Opo,"* the Tagalog term for yes, used as a sign of respect when responding to an older person.

She seemed pleased and amused as she led me to the escalator along with other fellow passengers. We went through a series of corridors and hallways until we arrived at the Customs and Border Patrol gate. There, a long line of passengers was moving like a lazy snake, slowly and quietly inching its way to the other side of a set of glass doors.

I took my place in the long line behind the old lady. She seemed strong for her age and quite cheerful. She did not whine or get grumpy, despite the long wait. Except for the occasional crying and laughter of little children in the line, our group was pretty quiet. Everyone looked tired but tolerant, patiently accepting what they had to go through as required by the law.

Finally, my turn came to face the immigrations officer. An older gentleman, the officer sat behind the booth and asked about my travel plans—where I was going, and what the purpose of my trip was. I suddenly became sentimental as I told him I was going to Houston to visit my cousin's family and my fiancé.

A gush of excitement shot up to my heart, and I caught myself smiling dreamily.

Wait. Control your emotions, Janelle. You do not want the officer to think you're a nutcase and deny your entry to his country, I told myself quietly.

I smiled and composed myself, careful not to show my anticipation, holding in the excitement brimming inside me. Yet my reverie continued.

I'd finally see my favorite cousin and his family again. And in just a few days, once I've recovered from jet lag, I would give my fiancé the biggest surprise of his life.

"Maria Janelle Marquez. Enjoy your stay in Houston."

The officer's words snapped me out of my daydream. He smiled warmly and handed back my passport, officially stamped with my date of arrival.

I had been approved entry into the United States.

I smiled back at the officer, thanked him quickly, and rushed to the other side of the terminal to collect my luggage. There, the old lady with the gold-rimmed glasses was surprisingly waiting for me. She told me she was on her way to Maryland to visit her grandkids, a mixture of joy and sorrow as it may be the last time she would travel to the United States. She said she had been in and out of Maryland for years but now that she was much older, she was afraid her daughter and her husband may send her back home to the Philippines for good.

It was strange.

Within a span of five minutes, the old lady described her fourteen-hour journey to me, occasionally giggling like a young woman narrating her love story. Somehow, we found a connection not only because we belonged to the same race, but because we were both fortunate, having had the opportunity to come to America, crossed the seas safely, and passed through airport security fuss-free.

Then she told me her secret.

Chapter 3

She said her name was Juanita, but I may call her Lola Juani—pronounced Hwanee—for short. *Lola* is the Tagalog term for grandmother, or someone who looked old enough to be a grandmother and did not have a problem being addressed as an old lady.

She looked around us, making sure no one was looking before she showed me a clear plastic bag full of white-colored pastries. She said she wanted to sneak some of her homemade rice cakes inside the plane on her way to Maryland, to snack on while waiting for her daughter to pick her up at the airport. She prayed airport security would not find out.

We had a name for those rice cakes in the Philippines. We called them *puto*. I had been told, however, that *puto* was an offensive term for Hispanics, as the word represented a male prostitute.

I cringed.

The Philippines was colonized by Spain hundreds of years ago. I wondered if our ancestors back then had adopted the Spanish language and twisted the meaning of some of the words, either due to ignorance or out of revenge against some of the *conquistadores'* rotten apples, who were said to have inflicted much damage against native Filipinos and their resources.

With one eye on the customs officers inspecting the passengers' belongings thoroughly, with large trash cans located everywhere to accommodate prohibited goods, I was positive Lola Juani's *puto* would make it to Maryland. Dry foods should be able to pass airport inspection if packed properly.

I wished the old lady good luck. It may seem weird now, but I did give her a tight hug before walking away to fetch my own luggage. I hoped her daughter and her daughter's husband would not send her back to the Philippines, against her will, for good. Lola Juani had extraordinary spunk—a huge amount of vitality about her that I rarely found in anyone, even those much younger than her. It would be unfair if that *joie de vivre* was wasted and the old lady lived the rest of her life brokenhearted.

I started walking slowly towards Gate 17 where I boarded another plane, headed to my final destination—Houston.

***

I shivered from the cold temperature, desperate for warmth, wondering how much longer I had to wait before my ride arrived.

"Yaniyaniyaniyaniyaneee!"

I jumped at the sound of a strange voice chanting behind me. It sounded masculine and dwarfish, like Alvin the Chipmunk trapped in a vacuum cleaner.

Instinctively, I grabbed my coffee cup. I made sure the brittle straw in the cup was strategically facing outward, ready for the mysterious creature that may jump at me. I planned to pierce the creature's eyeball first, before damaging its crotch with my knees.

Okay, okay, I thought. I didn't really want to pierce the creature's eyeball. That would be gross. Besides, I couldn't imagine the gore splattering all over my favorite sweater and potentially my new pair of boots. That would be Plan B. Plan A would be blinding the creature with my frozen coffee, and then hitting the so-called "family jewels" with my knee, hard enough to make him cry like a baby.

I waited for the perfect timing. The *Voltes V* theme song from my favorite childhood Japanese cartoon strangely popped into my head. I was getting distracted, but I didn't give in. I heard the mysterious voice again, sounding much closer than before. I tightened my grip on my coffee cup. When I was ready to launch my attack, I slowly turned around to come face to face with my adversary.

"Tita."

Standing right in front of me, at my waist level, was a little girl. She was wearing a fluffy pink coat with faux fur draped around her body, partially covering her tiny face. Underneath her coat was a chunky powder-blue scarf hanging loosely from her neck, stretching all the way down to her cream-colored boots, which I'd got her for her birthday.

That was the giveaway.

The little girl, bundled up in her warm and cozy ensemble, was my adorable niece, Sophia. I smiled as I realized my niece, who had never been to the Philippines, knew the Tagalog word *Tita*, meaning "aunt."

In the Philippines, at least where I grew up, we referred to the children of our cousins as nieces and nephews. I had heard in other parts of the world, Western countries in particular, people refer to the children of their cousins as "first cousins once removed."

I stepped closer to Sophia and gave her a hug as soon as I confirmed her identity.

"It's beautiful. That would look perfect on my back," the six-year-old diva cooed at me, batting her long eyelashes dramatically, her tiny hands resting on her hips with her elbows sticking out like nobody's business. Evidently her full attention had already shifted to my backpack. I looked around us carefully, knowing the owner of the mysterious voice chanting eerily just a few minutes ago may still be lurking around, waiting for the right time to attack.

Sophia took the pink Hello Kitty backpack from my back and started giggling, thrilled with her acquisition. "You're the coolest, Tita Janelle," she said, giving my hand a tight squeeze as she melted my heart with her charming character.

"Sophia, baby, who are you with? Is Grandma with you?" I asked her, feeling confused. My aunt was supposed to pick me up at the airport, but she was nowhere in sight; a rather unusual scenario for a dependable I-want-to-save-the-world person like her.

"Daddy, it's time to come out now!" Sophia screamed her lungs out.

In an instant, my cousin Wooly came running out of nowhere, scooping up my niece into his arms. Sophia covered her daddy's ears with her pudgy hands, and the duo started laughing. I looked at father and daughter for a moment and smiled, wondering what it would feel like to have my own family, and what my future kids with Anthony would look like.

Out of nowhere, a little boy stood next to me and gave me a peck on the cheek. I felt shock and amazement at the same time.

"Kenny?" I asked hesitantly.

Sophia's older brother, my nephew, was ten years old already and would be about the same height by now. His name was Kenneth, but I liked to call him Kenny.

"Hey, Tita Janelle. It's Kenneth, not Kenny. How was your flight? How's the fam in the Philippines?" he asked. As I was about to respond, a high-pitched voice nearly shattered my eardrums.

"Yaniyaniyaniyani!!!!"

I turned around abruptly. Like a silly movie trailer in slow motion, I saw my cousin's mouth moving, his pearly whites lighting up his handsome face, making his eyes look even smaller.

So there goes the mystery voice, I thought.

It was Wooly. He was the creature—the same one eerily chanting, saying my childhood nickname, Yani, over and over with his creepy voice—hiding somewhere behind me. It had scared me to death. I couldn't believe I hadn't recognized my silly childhood nickname.

I smiled to myself as the picture of Wooly, coffee-drenched and with a Starbucks straw piercing his face, flashed in my head. Imagine if I had launched my *Voltes V* attack, not knowing it was my cousin's face I was about to damage in the process. The kids would have been traumatized.

"What took you so long to get here? We're starving," Wooly said in his normal pitch, as if nothing had happened. I smiled at my cousin as my mind took me back to my adventure, back on the plane on my way to Houston.

Chapter 4

My flight from Detroit was delayed for two hours because of a storm.

I remembered the passengers on the plane being extremely quiet. They closed their window shades and tried to catch some sleep while I did the exact opposite. I opened my window nonchalantly to take a peek outside to see what was holding us up.

I almost fell out of my seat.

The clouds beneath the plane were as black as charcoal, looking ominous and frightening. All of a sudden, our plane began piercing through the clouds like a dull knife slicing a thick slab of bread. We made our slow descent, mildly shaking at first, and then our plane started dropping—once, twice, thrice, like a gondola breaking free from its latch on a Ferris wheel.

The experience was inexplicably terrifying. A gnawing feeling of powerlessness took over me. I felt stupid for not drafting my last will when I'd had the chance. But then again, what normal mortal would have the time to draft a will? I'd known of a lot of lawyers who didn't even have one.

Meanwhile, in the cockpit, our pilots seemed to have realized fighting nature was a bad idea. Our plane hovered above Houston for at least another hour, waiting for the green light from the control towers so we could land in one piece. When we got the green light, our plane had to make a pit stop at the Dallas airport to refuel.

We stayed inside the plane for about an hour, and none of us were allowed to get out. To kill time, my fellow passengers began calling friends, families, anybody, using their cell phones. Not having a cell phone, I stared out my window, seeing nothing but wide-open spaces. It was by far the biggest parking lot I had ever seen in my life.

When I got bored, I got up from my seat to stretch my legs for a few minutes and then headed to the plane's lavatory.

In the Philippines, we referred to lavatories as "comfort rooms," or CR for short. If you wanted to be a cut above the rest, you would refer to them as powder rooms or ladies' rooms or men's rooms, or lounge areas. The possibilities were endless.

A brown-skinned, middle-aged man caught my attention. He was standing by the lavatory on the opposite side, waiting for his turn to get in. He was talking on the phone, telling the person on the line that he had brought *pasalubong*.

I stopped dead in my tracks.

Pasalubong is the Tagalog word for treats or gifts, brought back by someone who just came back from his or her travels.

I remembered the lovable Lola Juani, who I met in Detroit, and thought a much-needed conversation with a fellow Filipino—someone who understood my native language—would be a great idea to keep my spirits up.

I approached the man casually, smiling warmly as I headed in his direction. "Hello, sir. Are you Filipino?" I asked enthusiastically. The man looked at me with curious eyes. He then shrugged his shoulders, dramatically it seemed, and his lips slowly curled into a smile. Finally, with a twinkle in his eye, and pride and joy written all over his face, he said, "I used to be."

I smiled back and nodded in acknowledgment before silently walking into the vacant lavatory on the opposite side. I closed the door behind me, washed my face with cold water, and tried my best to scrub off the image of my proud *kababayan*, my countryman, who was officially responsible for my first culture shock in America. I couldn't believe he boldly told me he was a former Filipino.

How could you possibly undo your race? I asked myself, heaving a sigh, dismissing the man's shocking revelation by giving him the benefit of the doubt. I tried to convince myself our conversation was merely muddled by a language barrier. He probably meant he was not a Filipino citizen anymore, because he had already been a naturalized American citizen.

"*Pwede,*" I told myself in the mirror with a shrug before heading back to my seat. That would work.

***

I caught myself staring blankly at my cousin and his two little kids as I drifted back to reality. A cold gust of wind hit my back, sending chills down my spine—literally. I quickly scrapped the idea of narrating my travel tales. Wooly and the kids were starving, and I was on the brink of catching pneumonia.

I gave my cousin a high five. I wanted to ruffle his hair like I used to when we were little kids, but I realized that wouldn't have been a good idea. The guy was almost six feet tall, a phenomenon that skipped my side of the family.

"Our flight was delayed because of the storm," I said nonchalantly. "Let's get the kids out of here. It's freezing. By the way, what happened to Tita Girlie?" I asked Wooly, referring to my aunt who was supposed to pick me up.

"Mom couldn't come because of work. She may not be able to cook dinner for us tonight either, because she had to cover an extra shift at the hospital," Wooly explained.

My aunt, Wooly's loving mother, was a registered nurse who worked at the Medical Center. Houston was home to the largest medical center in the world, and many Filipinos who lived in Houston were in the medical field.

"We're going to have to eat out," Wooly said.

"Ooh. Can I play in the playground?" Sophia asked excitedly.

"No way. It's Tita Janelle's first day in Houston. No fast-food tonight," Kenneth teased his little sister.

Wooly winked at me as he scooped his daughter up, while Kenneth stood next to me like a perfect gentleman.

"C'mon, Yani," Wooly said. "Let's go get you some serious calories."

Chapter 5

Wooly's favorite restaurant only took reservations for dinner, and we didn't make it on time.

We were initially booked to have dinner at a fine-dining Brazilian restaurant, famous for its mouthwatering all-you-can-eat steaks. According to Kenneth and Sophia, their dad was a T. rex in human form.

"So, are you a Brachiosaurus, Tita?" Kenneth asked me casually as we drove to the restaurant.

"Brachio soy sauce?" I asked in confusion.

"No. A Brachiosaurus. A dinosaur that only eats plants," Sophia said, giggling.

"Oh, okay. I guess I can be. I don't want to be a T. rex," I said, disoriented, imagining the ugly dinosaur head with unflossed teeth wobbling on my neck. But before my creative mind could wreak more havoc on my imagination, my cousin interfered.

"Okay, y'all. Fasten your seatbelts. We're not fine-dining tonight. We're going somewhere else."

Somewhere else turned out to be an eight-dollar buffet restaurant serving a variety of cuisines from different cultures all around the world. I noticed in that restaurant, that Asian cuisine generally pertained to Korean, Japanese, Vietnamese, and Chinese.

According to Wooly, there was a place in Houston called Bellaire that looked like a bigger version of anybody's Chinatown. He said he'd take me there one time for some authentic shrimp dumplings and my favorite flat rice noodles.

The buffet restaurant we had dinner at was packed, and judging from the amount of people dining inside, the restaurant's patrons seemed to like what the chefs were cooking in the kitchen.

As we were seated at our designated table, I was overwhelmed by the amount of food piled up in every corner of the restaurant. I saw a steak station, a soup depot, and a meat and fish section with every side dish imaginable. There were mashed potatoes, french fries, corn chips, vegetables, pasta, rice, bread, tortillas, and tacos. On one side was a long salad bar, which was quite deserted compared to the busy and crowded bar designated for cakes, ice cream, and all kinds of dessert.

I wasn't really hungry.

During my flight going to the States, we were served breakfast, lunch, and dinner at odd hours, depending on which time zone our plane was on, which pretty much messed up my system. Imagine having dinner and then being served breakfast three hours later.

I went to the salad bar, just so I did not waste my cousin's eight bucks. One quick look at the floating pineapples in hazy water, though, changed my mind.

Back in the Philippines, there was a fast-food restaurant famous for its salad bar and for a few pesos, anyone could build a salad tower. Their salad plate was small, but customers could bank on their creativity, strategically building their salad vertically, and stacking the ingredients on top of each other in a perfect rectangle. I tried doing that many times, but mine always caved in. My foundation for my salad turned out to be weak because I'd put on too much pineapple.

The floating pineapples on the salad bar, lurking in the muggy water at that eight-dollar buffet restaurant did not get my vote. I made a mental note to ask Kenneth what the dinosaur equivalent of a pineapple monster was.

I moved on to a different bar and got myself a piece of fried chicken and some mashed potatoes. Gone was the Brachiosoy-sauce-plant-eating dinosaur that my niece and nephew had believed I was. I got extra brown gravy on the side to dip—more like dunk—my chicken into, to find out if their gravy was better than what some popular chicken places in the Philippines served.

I heard most chicken places in the United States did not serve fried chicken with steamed rice or brown gravy, unless customers ordered mashed potatoes with brown gravy as a side dish.

That's not fun, I said to myself.

On my way back to our table, I looked around at the people piling food on their plates like there was no tomorrow. I saw plates overflowing with food on top of plates already filled with so much food, and observed a waitress throwing leftovers that looked like they were not even touched into the trash can she was pushing around in her cart.

I noticed several people who could barely fit into their clothes and remembered what I'd read on the Internet.

Obesity was one of America's biggest problems. I wasn't sure if that was caused by certain medical conditions or because the majority of the country's population just had way too many choices.

I thought about the Philippines.

In the streets of Manila, and practically anywhere in the country, it was hard to miss the little kids and their poor families who had nothing to eat. It was a major culture shock for me to know that places of excess like that eight-dollar buffet restaurant existed, while somewhere on the other side of the world people were starving.

Before depression took over me, I hurried my way back to our table. I noticed Sophia and Kenneth were tearing up their dinner rolls and couldn't help but feel guilty for making them wait for me at the airport that long. Wooly, on the other hand, had a plateful of greens and steaks generously seasoned with salt and pepper on the table in front of him. On another plate were several dinner rolls he had already spread butter on. He had his iced tea already sweetened, with a slice of lemon swimming inside the tall plastic cup, and a plate of cookies and miniature cheese cakes were chilling next to it, ready to be devoured.

That was how Wooly had always been since we were little kids. He'd always wanted to enjoy his food, and would not begin eating until everything was set up. He reminded me of Barbara Streisand in *The*

Mirror Has Two Faces. I tried to recall if, in the movie, the actress had indeed cut her salad methodically into tiny pieces and speared it with her fork to create the perfect bite.

Wooly glanced at me quickly and told me to eat my food before it got cold. He also warned me in between bites not to get too full on sweets, because there may be a surprise waiting for me at his parents' house. I smiled broadly to show my genuine appreciation for everything Wooly and his family were doing for me. I would be their guest for a little over a month, and for that, I volunteered to babysit Kenneth and Sophia in the absence of their mother, who was in Japan for a business trip.

***

Charm, Wooly's wife, was an accountant who was recently sent by her employer to conduct training in their newly opened office in Tokyo. She was a Filipino immigrant in transition, at a crossroads, still torn between managing a blossoming career in finance and being with her children to take care of them twenty-four hours a day, seven days a week. One of her frustrations was not having a maid to take care of housekeeping for her, or a nanny to take care of the kids' needs while she was busy at work. She grew up in the Philippines with maids, and felt living in America to raise her kids—while doing household chores and maintaining a successful profession—was her punishment for having the luxury of maids all her life, before she decided to "jump off the cliff" like I did.

Charm was undoubtedly overwhelmed, and it affected her character. She set unrealistic expectations for herself and would get depressed when she couldn't accomplish her goals. She hated business trips because that was time spent away from her kids. But she didn't have a choice. There was no way she would give up her career. Before she left for Tokyo last week, she sent me a long and detailed e-mail, followed by

26

a phone call on how to take care of Kenneth and Sophia on a daily basis—complete with a list of clothes they should be wearing for specific occasions. We also had a phone conversation a few days before I left for the States, just to repeat what she'd already told me in her e-mail.

I honestly thought Charm was being silly and overprotective, but then again, she was the mother of the kids I was going to babysit, and I felt obliged to listen to her. Before our phone conversation ended, I assured Charm everything would be okay.

***

Sophia and Kenneth had just finished eating their dinner at the buffet restaurant and were entertaining each other—Wooly and I included—with their interesting conversation.

Kenneth: "My favorite number is 100."
Sophia: "My favorite number is 128,598."
Kenneth: "Seriously?"
Sophia: "Seriously with a double serving of strawberry and vanilla ice cream with cherry on top."

Wooly and I looked at each other. My cousin whispered to me that if we showed any reaction, Sophia would start to whimper like a hurt puppy, so we were careful not to laugh.

I quietly dug into my plate as I tried my best not to worry about Charm's expectations of me. Offering an apology to my half-eaten chicken, I quietly recited my babysitter's mission slogan.

Sisiw, I said to myself.

In Tagalog, *sisiw* is an idiomatic expression—a slang word that figuratively means "piece of cake" or "easy" or "a walk in the park" or "I can do it with a double serving of strawberry and vanilla ice cream, with a cherry on top."

Chapter 6

It was close to midnight.

I heard a steady buzzing sound from the spacious kitchen where my uncle and aunt, Wooly's loving parents, were cooking up a storm.

A fancy-looking white machine sitting on top of the kitchen counter, which looked like Cinderella's carousel moonlighting as a popcorn maker, caught my attention. It was pretty bare except for the few gold trimmings engraved on the side. Inside the glass case was a big mound of fine crushed ice that looked like snow.

It suddenly reminded me of the patches of snow covering the ominous mountain peaks in Japan, visible from my window as our plane took off from the airport on our way to Detroit more than fourteen hours ago, and it gave me the creeps. Nature, for all its indisputable beauty, scared the heck out of me; a wondrous fixture of Earth that bares its true colors when disturbed. It would tear up our planet and destroy everything in its path, as if we didn't matter.

"Do you like my new snow cone maker, *iha?*"

I snapped out of my trance as I heard a familiar voice in the background. I turned around and saw my favorite aunt standing poised by the oven, wearing her red and white checked apron and smiling sweetly at me. My aunt had always referred to me as *iha*—our family's version of the Spanish term *hija*, for daughter.

I ran to my aunt and gave her a tight hug. With my three-inch boots, I was almost the same height as her.

"How was your trip? I heard your flight was delayed for two hours. *Hay naku*, I had to work early this evening at the hospital, so I wasn't able to cook dinner for you. I have to call your mom later, because

I know she'll be upset when she finds out. She wanted me to cook *chicken adobo* for you."

My aunt was rambling as I glanced into the living room. I saw Wooly and my uncle carrying Kenneth and Sophia in their arms, carefully taking them to their designated room in the house. The kids fell asleep in the car on our way to my aunt and uncle's house from the buffet restaurant, where we had dinner earlier.

"Thanks, Tita. I'm just glad I made it here in one piece. What's cooking in the oven?" I grinned as I smelled the sweet aroma of caramelized sugar and cinnamon. My aunt ran to her stove and fumbled for her kitchen mittens. She opened the cover of her steamer and turned off one of the knobs on the side of her immaculately clean oven.

She was making *leche flan*, my all-time favorite Filipino dessert. Some called it caramel custard. It was a delicious flan made from milk, eggs, and sugar. The soft, heavenly caramel on top—or bottom, depending on how you liked to eat it—and syrup were my favorite.

In the Philippines, *leche flan* was served mostly during special occasions such as birthdays, weddings, and christenings aside from Christmas and New Year's Eve, but it was most popular during town *fiestas*, annual festivities celebrated by Filipinos living in small villages or towns, to commemorate their patron saints. We inherited that tradition from our ancient Spanish conquerors, who were Roman Catholic.

My Tita Girlie—short for Felicidad—was my mother's fabulous twin sister. Even in their mid-fifties, both women still had healthy, lustrous locks on their no-nonsense heads, prominent European noses, slender figures, and deep-set hazel-brown eyes. They got those foreign features from my grandmother, who went a notch stranger by having green eyes. My grandmother's grandmother was married to a Spanish *mestizo*. Unlike my prim-and-proper-bordering-on-square-but-still-lovable mother though, my aunt was more hip, more stylish, more fun-loving, and more approachable. She was the one who sneaked chocolate ice cream cake and iced candy into the kitchen for my cousins and I to feast on, back when we were still little and had nothing to do during uneventful summer nights in our small town in the Philippines. She would always be there to give us snacks after a game of *taguan, step no,* and *tumbang preso* which were Filipino innovations of universal childhood games such as hide and seek, hopscotch, and, well, probably kickball.

My Tita Girlie studied to be a nurse when she was younger. She immigrated to the United States a few years after passing her qualifying exam to become a registered nurse in America, with the goal of earning more for her family. My aunt petitioned her husband and her only child, Wooly, to the United States five years later. Unfortunately, in the Philippines the noble nursing profession did not pay as much as it did overseas, a sad reality that had yet to improve.

My mother, on the other hand, pursued the study of law and later became a respected lawyer in our community. My mother did not see the need to go to the United States to earn more for her family like her twin sister did, as her earnings from her profession, combined with my father's earnings, were enough to give me and my siblings a relatively comfortable life.

"Ready *na ba ang halo-halo*?" My uncle stepped into the kitchen to assume his role as ice crusher. He asked if the *halo-halo* was ready.

Halo-halo was another favorite Filipino dessert made of shaved ice, evaporated milk, and an assortment of fruits, gelatin, sweet beans, rice flakes, and *leche flan* with ice cream on top.

Apparently, my aunt was making *leche flan* as well as *halo-halo* to my taste buds' delight. My uncle put several more cubes of ice in the snow cone maker while waiting excitedly for my aunt to take out the freshly made *leche flan* from the refrigerator.

My uncle was a stay-at-home husband who had retired a few years ago due to impaired vision. He used to work as a sales person in the men's shoe department in one of the malls in the area, but he quit after a few years.

My uncle's real name was William, and Wooly was named after him. I called my uncle Tito Boy.

In the Philippines, for some reason, almost every family had a Tito Boy.

Boy had probably been a popular name back in the day when it was the Americans' turn to govern our country. Most Filipinos had probably been fascinated by American English, and maybe the word "boy" was one of the first English words that got stuck in their heads.

My uncle's nickname had always been Boy, even before he met my aunt whose nickname had always been Girlie. It was weird how fate exhibited a rare sense of humor every now and then.

Boy and Girlie had married each other after dating for two years, right after my aunt graduated from college. My uncle was eight years older than my aunt. My grandmother had not approved of the marriage, but my uncle, who had a kind heart and a sunny personality, won over my grandmother and every single family member on my aunt's side of the family.

Tito Boy was a geodetic engineer back home in the Philippines, but he did not pursue a career in the States when they immigrated.

I heard my uncle came to Houston as a tourist, but for some reason he overstayed and exhausted his limit as a visitor. He was referred by their fellow Filipino friends as "TNT," for *Tago ng Tago*, a comic slang popularly used to label illegal Filipino immigrants abroad.

Fortunately for my uncle, he was part of the United States' amnesty program years ago, which pardoned responsible illegal immigrants in the States and awarded them American citizenship. After working briefly as a sales attendant in a popular mall's shoe department in Houston, he eventually quit to stay at home full-time, mainly to save on day care fees and to make sure the best care was given to their only son. My uncle made that choice when Wooly, who was still in grade school, did not have anyone to stay with after school.

Being the breadwinner of the family, my aunt worked several shifts at the hospital as a registered nurse to not just pay the bills, but also to have some extra money for family vacations and savings. She didn't have the opportunity to fully take care of Wooly, even on her days off. Her time off was spent taking care of household chores, errands, doctor's appointments, and, well, getting her much-needed sleep.

My uncle didn't have a problem with being a house husband at all. Cheerful by nature, my uncle didn't have an inflated ego. He was completely fine with not being the one who brought home the bacon. Mopping the floor was not a demotion to him, and he actually preferred housekeeping over getting enslaved by his previous profession. Being at home, he was able to enjoy fixing the house while watching television. He did the laundry, dishwashing, house cleaning, running errands, and of course, attending to his young son's needs as nanny and chauffeur.

As I sat in a chair at my aunt's breakfast area, I noticed my uncle and aunt's house was spotless. I suspected my uncle had evolved into an obsessive compulsive neat freak like most housewives do over time, because everything in the kitchen seemed to be in its rightful place.

I looked at my uncle's back. I felt if I moved the salt shaker on the breakfast table two inches away from where he had originally set it, he would quickly slide it back in place when I wasn't looking.

I glanced at the calendar behind the open pantry door.

Four more days to go before Anthony found out I was in town.

Chapter 7

Wooly tiptoed into the kitchen after putting Kenneth and Sophia to bed in their temporary bedroom.

Since Wooly was an architect with no definite schedule, Tito Boy offered to take care of the kids until Charm came back from her business trip. Part of my role was to relieve my uncle of his babysitting duties, whenever he wanted to take a break and go fishing with his friends.

"Is the *halo-halo* ready?" Wooly repeated, not knowing what my uncle had said.

"Ready," said my aunt, who was already preparing to scoop the crushed ice from Cinderella's carousel.

I helped Wooly set up the *halo-halo* cups on the breakfast table.

We put two scoops of cooked mongo beans, *nata-de-coco*, tapioca, slices of jackfruit, and sweet cardava bananas in sweet syrup, white beans, rice flakes, and purple yam in each cup. My aunt put the crushed ice on top and doused the ice with evaporated milk. She finally layered the top with a generous serving of *leche flan* and its sweet caramelized syrup.

Wooly, Tito Boy, and Tita Girlie went over the top by putting vanilla and *ube* ice cream—a Filipino dessert made from purple yam—on top of the *leche flan*.

I didn't like ice cream on my *halo-halo*. I preferred the original set-up like those being sold in our neighborhood when I was still a child. Back then, a metal ice shaver was used to crush and scrape ice manually from a big block of ice, which was covered in clean cloth and placed in a cooler so it didn't melt.

I smiled as I took my first bite of my aunt's homemade *halo-halo*. It was a piece of heaven on earth. The sweetness of the *leche flan* and the milky taste of ice, combined with the crunchy rice flakes sent my senses to that warm, cozy place everyone calls home. At the back of my mind I knew I still had to call my parents and my siblings before I went to bed that night. I still had to unpack and set up my temporary bedroom that would be my home for five weeks. I still had to shower and scrub off the travel germs that probably got stuck on my skin during my flight.

But all that could wait.

When I finished my cup, I took my boots off casually and let them slide on the kitchen rug under the breakfast table, then I propped my legs up on my chair like a street guy drinking beer at a small *sari-sari* store in our neighborhood back home.

A *sari-sari* store was what we called a convenience store in the Philippines, located in a subdivision or neighborhood, where basic groceries were sold by the packet.

"*Ang sarap, Tita. Isa pa nga.*" I addressed my aunt in Tagalog, asking for one more cup of her delicious ice concoction.

My cousin, who could understand Tagalog but couldn't speak the language, got up and obliged. He made us another cup each and then sat next to me as he devoured his second serving.

As I was about to take one more bite from my freshly made cup of *halo-halo,* my uncle jumped from his chair and asked excitedly, "Janelle, *iha,* deed your daddy send me my box crotcher?"

I looked at my uncle intently, trying to figure out what he'd just said, but nothing came up. I waited for the light bulb to suddenly pop up in my head, but my brain was getting frozen from the icy dessert I was probably having an overdose of.

What in the world is a box crotcher? I wondered.

"Dad, you meant back scratcher," Wooly laughed as he scolded his dad lovingly. Tito Boy nodded in agreement, unfazed by his casual sabotage of the English language.

"That's what I said. *Napadala ba ng* daddy *mo yung kamay na pang-kamot ko sa likod* from Baguio? I requeysted that from your dad. That's my pey-vorit scrotcher. *Aba, wala n'yan dito.*"

36

I looked at my uncle and nodded.

He'd asked if my dad had sent him the back scratcher from Baguio that he'd requested. My uncle said the back scratcher from Baguio—a tourist destination in the Philippines where one can buy one of the best, if not the best, wooden back scratchers in the country—was his favorite, and it was not sold anywhere in Houston.

"*Opo*, Tito Boy. It's in my luggage," I answered.

I set my unfinished cup of *halo-halo* on the breakfast table and hurried to get up to open my suitcase sitting in the living room. After several tries, I dug out the mysterious long wooden arm that my mom had packed the night before I left for the States. There was a note on the white tissue paper covering the package.

It read "For Tito Boy."

I looked at the wooden arm one last time before handing the treasure to my uncle.

"Good. *Salamat, iha,*" my uncle thanked me in Tagalog for his box crotcher several times before disappearing into the hallway to try it on his back. My aunt and Wooly started cleaning up in the kitchen after I finished the remaining *halo-halo* in my cup. I offered to help by washing the dishes.

"That's okay*, iha.* You need to rest already so you can get some sleep. If you want to call home, just do it tomorrow. I already told your mom we have you in the house. I have phone cards and a long-distance line. Just take your pick. And as for Anthony, don't worry, we won't tell him you're here already. I don't understand why you're keeping it a secret, but I trust you, Janelle. Just let us in on the plan, okay?" My aunt was multi-tasking again, talking to me while loading the dishwasher and rearranging her fridge.

"*Naku.* Did you bring *polvoron,* Janelle?" my uncle asked as he popped up from nowhere. "Last week, my friend almost went to prison for that."

I remembered packing a few boxes of *polvoron,* a Philippine delicacy, in the luggage because the US Customs did not prohibit such commercially packed pastries. I looked at my uncle, alarmed, waiting for his *polvoron* horror story.

"Tomorrow *na lang, iha.* I'll tell you the story tomorrow. I know you're jeyt logged," my uncle said with a concerned look on his face.

I looked at my uncle's lips in confusion but only for a few seconds.

He would pretty much be my buddy at the house while babysitting Kenneth and Sophia, so it would help me a lot if I could decipher his jargon as quickly as I could, I thought.

I was slowly figuring him out. I knew he meant jet lagged.

"Yup, Tito Boy. I'm going to rest now. Don't forget to tell me about the *polvoron* story tomorrow," I told my uncle. I smiled at him as I got up to gather my luggage. I gave my aunt a quick hug and my cousin a high five before crossing the living room to get to the hallway leading to my designated bedroom in the house. As I headed to the right side of the hallway, I heard my uncle's loud voice behind me.

"Your beydroom is on the left, ober deyr," he said.

When I turned around to look at my uncle, his hands were busy scrubbing the sink, so he had to make facial gestures using his tightly shut mouth to point to the left of the hallway, to show me where my bedroom was. I raised my right hand from the hallway in acknowledgment as I redirected myself to the correct room.

I felt incredibly exhausted.

After I hit the shower, dried my hair, and changed into my pajamas, I passed out in my bed. Before I fell asleep, however, I managed to set the alarm clock on my bedside table so I could force myself to get up the next day and fix my messed-up body clock. My bed was soft and warm, and smelled of lavender fabric softener. It didn't take long before I dozed off to dreamland.

In my sleep, I thought I saw the wooden box crotcher running around the snow-paved garden, along with the powdery pastry that came out of the snow cone carousel, but it didn't make it to customs security because the *puto* got in the way. The customs officer smiled and stamped the passport, while the Asian flight attendant handed him airplane delicacies in a pink Hello Kitty tray, as the pilot got out of the plane with the old lady with the gold-rimmed glasses, saying she wanted to sleep but couldn't because my book was too heavy, and she was begging the older lady seated next to me to stop the plane from shaking.

Then she told me a secret.

She said she was jeyt logged.

Chapter 8

The loud crowing of a rooster woke me up.

The sound was strangely coming from behind the wall of my bedroom, and it was getting louder by the second. I pinched myself lightly just to make sure I wasn't dreaming.

I'd always been a light sleeper, and the slightest sound—even that of a feather touching the floor—would surely wake me up. At the same time, rousing from sleep—even from my deepest—had never made me disoriented or unaware of my current situation. So yes, I was fully aware that I was in my aunt and uncle's house in America for a short visit and they didn't have a rooster, let alone a crowing one, inside their immaculately clean home. I was still sleepy, but my curiosity got the better of me, so I stood up and drew the window blinds. I gasped in horror at the looming darkness staring back at me.

"*Gabi pa?*" *It's still night time?* I asked myself in confusion. I turned around and looked at the bedside clock, which was pushed to the edge of the nightstand away from my bed. It said eleven o'clock. Judging from the darkness outside, it seemed I overslept by almost a full day and night, since I went to bed the night I came to my aunt and uncle's house after being picked up by my cousin and his kids at the airport.

Well, so much for setting the alarm clock to fix my jet lag. My body clock got even more messed up, I said to myself.

I ran to the adjoining bathroom to fix myself before heading out to face whoever was still awake in the house, and stop that annoying rooster from disturbing the peace. I smiled sheepishly at my silliness, though.

Who am I fooling? I'm not a pet person. I can admire cute animals from a distance, but I'd never consider getting a pet for myself. I was chased by two dogs a long

41

time ago, when I was very little, and I was traumatized; if I do happen to see that mysterious rooster, I'll probably faint, I thought.

I dressed in my favorite sweats. Anthony gave me the cute Victoria's Secret sweats when he went home to the Philippines last year to visit me, just a few days after we got engaged. He knew I liked lavender and pink. The colors of the sweats actually inspired me to pick lilac and silver as our wedding motifs.

Speaking of Anthony, I still had to figure out how to surprise him, but I hadn't come up with the perfect plan just yet. I knew I had to plot thoroughly, with the help, of course, of his friend Camilla.

Camilla was Anthony's best friend who also lived in Houston. She was his longtime college buddy and family friend. I put an imaginary bookmark in my head to call her in the next couple of days.

But first, the rooster.

I slowly opened my bedroom door and poked my head out to see if there was anyone around the living room area. Nothing was moving. I tiptoed my way into the kitchen without turning the lights on, to conceal my presence and to not scare the rooster away. I surveyed the breakfast area all the way down to the dining hall, but nothing seemed suspicious. Suddenly, I heard heavy footsteps coming from behind me. I closed my eyes and braced myself for what I was about to face, but before I could even move a muscle, bright lights suddenly flooded the kitchen and the living room. I froze where I was standing, temporarily blinded. I heard a man's wail as I struggled to open my eyes, my heart furiously beating.

"Janelle, my gash, *iha! Ano ka ba?* You skurd me. I almost had a heart attack. It's meydnight. What are you doing deyr in the dark? I thought you're a rubber."

That was my uncle.

I looked at him half-embarrassed, half-amused. He was in his pajamas, with his fist tightly clasping his cellphone, aiming it like a weapon at his unknown "rubber." When I looked at his cell phone, something clicked in my head. The sound of the crowing rooster was coming from his cellphone. I walked towards my uncle slowly, without taking my gaze off his electronic device.

"Janelle, *iha,* is deyr something wrong?"

My uncle spoke in between yawns. I could tell he was rudely awakened by my midnight stunt.

"Did you want to kowl your boyfreynd? Here, you can use my cell phone."

Tito Boy sounded confused.

"Oh, no thanks *po,* Tito Boy. What's that sound?" I asked as I tried to look at what was going on with my uncle's cellphone.

"Oh. Did you like it? That's my alarm clack. *Nagigising ako talaga sa manok na 'yan.* Okay, *di ba?*"

Tito Boy explained to me that the sound of the crowing rooster was his alarm clock.

"Just like in the Philippines in my *lolo's* farm."

Lolo is "grandfather" in Tagalog.

My uncle chuckled as he began reminiscing about his childhood days at his grandfather's farm in the Philippines, where he grew up. He said he used to wake up in the morning to the crowing of real roosters on the farm. I smiled at my uncle and nodded politely.

"Janelle, you can stay in the kitchen if you like. *Gutom ka ba, iha?* If you're hungry, you can just get anything in the Frigidaire. It's free." Tito Boy continued to chuckle as he spoke to me.

I realized my uncle and aunt's refrigerator in the kitchen was not a Frigidaire, but a different brand, yet my uncle referred to it as a Frigidaire, the common term or slang used by Filipinos in the Philippines when referring to any commercial brand of refrigerator. We generally tended to refer to generic things using commercial brands—Colgate for toothpaste, Coca Cola for a carbonated drink or soda, and the list went on.

"Did you know you slept the whole day and night? *Ang galing mong matulog, iha.* You're a deep slipper. Your Tita Girlie is on her way home *na*. She has *pancit*, your feyvoreet noodles. I am going back inside. Okay? Goodnight. *Mag-ilaw ka, talaga itong batang ito, oo*. The lights are free. Open them," my uncle continued, telling me that it was okay to turn the lights on.

"Yes, Tito Boy. Goodnight. I'll wait for Tita Girlie in the kitchen. You're right. I'll go get some snacks. I'm hungry *na po*," I said politely.

"Okay, Janelle. *Bun appetit*," Tito Boy said before disappearing into the hallway. I smiled while shaking my head. My uncle just spoke French to me with his endearing Filipino accent.

Bon appetit to me, I thought.

I headed to the kitchen and fixed myself a peanut butter sandwich, ditching the jelly.

In the Philippines, we usually dunked our favorite local rolls, called *pan de sal*, in a jar oozing with soft and creamy peanut butter goodness. Ludy's and Lily's peanut butter, a local brand, were a staple on my family's breakfast table back home. In some instances, Filipinos dunked their favorite bread in their beverages. I'd seen my own grandmother dunk her little round, flaky, light cookies called *paborita* in her cup of coffee, chocolate drink, and even in her soda, which she lovingly called *sarsaparilla*.

I opened my aunt's pantry to get the medium-sized jar of Jif crunchy peanut butter but didn't touch the jar of strawberry jam sitting next to it. I wondered where my aunt bought the couple of jars of strawberry jam on her shelf. They were imported from the Philippines, where the beautiful Baguio City was located.

Baguio City is one of the top summer destinations in the Philippines. Located atop mountains, the temperature there is cold enough for people to grow strawberries on their farms.

I took my sandwich plate to the breakfast table to enjoy my feast. Along the way, I grabbed a pen and a stash of paper so I could brainstorm and write down my plans for my big surprise for Anthony. As I was about to write down my plans, though, I heard the fake rooster crowing its lungs out again. As I wrote down Anthony's name on the sheet of paper in front of me, I heard my uncle's rhythmic snoring seep out of his closed bedroom door.

Tito Boy said his rooster alarm clock woke him up all the time. From the sound of it, its mechanical crowing seemed to have become his lullaby.

After a few minutes of munching on my peanut butter sandwich, I caught myself half-asleep, staring at my sandwich crumbs. I let out a big yawn as the rooster seemed to also lull me to sleep. I got up and threw my leftovers in the trash can and washed my plate and silverware. I dried my hands on the kitchen towel and started turning off the lights one by one as I headed towards my bedroom. I knew my aunt wouldn't mind if I didn't wait for her.

I methodically headed to the bathroom sink and brushed my teeth, went to my bed, and turned on the TV. I looked past the screen, though, as my restless mind tried to figure out what I wanted to do.

I knew I didn't want to go back to sleep. I wanted to stay awake until it was time for me to get up and get ready for my first official day in the Houston sunlight. But then I heard the fake rooster crowing again, and with its weird, almost evil spell, I slowly drifted off to sleep.

Chapter 9

He lazed outside the little Mexican restaurant, a slim cigarette in one hand, as he stood by the patio and watched a crowd of busy shoppers walk by.

Suddenly, a tall shadow sneaked up behind him. The shadow transformed into a good-looking, brawny man wearing a tight muscle shirt. He quickly grabbed the hand of the man with the cigarette and gave him a gentle peck on the cheek. The man with the cigarette rested his head, apparently, on his lover's shoulder, wrapping his arm around his waist like a princess clinging for protection. The two men exchanged meaningful smiles before walking hand in hand back into the restaurant.

I bit my lower lip as I watched the men's backs disappear from a distance. That was a full five minutes of culture shock, not because they were both men, but because they were bold enough to display their affection in public.

In the Philippines, my peers called that PDA—Public Display of Affection—which not a lot of people would dare do for fear of ridicule. Filipinos, especially the older generation, were conservative and known to profoundly frown on vulgarity.

If my grandmother had seen what I'd just witnessed, she would have approached the two men and sat down at their table in the restaurant to give them a lecture on propriety.

I looked around to see if anyone was as shocked as me, but surprisingly, even though there were a handful of people who saw what I saw, none of them seemed to give a hoot about it. I suddenly missed Jay Anne, my best friend and, needless to say, my top-notch coworker in the advertising agency in the Philippines that I had momentarily left behind.

In our advertising agency, we thrived on new blood. Among those brave enough to join the glamorous geeks of our company, applicants would likely get hired if they were young, smart, good-looking, creative, out of this world, or all of the above, but most especially if they were out of this world—whether they were straight or not, or somewhere in between. In fact, the more they stuck out from the crowd like a red Gummy Bear in a box of Chocolate Kisses, the better.

Jay Anne, my eclectic, fuschiaphobic, Prada-diva friend, was the bright-red, sticky Gummy Bear in that box of chocolates, and one of Philippine advertising's most celebrated and respected copywriters.

Between the two of us, Jay Anne was the more sensitive, the more compassionate, and the easier one to get along with. When life sucked, when I couldn't seem to get my act together, when I was about to give up, Jay Anne would always come to rescue me from my own foolhardiness, brimming with wisdom and humor and toting a plateful of cheese, a bottle of wine, a box of tissues, and a cup of tricks. Once in a while I'd feel inadequate for making stupid decisions. Oftentimes, I'd get frustrated for not finding the right answers, even to my most trivial problems. But the feeling would always go away, replaced by gratitude for having a friend who I knew would always be there for me, no matter what.

But interestingly, even though we were the best of friends, Jay Anne had never discussed romantic relationships with me. They had always been protected territory, a closed book, which I was never given the key to. I never asked why. I'd come to accept it as one of the strangest aspects of our friendship—our unwritten pact, bound by respect and sealed with love.

Like my grandmother, my best friend would have frowned at the two flamboyant men holding hands like lovers in the Mexican restaurant.

Jay Anne's real name was Jericho.

Fortunately, his family embraced his sexual orientation unlike other gays like him who were not as lucky.

Yesterday Jay Anne sent me an e-mail, but I was too tired to read his message. I promised myself I'd check his message and the rest of my messages in my inbox when I finally got back at my aunt and uncle's house from our shopping trip in the mall. I needed a good diversion for my current frustrations.

I'd been calling Anthony's best friend, Camilla, the whole day, but she never picked up. When I tried to leave a voice-mail, some guy did the automated greeting for her which, by the way, was strange. I didn't think Camilla had a boyfriend or a male friend in Houston other than my fiancé. At least that was what Anthony had told me. But I wasn't really that close to her, anyway. We were just civil to each other most of the time. If it weren't for Anthony linking us together, I didn't think we'd be friends at all.

Camilla was mysterious, reserved, calculated, and a know-it-all. But I had to talk to her. I missed Anthony so much, I was already tempted to abandon my plan to surprise him.

Actually, I'd been tempted several times since I had arrived in Houston to just give him a call and tell him where I was so he could pick me up. So we could finally spend time together. I was already excited to give him my gift—a huge box of his favorite local chocolates from the Philippines, called Choc Nut. I arranged more than a hundred of them in a cute little red box that had been sitting in my room since I invaded my aunt and uncle's guest room.

But I had to stick to my plan.

If my plan went smoothly, it would be the last time I'd be sneaking up on Anthony as his girlfriend, because in a little over a year from now I would be his wife, and there'd be no more need for pulling surprises.

I glanced at the huge clock on the wall by the busy food court. I'd been waiting for my uncle and aunt for a quarter of an hour already while they went shopping at the famous Houston Galleria Mall.

The Galleria Mall was an indoor mall in Houston, and was one of the most famous tourist and local destinations in the city. It was also frequented by celebrities visiting from all over the world. It was huge and modern, with many shops for famous high-end brands.

I noticed the shoppers in the mall seemed to come from all walks of life, but most of them were dressed to the nines, garbed in the latest fashion. I made a mental note to send an e-mail to some of my coworkers in the Philippines, who previously told me to watch out for Houstonians dressed in cowboy hats, starched jeans, and pointy leather boots. I'd tell them there was nothing Old West about the Galleria Mall, nor the people strolling around. There was some Americana-inspired décor and fashion, but nothing came close to what many of my coworkers in the Philippines had pictured Houston locals would look like.

My uncle told me there was a famous event in Houston, held annually, called the Rodeo, where people showed up in their best western outfits to relive the romantic Old West. Other than that, it was generally pretty conventional fashion for everyone in the Houston metropolis all year long.

A smiling middle-aged man suddenly emerged from out of nowhere carrying an armload of shopping bags and a cup of smoothie with a bright orange straw glued to his lips. Next to him was a jovial woman looking relaxed in her royal blue scrubs, carrying a bag of humongous soft pretzels.

I looked at the couple and recognized them immediately—my uncle and aunt.

"Janelle, come on down!" my cheerful uncle said. "Homeward bound."

I quickly fixed my bright red beanie, to tuck my stubborn hair inside and cover my freezing ears. Wearing the hat was my strategic way of making sure my aunt and uncle would see the top of my head in the mall amidst the thick weekend crowd. I then picked up my shopping bags with one hand and tightly held onto the three shimmering silver balloons I had bought for Anthony with my other hand, and happily trotted behind my aunt and uncle on our way to the parking garage.

I could sense myself grinning from ear to ear while walking, oblivious to the people around me who probably thought I was a loony or an idiot, but that didn't matter. All I cared about was the thought that Anthony—my future husband—was about to get the biggest surprise of his life.

Tomorrow.

Chapter 10

I had the privilege to witness the mind-blowing guessing game of the century that would give Alex Trebek's famous game show, *Jeopardy*, a run for its money.

> Sophia: "I'll give you a hint. It's small and it's gold."
> Kenneth: "Hmm. Give me another hint."
> Sophia: "Okay."
> Sophia: (mouthing the words slowly as if she was talking to a two-year-old) "It's so, so small, and it's really gold."
> Kenneth: "That's the same hint."

I wanted to roll on the kitchen floor laughing, but instead I had to be careful not to show my facial expression to my niece and nephew who were still conversing, poker faced, like nothing hilarious had just transpired between them. Sophia was holding a crumpled Christmas tree ornament in between her chubby palms. It was concealed under the breakfast table while her clueless brother tried to guess what her "so, so small and really gold" secret item was.

I drank my glass of cold water in three gulps while fanning my flushed face with a flimsy plastic coaster I found in the kitchen, until my nerves calmed down. I heard Wooly giving my uncle last-minute instructions on the kids' bedtime schedule. I quickly went to the front door to wait for Wooly, after giving Sophia and Kenneth a peck on their cheeks.

***

That was exactly half an hour ago, when I was still in good spirits, proudly convinced that I was ready to launch my spectacular surprise for Anthony.

I was in the parking garage of Anthony's high-rise apartment, currently hyperventilating inside Wooly's car with my polite and not-so-patient cousin who was left with no choice but to be my designated driver. It was eight o'clock in the evening. Anthony should have been home already.

Since Wooly gave me his I-am-bored-beyond-belief-will-you-please-get-out-of-the-car look, I had no choice but to unfasten my seat belt, pat my stubborn hair, put on my lip gloss, and grab the silver balloons and the red box of Choc Nuts I had brought for Anthony.

In less than two minutes I was standing next to Wooly's car, all prepped up. Strangely, the image of the crowing fake rooster hiding in my uncle's phone crept inside my head like an omen for a brief second. I shook off the negative vibe at once and gave my cousin the brightest smile any dentist would die for. Wooly gave me the thumbs-up as he settled himself comfortably in the driver's seat, preparing himself for the most boring fifteen minutes of his life. He told me earlier he preferred to wait in the car for me rather than come back after an hour or so to pick me up.

I started walking towards Anthony's apartment as I set out on my mission, slowly, with trembling knees and frigid hands, gasping for air every few seconds. I paused to catch my breath when I finally reached the third floor. I walked to the fifth door on the right side of the hallway, reaching deep in my pocket for the shiny silver key hanging from a pink Sanrio key chain.

Anthony had given me that key—his key to his apartment—as his birthday present for me a year ago. He even gave me his apartment's security code just in case for some bizarre reason I decided to drop by his place in Houston. The thought was crazy back then, and we had a good laugh about it, but the idea served as the foundation for my lofty quest to turn a highly improbable scenario into a beautiful reality someday.

Well, guess what, I thought, *someday had just arrived.*

The silver key felt cold between my fingers as I turned it carefully to unlock the front door of Anthony's apartment. I twisted the knob slowly and gave the door a slight push.

A sliver of light escaped from within.

I braced myself for the sound of the security alarm announcing my presence as I frantically surveyed the small hallway inside Anthony's apartment, to pick the perfect spot to hide. But strangely, the security alarm did not go off.

On one hand, I was appalled that Anthony had compromised his safety by forgetting to activate his security alarm, yet on the other hand, I was relieved he had, because I was able to get inside his apartment without much difficulty.

My feet began to feel like rubber trapped in clay. My heart was beating fast, and beads of sweat were beginning to form on my forehead. Every movement I made, even the sound of my breathing, seemed to create an imaginary crashing sound in my ears. I closed and locked the door behind me gently before stepping inside the spacious living room. I jumped when I heard what sounded like a bunch of chimes disturbed from slumber, but then, before I could even think of screaming in panic, the sound was quickly subdued, drowned by the melodic rhythm of a Kenny G classic streaming softly through the walls.

The music seemed to come from a small room, a bedroom perhaps, hidden behind the tiny kitchen.

If it weren't for the night-light illuminating the hallway and the dull light escaping from the room where the music was coming from, Anthony's apartment would've been in total darkness.

My adrenaline rush started to kick in. I couldn't believe I was inside my fiancé's apartment and seeing his living space for the very first time. I tightened my grip on my balloons, careful not to get the strings entangled with anything fragile that may fall and come crashing on the floor.

Even in the dark, Anthony's apartment looked tastefully decorated. But it didn't feel cozy inside. From the little light that illuminated sections of the apartment, I could see bits and pieces of the kitchen and the living room. The floor was partly wood and partly covered with carpet. The furniture seemed oddly spaced apart. Vases of different sizes were scattered on the floor, and several picture frames lining the shelves had no pictures displayed.

If I were a stranger, I would've suspected the person living in that apartment hardly stayed in. I wished I could inspect my fiancé's pantry, fridge, and closets, but that was not my priority at the moment.

Through the light in the room by the kitchen, I saw a clear vase filled with fresh pink roses submerged in water. It was sitting proudly on the breakfast table, out of place in the company of cups and saucers filled with what looked like bread crumbs. Somehow, the crumbs did not make it to the trash can sitting conveniently in a corner.

The potent smell of brewed coffee lingered in the room. I noticed a few coats resting on the backs of the chairs by the breakfast table, but I had difficulty counting how many and what they looked like. On the floor in the kitchen, unopened boxes of different sizes were stacked carelessly by the sink.

A cluttered bachelor's pad with fresh pink roses. Who would have guessed? I thought.

I continued to walk until I was just a foot away from the room by the kitchen. It glowed eerily in front of me, like a blazing torch guarding a medieval fort.

I was quite certain that was Anthony's bedroom.

I noticed the door was left wide open, and soft, instrumental music was playing inside. I walked closer to the room, pausing by the entrance, hesitating for a second as I tried to keep my balance. I held onto the red box and the silver balloons as I realized I was about to conclude my mission.

There was no turning back.

Brimming with excitement, shaking in anticipation, and struggling to contain a heart and mind that wouldn't be calmed, I slowly walked inside.

Chapter 11

He opened his eyes.

I stood by the foot of the bed, looking at his face. My eyes were fixed, not blinking. He got up and screamed my name in shock, but I had already managed to leave his apartment by the time he was able to get off the bed to validate what had just happened.

I had never seen Anthony so pale and shaken in my life. It was a dreadful sight and definitely not the kind of welcome I had anticipated for my first, and maybe last surprise for him.

My face froze in anger as I headed back to Wooly's car. I tried to block off the image of Camilla's naked body appallingly displayed in its perverse glory as she comically jumped off the bed to catch the silver balloons that escaped from my hands. The balloons drifted off to the ceiling in Anthony's bedroom, eventually getting caught in the ceiling fan. I remembered Camilla's attempt to cover her nudity with her long, curly hair with no luck as she glared at me like a wounded animal in a cage.

I still couldn't believe I caught my fiancé and his best friend in the same bed together—stark naked.

I continued to walk back to Wooly's car in the parking garage, crying and laughing at the same time. I thought I heard Anthony's voice calling my name from afar, but I quickly dismissed it. My mental faculties had already shut down.

I tapped on Wooly's car window when I reached his parking spot. My cousin unlocked the door while looking at his watch, disoriented. I quickly got inside the car and told him we needed to leave immediately. I asked him to start his car and drive away as fast as he could.

"What's going on?" Wooly asked me for the nth time as we drove past a busy intersection down a street called Westheimer, but I couldn't find the words to describe what had taken place in Anthony's apartment. I kept quiet as we drove through the evening traffic, containing my emotions as we passed modern tall buildings, restaurants, and retail establishments along a posh-looking avenue.

I saw a round silver piece of metal that looked like a gigantic silver wedding band in the middle of a busy intersection, suspended about twenty feet above the four traffic lights that faced each other. The impressive silver piece of architecture, which I had never seen anywhere else in the city, was seemingly bound by invisible wires and bore the name of the street. Engraved on the huge metal ring were the words Post Oak Boulevard.

The modern boulevard reminded me of Ayala Avenue back home in the thriving business district in the Philippines, where the advertising agency that I worked for was located.

I continued to stare out my window, still unable to talk or even look at my cousin.

We passed by a strip of residential areas along a quiet street called San Felipe, just a few blocks away from Post Oak Boulevard. Some houses were elegant and well-kept—a sight to behold with their unique architecture and perfectly landscaped lawns—while the rest of the houses looked like modern palaces hiding behind lush trees, trimmed hedges, and lofty fences. I saw a young couple waiting to cross the street, holding hands, keeping each other warm, shielding each other from the cold wind.

Suddenly, I heard myself rambling in between sobs. "He was sleeping in the bed. He saw me and he screamed. You know what? I left my balloons. I wanted to take them back to your parents' house so I could give them to the kids, but they were caught in that stupid ceiling fan, and I just left that place in a hurry because it was too dark, and I didn't want to come out of the wrong door, but I really tried. Damn it. I left the red box. I wanted those Choc Nuts."

Wooly kept himself focused on the road, glancing at me from time to time. When we stopped on the red light, he spoke. I could sense anger in his voice. "What happened in that apartment? Did Anthony try to hurt you?"

Try is an understatement, I thought. Anthony may very well have hurled a million ice daggers at me, because the pain was as unfathomable. To add insult to injury, he brought along an evil witch so they could hold hands while enjoying my anguish.

I clenched my fists as I remembered the gold necklace Camilla was wearing. It dangled like crazy on her neck when she jumped off their love nest to get the balloons off the ceiling fan. I gave that necklace to Anthony for his twenty-fifth birthday, but I realized he was a cheapskate, re-gifting what I'd invested my time and savings on, to that unworthy, callous, and dirty snake. I closed my eyes and quietly cried. Wooly didn't say anything but continued driving.

When I opened my eyes, a big lit OPEN sign was literally flashing before me.

Bubbly Tea House.

That's what the sign said on the other side of the glass windows of the small establishment my cousin had methodically parked his car in front of.

Surrounded by small restaurants and diners serving po'boys and deli sandwiches and Mediterranean and Hispanic cuisines, Bubbly Tea House looked like a quaint diner. Some chrome metal chairs and tables were set outside to accommodate those who wanted to enjoy their drinks *al fresco.* Its patrons were young, mostly Asians hanging out in groups, chatting and seemingly having a good time.

I wondered if the "bubbly" establishment had room for sourpusses like me as I listened to the rambling monologue in my head.

So what if I was cheated on? After all, my ex-fiancé was only thousands of miles away from me, far away enough so he could freely walk around with his pants down. Apparently, I'd just become part of the statistics, one of many men and women victimized by blindly trusting in long-distance relationships. And to think, I thought we were different—as in going-to-the-aisle-together-and-slicing-a-piece-of-the-four-tiered-cake-and-setting-the-white-doves-free-during-the-lavish-hotel-reception different.

Wooly was looking at me patiently while I processed my thoughts.

"Let's go inside, cuz. You'll love their tea. One sip will get you through whatever you're feeling right now. This is my favorite place when I need to de-stress. Wanna check it out?" he said, smiling a little awkwardly.

I realized Wooly was far from the Chipmunk-sounding prankster who fetched me at the airport just a few nights ago. I had to smile and give him a pat on the back. I was glad I had listened to him when he insisted earlier that he wait for me in the parking garage of Anthony's apartment, instead of just dropping me off. I didn't think Anthony and Camilla would have taken the trouble to entertain me while I sat aggrieved in their living room waiting for my ride home, anyway.

I held back the tears in my eyes.

"Okay," I told Wooly. "Let's go get some bubbly tea."

"Bubble tea," Wooly corrected me kindly, winking at me.

Chapter 12

It was close to midnight five years ago when my father's landline in his small office at home started ringing.

The endless ringing competed with the loud noise outside from the hundreds of fireworks and firecrackers lighting up our little festive neighborhood. I grabbed the phone absentmindedly, a bit annoyed by the unwelcome phone call from the anti-social caller who seemed to have forgotten to check the calendar. It was New Year's Eve, for crying out loud.

But as soon as I heard the sweet, cool, familiar voice on the other end of the line, my heart melted. It was Nick, my college boyfriend, calling to let me know he was unable to spend New Year's Eve with me. Amazingly, before I could even open my mouth to ask what was going on, Nick went on a long and unexpected monologue. He sounded confused yet persistent, reaping ideas from his garden of new-found wisdom. Slowly, he began to reveal what had been going on in his life all along, without my knowledge.

According to Nick, he had met someone special. He said he didn't want to hurt me, but he could not lie anymore. He said he was in love with her.

I wanted to kick Nick for his timing.

Seriously, I thought.

I wondered who had given him the license to blurt out all his pent-up feelings to me on New Year's Eve. It wasn't as if his world would end if he had waited and pretended everything was okay for just one more night so we could, at least, enjoy the festivities.

The phone receiver felt hot on my ear, burning my skin with every sound Nick made on the other end. A dark cloud seemed to hover

over the top of my throbbing head as my heart shattered into a million pieces.

There I stood, in the middle of my father's office, staying strong like a soldier, too proud to go down as I listened to my boyfriend of three years try his best to justify why he had to end our relationship.

When Nick finished talking, I had nothing to say. There was only silence—that long, awkward, uncomfortable sound of nothing. Yet I found comfort in silence. It soothed my pain, pacified my revolting senses like a warm cup of soup, an essential source of sustenance on very cold nights.

Before I hung up, I told Nick I would try to understand what had happened to us, and I wished him good luck. But as soon as I put the phone receiver back on its cradle, I quickly crawled under my father's desk, crying endlessly until my tear glands dried up, holding myself together until I stopped shaking.

***

It was my very first breakup from my very first relationship.

Amazingly, my younger mind processed the pain fast. In less than two weeks, before Nick could even dare ask how I was doing, I'd already been healed, bouncing back like a carefree child on a trampoline.

But tonight, it was a little different.

Looking around in the dark tea house full of strangers talking among themselves, their voices drowned out by the blaring 80s music playing in the background, I didn't feel like the proud soldier who refused to go down five years ago. In fact, the weight of my first breakup with Nick seemed to have added to the heavy load I was carrying from what transpired in Anthony's apartment just an hour ago.

"It Might Be You" softly streamed from the speakers, an 80s Stephen Bishop classic that Anthony sang to me when we started dating two years ago.

Really, I thought.

Suddenly, my feet felt like jelly, my knees started shaking, my mouth felt dry, my eyes burned, and my chest literally ached with every breath struggling to escape from my lungs. I looked at the door as I grabbed my purse. I wanted to run somewhere and hide, far away from everything that tormented me.

"Here you go," Wooly told me as he handed me a drink. It looked like coffee smoothie with little black round balls and diced jelly settling at the bottom of the medium-sized plastic cup.

Wooly handed me a fat straw and motioned for me to follow him to a booth in a corner by the window overlooking the parking lot.

"That's cappuccino with coffee jelly and tapioca. That's bubble tea to some people. Over here, they call it *boba* or milk tea or pearl tea, the bread and butter of Bubbly Tea House. In the Philippines we call them tapioca balls, or *sago,* I believe. Here, stab the plastic cover on top with the pointed end of the straw. This drink is cold. No sugar added. Tell me if you like it. It's my all-time favorite flavor, but I have to stay away from coffee right now. Not good for my beautiful body," Wooly explained, winking at me and patting my head like he used to when we were kids.

"And if you care to know, I got myself a red bean smoothie with fruit jelly. No tapioca and no sugar. This is my latest discovery and current flavor of the month. Cheers!" Wooly continued.

I smiled as I realized my cousin had always been the big brother I never had.

Wooly moved to the States twenty-five years ago, when he was only six years old. He came back to the Philippines to visit us five years later with his parents, and from then on, their family would visit every other year, usually in the month of June during his summer break from school.

Unlike in the United States, the Philippines' summer break fell between the months of March, April, and May. Although we only saw each other every two years, Wooly and I developed a strong friendship, eventually becoming cousin-best-friends. When he was in the Philippines back when I was in grade school, he would be my body guard, always there to come to my rescue when some bored kids in the neighborhood wanted to bully me.

When Wooly married his wife, Charm, who he met in the Philippines when he was only seventeen, I was one of the bridesmaids during their church wedding. They tied the knot shortly after his twentieth birthday in a small parish church in Tagaytay City, a romantic summer getaway in the Philippines.

I took a deep breath before taking a tiny sip of my cold cappuccino *boba* drink. It was a little richer than what I used to drink back home in Manila, but the black coffee jelly and tapioca balls were cooked just right, blending perfectly with the strong, rich taste of sugarless coffee.

I took another sip. It was a piece of heaven on earth.

Just like the good-looking Cutie Pie headed to our table.

Chapter 13

Mr. Cutie Pie walked to our booth.

He looked at me briefly, then switched his gaze to my unsuspecting cousin. When he finally reached our booth, he tapped my cousin's shoulder. Wooly jumped. When he saw Mr. Cutie Pie, he got up from his chair and the two men bumped fists.

"Dude. Wassup?" Wooly said with a grin on his face.

"Didn't see your car, bro. Where'd you hide it?" Mr. Cutie Pie said smiling broadly, showing his perfect set of pearly whites.

The lights in the tea house were dim, so it was easy for me to check out Mr. Cutie Pie without my cousin noticing.

He looked Asian but mixed. Half-Korean or half-Japanese, perhaps. He was wearing faded jeans and a simple T-shirt, but for some reason he looked dressed up. His nose was thin and high-bridged. The shape of his face was oval, yet a bit square-ish. His facial features were masculine, but there was a slight trace of femininity about him. His hair was rich, cascading past his shoulders, layered, and streaked with blond highlights. He was almost as tall as Wooly, slim bordering on lanky, but his toned arms suggested he spent a good amount of time working out in the gym. His body was fit and athletic but not bulky.

I looked at his eyes. There was something different about them. They were shaped like almonds, draped with thick and long eyelashes.

I glanced at Wooly and didn't realize my cousin had been staring at me while I was checking out his friend. I felt so embarrassed when I saw him looking at me as if I just turned completely psycho.

"By the way, this is my little cousin. Her name's Janelle. She's the one I was talking to you about. She just came in a few days ago from the Philippines. Just a couple of days after Charm left for Tokyo." Wooly explained the dork sitting across from him to his gorgeous Cutie Pie friend.

"Hey. How was your trip, Janelle?" Mr. Cutie Pie asked. As I looked at his lips while listening to his voice saying my name, I was mesmerized. He reminded me of the Asian guitarist from my favorite 90s band, The Smashing Pumpkins. I tried to recall the guitarist's name.

James Iha, I thought.

"Janelle, this is James," I heard my cousin say.

I almost choked from the tapioca ball sliding down my throat. *How in the world did they have the same name? I must be going nuts already,* I thought.

James looked at me strangely, probably wondering if he should shake my hand or slap my back to get the tapioca ball out of my throat.

"James is a good friend of mine, and a fellow architect from work," Wooly told me with a puzzled look on his face.

I smiled at James shyly, and in an awkward voice, I said, "Hi."

I didn't know if I should hit my head on the wall to bring myself back to reality, or tell Wooly to cut the chitchat so we could head back home already—so I could cry all night about my misery—instead of gawking at his architect friend like a star-struck weirdo.

James did not shake my hand. Instead, he turned to Wooly and casually explained what he was doing at Bubbly Tea House. He told my cousin he just stopped by to get a *boba* and was about to head out. The two architect-friends briefly said their quick see-you-laters before James started heading for the door. But just a few steps later, looking as if he forgot something, James glanced back and smiled at me.

I melted.

Discreetly and unintentionally.

When James turned around to head out of the tea house, I quickly rummaged through my purse pretending to look for something, anything, making sure my cousin did not notice the glow on my face. When my nerves settled, I let go of my purse and started to relax. I looked at my drink again, wondering what was inside my cup of smoothie. I turned it around slowly, inspecting the clear cup beaded with water from the crushed ice inside.

I took another sip.

So, I just got ditched by my ex-fiancé a few hours ago, but here I am feeling warm and fuzzy because a good-looking stranger smiled at me, I thought.

I began to wonder if it was too soon for me to feel better. After all, the tapioca ball trying to choke me was gone, I just met the delicious lookalike of my 90s celebrity fantasy, and I was halfway through my cup of cappuccino goodness, which was giving my system a welcome caffeine triple-kick.

I stopped myself from grinning as I noticed my clueless cousin was beginning to look at me funny. I smiled innocently. I knew I was acting stupid.

As I was about to take another sip from my *boba* cup, a light bulb lit up inside my head. I just realized my drink and I had something in common.

Considering I chose to run away instead of fight back and create havoc in Anthony's apartment after discovering my ex-fiancé was cheating on me, there was no other way to describe my reaction except that it was straight up foolish and dumb. I was clearly exemplifying the classic case of a *boba* drinking a *boba.*

In the Philippines, *boba* is the Tagalog term for a dumb female.

I frowned at the metaphor.

Oh well, I thought. *Cheers!*

Chapter 14

I woke up with a headache.

After Wooly dropped me off at my aunt and uncle's house last night, I went straight to bed without bothering to brush my teeth, take a shower, or even change my clothes. I felt the metal piece of my leather belt poking my waist and it was starting to hurt, but I still didn't move. There was something else hurting inside me, zapping my senses like a lightning bolt every few minutes, and it was making me feel nauseated.

I looked at the ceiling, fighting the urge to cry. I tried my best to refocus on what was left of my energy. I concentrated on my wrinkled clothes and the stale lipstick weighing heavily on my mouth. They were beginning to bother me, including the sight of the half-filled plastic cup of the cappuccino *boba* I left sitting on the nightstand before I fell asleep. I searched my mind to recall the dream—or nightmare—I had last night but couldn't remember anything.

The land phone on the nightstand started ringing. I let myself listen to the menacing ring tone a few more times before deciding to use it as an opportunity to finally get out of my spell. I grabbed the phone receiver and waited for the caller on the other end to speak first.

"Hey, are you awake?"

It was Wooly.

"Does it matter?" I asked weakly.

"Hey. I'm sorry you feel that way, cuz. Trust me. What happened to you and Anthony will make you a stronger person. We've all been there before," Wooly said kindly.

I had told my cousin everything that happened in Anthony's apartment on our way back to my aunt and uncle's house last night, right after we left Bubbly Tea House, and I was grateful for his company and wisdom.

"Guess what. I have something to cheer you up. I mean, it might. A little bit," Wooly added on the other end of the line.

"Thanks, cuz. You don't have to do anything to make me feel better. It's not your fault or mine. Life kicks us every now and then. As for me, I just have to suck it up and move on," I said, consoling my wounded self. What transpired in Anthony's apartment was still fresh in my memory.

"Well, tell you what. Why don't you stay at home today and recuperate? Dad went out fishing with his friends this morning. Mom has work and won't be back until midnight. And don't worry about the kids. I took them with me to my office. You have the entire house to yourself. You know the code to the security alarm, so you're good. Just don't open the door, even if somebody knocks or rings the doorbell. Call me when that happens, okay? Just relax for the day. Take care. I'll see you later tonight when we get back," Wooly said as if he was speaking to his own child.

"Thanks, cuz. You guys are awesome. I'm sorry this had to happen. I appreciate everything," I said sincerely.

"No prob. See you in a bit," Wooly said.

"Hey, wait. What was supposed to cheer me up again?" I asked. I knew I sounded like a brat, but I also needed a little bit of sunshine to look forward to.

"You're funny," Wooly said cheerfully. I could imagine him making a funny face on the other end of the line.

"You know me," I said, attempting to put a smile on my worn-out face.

"Well, you're gonna have to wait. Stay put until we come back," Wooly said, laughing.

"Fine."

"See ya."

"Kiss the kiddos for me, please."

"Will do."

I got up from the bed after I hung up and stretched my arms all the way up until my back and shoulders hurt. I needed the pain to wake up, and kick-start my brains to get going. I looked at myself in the mirror on the wall and was disgusted at my reflection. My hair looked like it was braided, blow-dried, and vigorously teased by a troll while I was asleep. My clothes were wrinkled, my left foot still had a shoe on, I was still wearing my jewelry, and my makeup was wiped off my face.

I quickly looked at the bed. I was appalled when I saw lipstick and makeup stains all over the sheets. I hurriedly pulled out the bed cover, stained by my makeup, from under the comforter and headed to the laundry area by the hallway. I dumped it inside the empty washing machine while inspecting the knobs and the green lights that turned on every time I pushed a button to make my selection.

"Okay," I said, the sound of my voice sounding weird in the quiet house.

"*Pa'no ba'to?* How in the world would I know how to operate this complicated machine?" I said, talking to myself out loud.

I surveyed the laundry area, looking at the sleek, silver-colored washing machine and dryer in front of me, admiring their beauty and technology. We didn't have anything like those back home. My parents' household help did our laundry manually, and if they ever used the simple washing machines we had, it was only for special occasions.

I suddenly remembered Miko's words of wisdom.

"Never touch anything that is alien to you."

My younger brother was twenty years old, but he still acted like a big kid when he was around the family. In fact, he only acted his age when he was in public or hanging out with his friends. But amazingly, he would come up with sound advice once in a while.

"That pretentious little bastard. I miss him," I muttered to myself.

Since I didn't want to create another mishap, I heeded Miko's advice and left the washing machine and the dryer alone. I thought maybe my aunt or uncle would teach me how to use them when they get back.

In the meantime, I could hear the phone in my bedroom ringing—off the hook. I quickly ran back inside to pick it up, but as soon as I saw the caller ID on the receiver, I headed straight to the adjoining bathroom and threw up.

My nausea had come back.

Chapter 15

"He wanted to taste all kinds of women before he gets married." The voice on the line was arrogant, unapologetic.

"Is that what you wanted to hear?" it continued.

I closed my eyes to calm my raging nerves as I recognized Camilla's twangy American accent. I'd always thought she was strange and cold and bitter, but never once did it cross my mind that the woman was outright evil.

She called my uncle and aunt's home phone through Anthony's phone line, perhaps because she knew Anthony's number was listed on my aunt's contacts, and that I would surely pick up the moment I saw the caller ID reflecting my ex-fiancé's name.

Camilla called methodically, letting the phone ring in bursts for several hours, perhaps taking advantage of my raw emotions. She gave me enough time to build my anger, which turned into annoyance, which then turned into a rage like a fireball shooting through the skies, razing in vengeance.

True enough, after much considering, I finally picked up. And lo and behold, sizzling with anticipation to blurt out her dramatic spiel, there was Camilla on the other end of the line, hissing like a snake, spitting on my bleeding heart, taunting my wounded ego.

She waited for me to speak first, but when she sensed I wasn't going to say anything, she went on with her speech.

"I want to make this clear. None of us knew you were coming to visit. We didn't plan for you to break in and find out what we were doing. We didn't intentionally flaunt our relationship to you. You're the one who plunged into your own misery by coming unannounced. Why would you surprise people like that? How selfish could you be? Did you think the world revolved around your happy little life? Anthony didn't cheat on you. He just realized what he really wanted for himself at the last minute, before getting married by mistake to you, and didn't have enough time and the right opportunity to break the news to you. You were thousands of miles away. It wouldn't hurt to wait for the perfect time so we could finally tell you the truth without bursting your rainbow-colored bubble.

"Did you notice the boxes and the clothes in the kitchen in Anthony's apartment? I was getting ready to move in with him so we could finally start a new life together. In fact, we just started celebrating, but you couldn't sit still in that third world country of yours. You had to fly in to surprise everyone, so you could insert yourself in people's lives. What was your purpose? Didn't you know people hid precisely because they didn't want to be found? Anthony hadn't called you for three weeks. Take the hint," Camilla nearly shouted.

I could hear her teeth grinding against each other on the other end.

"Camilla, I don't want to talk to you," I said coldly. "I don't know what *telenovela* you're addicted to, but you need to deliver a better script than what you just wasted my time with. If you're going to bother me and insert yourself in my life, you have to be prepared. You'll never know what I wanted to hear or wished to hear because newsflash, woman, it's none of your damn business. And before we end this worthless conversation of ours, I want you to tell Anthony that if he has any balls left, although I'm certain they're dangling without purpose in between his legs, he needs to be man enough to talk to me, face to face, not his stupid mistress." I was fighting back tears as I finished.

I didn't give Camilla the opportunity to speak again. I put the receiver back on its cradle softly, even though I badly wanted to smash it on the wall. I couldn't believe Anthony would settle for a woman who didn't have the moral capacity to know the difference between right and wrong.

Suddenly, I felt the burning need to clean the entire house. I knew it was a sign of imbalance somewhere in my system, but I didn't care.

I stood up from where I was sitting and hurriedly ran to the utility area to get my aunt's cleaning gadgets. As soon as I opened the cabinets though, I noticed the cleaning bottles and gadgets I saw when I arrived a few days ago were already gone. I quickly checked the kitchen counter. The knives stacked neatly in the wooden holder were gone, too. An imaginary light bulb suddenly lit up, and I had to shake my head.

My aunt and uncle must have thought I could potentially hurt myself after my traumatic episode last night, and they did their best to prevent me from doing something stupid I may regret later on.

I heard the security alarm go off.

I was about to have a panic attack when I remembered Wooly and the kids were already about to come back from Wooly's work. I looked at the kitchen clock and saw the time. It was past seven o'clock in the evening. I walked slowly to the living room to check if there was a burglar barging inside the door.

Because I was brave like that.

Or brainless.

I saw Sophia running to me from the front door, followed by her brother who smiled timidly when he saw me. "I missed you Tita Janelle!" Sophia screamed in delight.

Behind the kids, standing by the door, was Wooly holding a humongous brown bag. Next to Wooly was James, holding three bright pink balloons and a huge yellow stuffed toy. In his arms, resting comfortably and smiling from ear to ear as if amused by my haggard appearance, was the wide-eyed Pikachu.

Chapter 16

I looked at my "surprise" and smiled.

I slowly walked to the door, hesitating for just a teeny bit, undecided on how to thank Wooly and James for my neon pink balloons and the fluffy Pikachu.

"Thank you for holding my balloons, Uncle James. You're the best," Sophia said loudly as she ran back to the door to snatch the balloons from the hands of Wooly's architect friend. James knelt down to give Sophia her balloons, and my niece rewarded him with a big hug. He laughed softly as he tried to untangle his wrinkled shirt from Sophia's grip.

"Okay. Let go of Uncle James. It's my turn now," Kenneth said, grinning. He reached out for the fluffy Pikachu barely clinging onto James's free arm.

"Thanks for holding my Pikachu for me, Uncle James. You're awesome," Kenneth said as he gave James a high five.

"We're going to play now, Tita Janelle. See you guys later," Sophia said excitedly, zooming her way to the guest room as Kenneth tried to catch up.

"Sure, sweetie," I said enthusiastically, trying in vain to hide my embarrassment.

What in the world possessed me to think the balloons and the stuffed toy were for me? What's with me and surprises, anyway? I thought bitterly.

"Yan Yan! Come here. Guess what I got for you!" Wooly shouted from the kitchen.

"Yan Yan?" James asked, puzzled.

"That's my childhood nickname. My cousin loves to embarrass me," I said blushing.

"Oh. What's wrong with Yan Yan? You should hear what I call my little cousin," James said, grinning.

I smiled back but didn't say anything. James seemed easy to get along with and friendly, but I was still traumatized by Camilla's toxic phone call; I couldn't come up with a witty response. I casually walked to the kitchen while James followed quietly behind.

On the kitchen island, Wooly set up the goodies from his brown bag. He arranged fresh fruits, vegetables, seasoning, olive oil, packs of noodles, and lots of junk food. But something else caught my eye. Sitting on top of the breakfast table was a bright red bowl filled with golden brown *turon*, one of my classic Filipino favorites. A popular Filipino snack, *turon* was made of thinly sliced Saba bananas and sliced jackfruit, rolled in or generously sprinkled with brown sugar, wrapped in a spring roll wrapper, and then deep fried.

"Oh wow. Whose *turon* are those for?" I asked, afraid to assume again.

"They're for you. I bought them from a Filipino restaurant nearby. I know they're your favorite," Wooly said cheerfully.

"Thank you. I needed my comfort food," I said.

James smiled but said nothing.

"So, are you ready for dinner?" Wooly asked.

"Sure, but where to?" I asked back, knowing my aunt hadn't cooked anything for us before she went to work at the hospital that morning.

"We're having dinner here at home, courtesy of the best Japanese-American chef in town," Wooly said, winking at me.

"Uhmm. What chef?" I asked, puzzled.

"Master Chef Ren, the good-looking gentleman behind you," Wooly said, grinning.

I turned around to look at James, the only other person in the kitchen. He was sitting on a stool by the kitchen island, inspecting a

80

carrot. He smiled at me when he caught me looking from his face to the carrot he was holding.

"Don't believe the hype. Will is the president of my fan club," James said calmly, attempting to mock my cousin who was busy stuffing potato chips into his mouth.

I wanted to laugh but didn't feel comfortable enough to let my guard down. I looked at James's hazel-brown eyes. They looked as soft as pools of caramel and butter swirling in an almond-shaped lake, and they were drawing me in like a magnet.

"Janelle?" I heard James's voice.

Oops, I did it again, I thought.

"Sorry. What were you saying?" I apologized to James, feeling a bit flustered and hugely embarrassed.

"Nothing. I was just wondering if you have any food allergies," James said casually.

"Nope. Not me," I said quickly. "My tummy is happy, not very fussy."

Did I really just say that? I seriously need to get out of the kitchen and lock myself in my bedroom and never come out before I truly make a fool of myself, I thought.

"That's good," James said, smiling.

I smiled back, hoping he couldn't hear the monologue in my head.

"What do you say, bro? Should we start warming the stove already?" James asked Wooly.

With his mouth full, Wooly managed to give a thumbs-up sign as he prepared to drink his Coke in a tall, "sexy" glass filled with crushed ice.

Suddenly, frantic footsteps could be heard from the living room, behind the kitchen counter. As I started to get up from my seat to check what was going on, Sophia came running into the kitchen teary-eyed.

My niece quickly went to Wooly and started crying louder as her daddy picked her up.

"What's wrong, baby?" Wooly asked Sophia, looking worried.

In between sobs, my niece managed to respond. "Kenneth told me I'm Filipino."

Chapter 17

"Did you say you're crying because your brother told you you're Filipino?" Wooly clarified.

"Yes," Sophia whimpered.

"But if you're not Filipino, then what did you think you were?" Wooly asked again.

"I'm a princess!" Sophia said loudly as she grabbed her dad's shirt collar.

Wooly almost choked while James looked down at the floor, trying his best to hold his laughter. "This is the reason why Charm needs to quit her job and start focusing on raising our kids. I'm clueless about this," Wooly said softly while Sophia bawled on his shoulder.

I looked at Sophia as my heart melted. I had to do something. "Hey, Sophia. Do you like Disney?" I asked my niece when she stopped crying.

"Yes," Sophia said softly

"Really? I like them too. Which one is your favorite princess character?" I asked enthusiastically.

James and Wooly were quiet, wondering where I was going with my scheme.

"Cinderella, Tinker Bell, and Snow White," Sophia said excitedly.

"Tinker Bell is not a princess," Wooly said matter-of-factly.

I had to give Wooly the evil eye as he nodded apologetically, before proceeding with my script.

"How about Mulan? Do you like her?" I asked.

"Yes," Sophia said. "But she's not a princess," she added.

"True," I said. "But in her father's eyes, Mulan is a beautiful and brave princess, a delicate flower in their garden waiting to bloom in the spring," I added dramatically knowing I'd probably twisted the Disney script.

Sophia looked at me with renewed interest, excited to hear what I had to say next.

"Did you know Mulan is Chinese?" I asked.

"Yes. Kenneth told me she's Chinese because she was born in China," Sophia said.

"Right. But not only that. Her parents were both Chinese. That is their race, their nationality. People who were born to Chinese parents are called Chinese," I explained.

"Oh. So, is she a Chinese princess?" Sophia asked, her eyes wide and bright.

I said, "Correct."

Sophia looked at Wooly and said, "Lolo Boy and Lola Girlie are both Filipino, and my mommy's daddy and mommy in the Philippines are Filipinos, too. That's what they told me.

"So does that mean you and Mommy are Filipinos, too?"

Wooly gave me the thumbs-up discreetly as he answered Sophia's query.

"Yes, baby. That is correct."

"So does that make Kenneth and I Filipinos?" Sophia asked again.

"Absolutely!" Wooly said.

Sophia smiled brightly. "So am I still a princess, Daddy?" she asked excitedly.

Wooly was contemplative when he answered, "Always will be."

"So just like Mulan, I am a princess, too. Not a Chinese princess but a Filipino princess." My niece giggled as she came to her wonderful conclusion.

"The most beautiful and the sweetest Filipino princess ever," Wooly said poignantly as he kissed Sophia on her forehead.

"Thanks, Teacher Tita Janelle," Sophia said to me. "I'm going back to the playroom now."

I took Sophia back to the guest room where Kenneth was watching TV. I made sure everything was okay before leaving them to go back to the kitchen.

I found James and Wooly sitting by the breakfast table already, slicing and dicing the freshly washed vegetables. Wooly smiled at me appreciatively as I sat down with them to help.

"Very impressive. Thanks Janelle. You will be a great mom one day, or at least a counselor on good parenting," Wooly said.

I winced when I was reminded of my broken engagement with Anthony. I wondered how I'd even begin to cancel appointments for our upcoming wedding and inform everyone involved that no wedding would take place as planned, once I returned to the Philippines.

But my brain was exhausted, and my tummy was empty. *It's not the right time to be sad,* I thought.

"So, what's on the menu for tonight?" I asked cheerfully, eyeing the inviting bowl of golden *turon* on the breakfast table once again.

James looked at me thoughtfully while dicing the last of his potatoes, grinning before responding.

"Tonight, I'm making *yakisoba, donburi,* and my all-time favorite, chicken *adobo.*"

Chapter 18

The phone rang six times before my call was routed to the voice-mail.

"Jay Anne, it's me. Where are you? Send me an e-mail when you get this message and I'll call you back. It's cold in Houston right now. Freezing. I repeat. Freezing," I said before hanging up, feeling dejected as I stared at the desktop computer in my bedroom.

I dozed off on my bed. Half an hour later I woke up abruptly. I got up and turned on the desktop computer, logging on to my Hotmail account immediately, hoping my best friend had already responded to my voice-mail.

It turned out he hadn't.

Frustrated, I decided to compose a nice little e-mail to my friends and family in the Philippines instead, to describe my supposedly fun vacation in Houston, careful not to let them know about what was going on with me and Anthony.

I wasn't ready to disclose that ugly piece of information just yet. After all, the last thing I wanted was for anyone to feel sorry for me. There would be plenty of time and opportunities to explain what had happened to me when I got back to the Philippines. In the meantime, it was zilch.

I looked at the clock on the wall in my bedroom. It was thirty minutes past midnight, roughly an hour and a half already since Wooly and James left the house after dinner, but I could still taste James's wonderful cooking. My favorite was his beef *donburi*. James cooked the dish so well, the flavor of the garlic and soy sauce blended perfectly with the sliced onions and diced potatoes. Even the steamed rice at the bottom of the bowl was delicious.

I also finished a small bowl of James's *yakisoba*, my all-time favorite Japanese noodle dish, and still managed to save some room for his ultimate creation—the chicken *adobo*. James's version of our famous Filipino dish was not soupy, but it wasn't dry, either. The consistency of the ingredients was just right, and the flavors of sugar, garlic, soy sauce, and vinegar mixed well with the flaky chicken.

"Are you still interested in your surprise?" I remembered Wooly asking me during dinner.

"Oh. I almost forgot about that. Dinner was so good, I think I developed amnesia," I said, throwing a well-deserved compliment to the generous cook.

James smiled in acknowledgment.

Wooly cleared his throat before speaking.

"Well, my mom is throwing a party next week to introduce you to her friends. That would be next Saturday. It's supposed to be a surprise party to make up for all the birthday parties that she hasn't thrown for you since she left the Philippines to live here in Houston. I repeat. It's a surprise party, so you have to act surprised when that happens. It's quite a huge gathering, with over a hundred expected guests. Don't tell my parents and the kids I told you about it. I know you don't like surprises, so I'm telling you exactly when the party is going to happen," Wooly said, smiling.

"And since you've already been holed up in my parents' house for almost a week now, James and I thought we'd take turns showing you the city," Wooly continued. "I already talked to my dad about it, and he agreed to adjust his fishing schedule."

My cousin paused, looking at James as if waiting for his friend to say something.

James also cleared his throat before speaking.

"This is on me, and I would understand if you don't want to do it," James continued.

I raised my eyebrow, holding my breath.

"We need an intern at the office. I don't know if Will already mentioned it to you, but we have established a small architectural firm together, and we need extra help right now. Will and I would like to ask you for a big favor. If you're interested in helping us at the firm, you can come to the office on Monday and we'll show you around. Our office is nice, and the people who work with us are friendly. It's a good place to be at, when you're not out shopping. Not a boring moment, I promise." James smiled as he made his offer.

He continued to explain to me that while I was not allowed to legally work in the United States because I was only a tourist, I had a choice to help out. I wouldn't be on their company's payroll, of course, but James and Wooly would pool resources from their own personal funds so I could be compensated accordingly. It would be like earning extra shopping money for my two to four weeks' worth of helping out.

What am I supposed to do in an architectural firm, anyway? Would I work as a receptionist, a mail person, or someone helping in constructing studios? I wondered.

"That's great," I said, feeling extremely grateful for what the two men were doing for me. "Thanks ... I'm speechless. Thanks, cuz for telling me about the party. And as for the intern position in your office, I want more time to think about it. Would it be okay if I let you know tomorrow night?" I asked James, my face red from shyness.

"Cool beans," James said quickly.

"Cool beans?" I asked, confused. I looked at the plates on the dining table. I didn't see any cool or cold beans.

Wait. What did he say again? I thought.

Wooly laughed. "'Cool beans' just means everything's cool, like 'we're good,' or 'okay,'" my cousin explained, smiling broadly, trying to hold his laughter. I bet if James were not with us, Wooly would have been clowning around already.

***

I suddenly snapped out of my musing as I came back to reality. I was back in my bedroom again, looking at the screen of the desktop computer in front of me. I saw a strange e-mail in my inbox on my Hotmail account.

The subject read "Urgent. Work. R Account Related."

"R Account" was a special code for my dream account in the advertising agency where I was employed in the Philippines. Using codes was my way of communicating with my account team when we had to pass on sensitive information to each other. We also used codes when talking about top secret prospect information that we didn't want other people to know about.

I looked at the name of the sender of the e-mail and gasped. It was Jay Anne. I quickly clicked on the e-mail and read its content, as my heart beat faster than normal.

Jan,

R is no longer assigned to you as promised. The agency won the pitch the other day, and Jean gave the account to Mark, the newly hired Senior account executive on the South wing. Mark will manage the eight brands of the group, effective tomorrow. I think Jean had no choice. You're not physically here in the agency, and the group is pretty demanding. They needed to know ASAP who the official AE would be so they could meet and begin the transition. I'm sorry you lost your dream account. I know you'll hate me for saying this, but I truly believe you'll get another one. And as if that's not enough, your biggest account, Alpha 1 officially left the company two days ago. They were dissatisfied with media and creative. Somebody in your team dropped the ball and you weren't here to fix it. The group exploded and called it quits. In the meantime, Alpha 2 and Alpha 3 moved to our sister agency. It's a New York call. Headquarters' decision. Global alignment.

I know I've doused you with a bucket of frigid water, Janelle, but it is what it is. I know it sucks, but it's not your fault. It's just another terrible case of bad timing.

But don't stress. It's not the end of the world. You're getting married soon with the man of your dreams. That's more important.

I hope you and Anthony are okay as well as the rest of the family.

By the way, how did the epic surprise turn out?

Call me.

Jay

Chapter 19

Jay Anne picked up on the first ring. I called him after I read his e-mail.

"Jay Anne, I've only been gone for a week. How did everything … I don't get it. It feels like a bucket of bad news was hanging over the top of my head, and all of a sudden, as soon as I got here, the rope holding the bucket broke," I said plaintively as I stared at my bright yellow luggage resting in a corner of my bedroom with its back to the wall.

"I really don't know what to tell you. And you're right. As soon as you left, your fort surprisingly collapsed. It's strange. But don't worry about it. I'll keep an eye on your other accounts for you and talk to Jean every day until she calms down. You're still one of the best AEs in the agency, if not the best, and don't you forget that," he said reassuringly.

Jean was my boss—the vice president for account management in the South Division of the ad agency I worked for, who supervised our team. She was a gracious, loving, intelligent, and considerate lady who stood as our second mother at work. However, she was also the kind of person who would panic the most, sometimes unnecessarily, every time our team lost or gained an account. I could imagine her well-manicured fingers holding a slim cigarette as she drank her decaf coffee while walking back and forth in her little office, barking at our team, trying her best to squeeze out the answers from every clueless soul in that room. But she listened to Jay Anne, despite her panic attacks. Hopefully my best friend, who could literally sell ice to an Eskimo, would be able to convince Jean to calm down or to pull herself together at least, for one more month until I returned.

"Well, let's change the topic. What was your voice-mail about, my dear? Why the hell is Houston freezing? Last time I checked, you were basking in the sunshine, getting ready to surprise the love of your life. Are you and Anthony okay? Are you okay? What happened?" Jay Anne asked, concerned.

"It's complicated," I said softly.

Jay Anne was quiet on the other end, waiting for me to explain myself. When I remained silent, he took a deep breath before speaking.

"Jan, you and I both know there's nothing more complicated than the life that I live. Speak up, girlfriend. What's going on in Houston?" Jay Anne demanded. His voice sounded exhausted yet determined, a little imposing yet kind.

I remembered when I was the one consoling him a year ago after he lost a huge pitch for the agency, not because his creative board was dull—after all, he was only one of the most brilliant copywriters in the country—but because of office politics.

A week after he recovered from his loss, he wrote me a poignant letter to thank me for being there with him in his lowest moment.

He wrote:

"… but in spite of that, I'm still here. My world goes on, and I move along with it. And what makes it easier for me is having someone who understands me, who knows what I'm going through. You are that someone, my friend. You've always walked with me through my darkest journeys without a single doubt, even though you hadn't a clue where I was going …"

I sighed. I wanted to tell Jay Anne everything, yet I didn't know where to begin. I wanted to describe Anthony's shocked reaction, Camilla's catty voice, and their dark, cluttered apartment that haunted my memory and gave me nightmares, but I couldn't find my voice. And as if my heartbreak wasn't painful enough, the career that I'd built over the years had started crumbling in my absence.

If my relationship had still been in full bloom, my lost accounts wouldn't have been such a big deal. Who cared if my professional bubble got deflated if I was going to marry the man of my dreams, anyway? My blissful life with Anthony was my impenetrable bubble, and everything else outside of it was trivial. But the bubble had burst, and I'd lost my armor. It left me vulnerable. Suddenly, every little pain, however trifling, became unbearable.

I tried to speak but couldn't. In a second, like a stream of water aching to connect with the grander river, my tears flowed incessantly from my eyes. My emotions took over me. I sobbed on the phone, pouring out all my heartache to my best friend who was thousands of miles away from me. When I calmed down, Jay Anne took the liberty to speak first.

"Jan, I wish I were there with you. But unfortunately, I'm on the other side of the world. I can't do much right now except listen to you. You know I'm a very busy person, but what the heck; I'll stay on the phone with you for as long as you want me to. I'm not going anywhere, Jan. When you're ready to talk, I'll be here."

I closed my eyes. After a few minutes, I found my voice. "Jay, Anthony cheated on me. I caught him in bed with another girl," I said softly.

Jay Anne was quiet. When he finally spoke, his voice was firm. "Was it Camilla?" I was so shocked, I almost dropped the phone.

"How did you know?" I asked.

"Hmm. Do you remember the house key that Anthony gave you for your birthday last year?" Jay Anne asked.

"Of course," I said.

"If you still remember, the key didn't come in a box. Anthony gave it to you as it was, hanging on a key chain," he explained.

"Right," I said, puzzled.

"Well, it came with a box. Anthony just didn't give the box to you. What you didn't know was Anthony threw the box in your trash can at the office. He did that while waiting for you, before you two headed out to celebrate your birthday," he said.

"Okay," I said, trying to see where our conversation was leading.

"I saw the box, Jan, and I confronted Anthony about it. But of course, he laughed it off, saying it was just a prank. He explained the joke behind it so well that I felt stupid for even asking about it," he continued.

"I don't understand. What about the box?" I asked.

"Jan, your gift came in a little pink box with gold engraving. When I saw it … when I saw what was engraved on it, I knew why Anthony didn't give it to you," he said.

I could feel my heart beating faster, my face turning red.

"What was engraved on the box?" I asked.

Jay Anne drew a deep breath before speaking.

"For my Camilla."

Chapter 20

"Janelle, let's go."

I heard Wooly's voice on the other side of the door as I took off the last of my curlers from my hair. The sink where I was fixing myself was connected to the bathroom conveniently located next to my bedroom, which was also connected to the sink by the guest room. Wooly spent the night last night in the guest room.

"Coming! Give me five more minutes," I said, trying my best not to shout as I brushed my hair back in place. I had just finished setting my freshly blow-dried hair with hair spray, looking meticulously in the mirror, making sure my baby hairs were not sticking out as usual.

"Okay. I'll wait for you in the driveway," Wooly said.

I looked at my bedside clock as I grabbed my favorite Lacoste Sport shoulder bag. It was only five o'clock in the morning.

Yesterday—the day after I spoke with Jay Anne—I didn't have the energy to do anything else except browse through the *Harry Potter* book that I wasn't able to finish reading on the plane during my flight to Houston. My good uncle tried to cheer me up by inviting me to sing *karaoke* with him in the living room, but when he started singing Filipino love songs over and over and over, my depression began setting in, and I had to excuse myself so I could go back and hide in my bedroom.

My uncle probably got worried when I didn't come out of my bedroom to eat dinner, so he made an emergency phone call to Wooly so my cousin could come by and smoke me out of my cave. Wooly arrived at the house last night, shortly after eight o'clock. He brought me *tiramisu*.

I smiled to myself as I realized my cousin had always been successful at luring me out of hiding with food. And because I couldn't resist my favorite Italian dessert, I gave in. I was out of the bedroom and into the kitchen where Wooly was having dinner in less than five minutes.

"Hey there. I got *bistek tagalog* with freshly cooked rice and a slice of mouthwatering *tiramisu* for you. You can eat them in no particular order. I'm not picky. Have a seat," Wooly said.

Bistek tagalog is beef steak in the Philippines.

"You know me so well. Thank you, cuz," I said as I patted Wooly's shoulders appreciatively.

He then told me he was going to stay over at his parents' house for the night because he was going to take me to a car show the following morning. Since all I could do that day was plot the downfall of Anthony and Camilla in every fashion imaginable, I felt I could use a break and experience something I didn't have any passion for—cars.

***

I snapped back to reality when I heard the garage door opening. I realized Wooly was waiting for me outside in the driveway. I quickly turned off the light in my bedroom before gently closing the door behind me. I stepped out of the house quickly, knowing Wooly wanted to leave early. He told me the parking space at the car show could get pretty crowded as early as six in the morning. As soon as I emerged from the house, Wooly ran back to the house to arm it and lock the doors. While I waited for Wooly, I stood in the driveway rubbing my palms together to stay warm.

I noticed a black car behind Wooly's red sports car. Its engine was running. The person behind the wheel looked like a man wearing a dark beanie. His head was bent down as if he were fixing something on the floor of the passenger side of the car. When he lifted his head back up, he smiled and waved at me.

It was James. Even under the dim light in the driveway, I recognized the blond highlights sticking out of his hat.

"Get inside the car, cuz. We'll follow James," Wooly told me as he closed the garage door with his remote control. I stood mesmerized watching a remote-controlled garage door close on its own for the first time in my life.

I heard Wooly getting into his car, so I quickly got in the passenger side, pulling my red beanie closer to the back of my neck as the cold wind hit my exposed skin.

"What gathering are we going to again?" I asked, curious.

"It's just a car show with a bunch of people wanting to show off their cars. Our client hosts this event every quarter. Car clubs get invited to come for free, while our client pays the fee to hold the event in a big parking space, usually located in an outdoor mall or the top parking garage of a building downtown. You get to see nice cars, meet people from the car scene, and get introduced to potential clients who need architectural services while enjoying a cup of coffee. You'll like it, I think. Have you been to one before?" Wooly asked.

"Not really. I've seen a group of kids racing in Greenhills in the Philippines at one point, showing off cars that their parents probably own, but I don't think that's a big thing back home. At least, not in my circle. For one, there's not a lot of road space, and there's not a lot of sports cars," I said while stifling a yawn.

"I see. Does Anthony like sports cars?" Wooly asked casually.

I wasn't prepared to hear my ex-fiancé's name. It felt like my body froze in mid-air. Wooly noticed my discomfort and quickly apologized.

"I'm sorry. I still don't know why Anthony did what he did to you, but at this very moment, just an FYI, cuz, I would love to kick his ass," Wooly said without pausing.

I touched Wooly's elbow lightly to show my gratitude but didn't say anything.

"What kind of sports car are you driving? I haven't seen you drive this car since I came here," I said, changing the topic.

"It's a 1999 Acura Integra coupe. I don't drive it every day. I clean and polish it every month, but it only comes out of the bat cave when I'm racing or going to a meet," Wooly said proudly.

"You race? Like street race?" I asked.

"No ma'am. I used to be a street racer, but I now responsibly and legally race on the race track during events. I can't race in the streets no more. I'm a father now. I have too much to lose," Wooly said.

"That's good. What about James?" I asked.

"What about James? He drives a Mitsubishi Evolution VI. A high-performance sports car, a TME, turbo charged, five-speed manual," Wooly explained.

"Hmmm. Impressive. Does he race too?" I asked, unfamiliar with the car jargon Wooly mentioned. The closest I got to car racing was playing *Gran Turismo* on weekends with my younger brother.

"James races on the track more often than I do. I know he still races in the streets once in a while, but he's gotten so much better than when he was younger," Wooly answered.

"How old is he?" I asked.

"He's twenty-six," Wooly replied.

"Is he Japanese, Korean?"

"He's Japanese-American. His dad is half-Caucasian, half-Japanese, and his mom is pure Japanese," Wooly said.

"He's mixed?"

"Yeah. One-fourth Caucasian, three-fourths Asian."

"Is he married?"

"No. He's single."

"Does he have a girlfriend?"

"Not that I know of, but I could be wrong."

My cousin looked at me for a brief second with a grin on his face. "Wait a minute. Are you interested in James?" he asked.

"What do you mean? ... Oh, no you're not ... You're crazy. I just met him," I said, embarrassed, scolding myself in my head for asking Wooly such silly, intrusive questions.

Wooly looked at the road again, steadily following James's car in front of us. He seemed deep in thought, as if figuring out something that was bothering him. After a few minutes he smiled broadly, looked at me, and asked, "Would you consider going out with James?"

Chapter 21

James was treated like a rock star at the car show by women from all walks of life, in all sizes and packages. As soon as he parked his shiny black sports car next to Wooly's red coupe, women came flocking to him like metal to a magnet.

The bubbly groupies marched onto our spot to chat with the Japanese-American hotshot, even managing to wrap their snakelike arms around his shoulders to take pictures with him while gushing at his Evo.

Compared to the pretty, curvaceous, and tall women brimming with sex appeal who flirted with James, I looked like the ugly duckling watching by, sadly singing the 70s classic "At Seventeen," while sulking unnoticed in my dark lonely corner.

Contrary to what my cousin assumed, his chef-architect friend already had his hands full. With all the attention he was getting from all those gorgeous female car enthusiasts, Wooly's assumption that James may be interested to go out on a date with me just got thrown out the window.

Not that it really mattered. It was just my silly self-esteem getting in the way.

When your fiancé has just kicked you in the face by sleeping with another woman, all the pride and confidence you used to surround yourself with suddenly fizzles into thin air, leaving you with nothing but doubts and uncertainties about yourself. You then begin to question your attractiveness and whether or not you even had any to begin with. You become obsessed with your marketability, always wanting to know if you're desirable enough to attract the opposite sex.

That's what happened to me.

I had no intention of dating or going out with any guy, but after my breakup with Anthony, the realization that a good-looking, sought-after bachelor was not physically attracted to me was a huge dent on my ego and quite difficult to digest.

"Do y'all want to grab a cup of coffee first? There's a Starbucks on the other side. We can walk there quickly, get coffee or have breakfast, then we can walk around to see what everybody's got."

James's voice sounded relaxed, as if he hadn't just been mobbed. I was so deeply engrossed in my own musing, I didn't even notice that his female fans had already left. I also didn't know how long James and Wooly had been standing there next to me, waiting for my response.

"Tara let's!" I said.

The two men looked at me strangely, not understanding what just came out of my mouth.

"In Tagalog it means 'let's go,'" I explained with as much enthusiasm as I could muster. I didn't want James or Wooly to notice how insecure, ugly, and depressed those aggressive women mobbing James a few minutes ago had made me feel. I let the two men lead the way as I walked behind them, doing my best to catch up. James would look back at me from time to time, making sure I was still following behind.

After lining up inside Starbucks to get our hot cups of coffee, we headed out to the cold parking lot to look at the hundreds of show cars parked in every corner of the outdoor mall, with their owners standing proudly close by.

But the car show only lasted for two hours. By eight o'clock, many people were already heading out, including the owners of the cars who had lined up as early as dawn to wow the thick morning crowd.

The day started wrong for me, but I had to say I enjoyed the whole experience. I had the rare opportunity to see sports cars, vintage and modern, that I'd never seen before. It was fascinating to actually see and touch the red and yellow Ferraris, candy-colored Lamborghinis,

Porsches, Lexus's, and Audi sports editions, which I only used to see in my brother Miko's car magazines. James's Evo VI and Wooly's Acura Integra were a hit among car enthusiasts too, especially the younger crowd.

"Jan, I have to go to my client's office to pick up a document. It's quite a distance from here. Would you mind if James takes you home instead? I'll drop by the house to have dinner tonight with Mom and Dad and the kids when I come back from the gym," Wooly told me when we got back to our parking spot.

I looked at James, not knowing what to say.

"Sure, I can take Janelle home. Not a problem at all," James said to Wooly.

"Cool beans. I'll see you later, Jan. You guys take care. James, I'll call you later, man," Wooly said as he hurried to get into his car.

When Wooly left, James asked if I wanted to have breakfast first before he took me back to my aunt and uncle's house. "There's a breakfast place around here somewhere. It's only eight o'clock. We can grab a bite before heading home. Do you like pancakes?" James asked while opening the door on the passenger side of his car for me.

Before I could reply, two young girls wearing very short denim shorts and skimpy tank tops came by. They were giggling when they reached James's car.

"Hi, James! So glad we found you here. If you're free tonight, please drop by our event. Here's my card with my phone number. Let me know what time you'll be there so I can wait for you outside. The party starts at nine o'clock." The bedroom-voiced girl with the long hair handed her business card to James. She then looked at me from head to toe and smiled.

"Oh. I didn't know you were with your little sister. You can bring her too if you want, but I'm not sure if she's old enough. Call me, okay? See you later," the girl told James before heading out with her friend.

Chapter 22

The waitress brought our breakfast to our table. I didn't realize I was hungry until I smelled the inviting aroma of freshly cooked turkey bacon and scrambled eggs next to slices of ripe tomatoes, pineapple, banana slices, grapes, and oranges.

After the car meet and my not-so-pleasant encounter with the young woman who invited James for an event, my designated driver took me to a cozy western-themed restaurant that served breakfast as early as six in the morning.

It was warm inside, and the décor was classy. I felt comfortable sitting in front of my gracious companion, who was busy cutting his pancakes and bacon strips after dousing them with maple syrup.

James put his navy-blue beanie back on to cover his shoulder-length hair which made his soft brown eyes look even more prominent.

"How's your food?" James asked after taking a sip from his glass of orange juice.

"It's great. Thanks for bringing me to this place," I said.

"Sure. I don't come here often because it's too far from the city, but when the guys and I get together for car meets around the area, this is a good stopover. More expensive than the regular pancake place, but it's worth it," James said in between bites.

"I see. Do you also live in Houston?" I asked, curious. I didn't really know anything about him except he was one of Wooly's closest friends and business partner.

"I live in Sugar Land. It's part of the Houston metro area," he said.

"How far is that from my aunt's house?" I asked.

"Let's see. My apartment is about ten minutes away from my parents' house. My parents live in a subdivision that's about twenty minutes away from your aunt's house. So about thirty minutes. Will's house is on the other side, farther from where I live, but it's much closer to your aunt's house. Will's house being closer to his parents' works with your uncle's schedule, because Uncle Boy has to pick up Sophia and Kenneth every day from school," James explained.

"How long have you known Wooly? You seem pretty close to the family," I said.

"It's a long story, and I won't tell you unless you promise to split dessert with me," James grinned, teasing.

"Oh. Dessert after pancakes? Sure thing. I love sweets," I said smiling.

James called the waitress, who attentively rushed to our table. She was a pleasant-looking older lady wearing a blue dress and a nice little white apron. She smiled as she took James's additional order. When she left, James looked at me and began narrating his so-called long story.

"Okay. Well, I have an older brother. His name is Patrick.

"He's my one and only sibling. We were born in Brooklyn, New York, and grew up there until our parents decided to move to Houston. I was only twelve when I came here. My brother is five years older than me.

"Patrick met Will in high school, and they have been best friends ever since. They both went to college. Will studied to be an architect, and my brother went to med school. They both graduated a few years later. Will became an architect after passing the board, and my brother earned a medical degree," James explained.

I suddenly thought about my family in the Philippines. My older sister, Bianca—my over-achieving sibling—just passed the bar exam too, proudly following in the footsteps of our mother.

I looked at James as he continued with his story.

"A year or so later, my brother took his medical board exam and passed. He became an intern in one of the biggest hospitals at the

Medical Center here in Houston. That's where he met this Filipino guy named Greg, who'd just come from the Philippines. Greg was an older guy. If I remember correctly, he was at least five years older than Patrick. But anyway, Greg and Patrick became good friends. My brother introduced Greg to Will, and all three of them became inseparable," he said.

I noticed while he narrated his story that James seemed focused, as if being unable to recall every detail was a sin he didn't want to commit against his older brother. Suddenly he paused, looking at me.

"Janelle, I'm warning you. This is going to be a pretty long story, so bear with me," he said, half-grinning.

"Go on," I said, smiling.

"All right. So Greg was working then as a nurse at the hospital. Aside from being cheerful, my brother noticed Greg's impressive professional demeanor, not too common in many of the staff working at the hospital. My brother had also noticed how intelligent Greg's analyses of certain medical situations were, while they were on the same shift together.

"Eventually, Greg told Patrick and Will that he was a board-certified physician in the Philippines who wanted to practice medicine here in the States. When the guys asked why he was working as a nurse at the hospital, Greg said it was the fastest and easiest way for him to study, get another medical degree, pass the board, and practice as a licensed doctor here in America, if he got lucky," James narrated.

"Wow. Really? I didn't know a doctor would work as a nurse just to practice medicine legally in a different country," I said, amazed and shocked at the same time.

"I know, right? Pat and I couldn't believe Greg's story either," James said before continuing.

"Since we both grew up here, none of us were aware of what some people had to go through to get the privileges we enjoy and, you know, take for granted. Patrick was actually turned off by a few people who dismissed Greg's opinion because they thought Greg should confine himself to taking care of the patients' bedside needs. But Pat couldn't blame the staff. It's part of their system.

"But anyway, to make a long story short, Greg eventually earned his medical degree and passed the medical board on his first try. He became an intern at another hospital here in Houston for a year, and then decided to go to London because he was offered a job in one of the biggest hospitals there.

"After working for a few months in London, Greg asked Patrick if he also wanted to work in the same hospital in London with him. So after several drinking sessions with Will and my dad, Patrick was finally convinced to go to London. Pat now works with Greg in the hospital there as a neurosurgical resident in training." James paused to drink the remainder of his orange juice while I contemplated Greg's inspiring story.

"Oh. By the way, Pat met his fiancée at the hospital, too. She's a younger nurse, and they're getting married next year. And Greg now lives with his wife and kids in London. He petitioned them from the Philippines," James said after putting his glass down and wiping his mouth with his napkin.

"What a great story," I remarked, trying my best to conceal my emotions. Happy endings tended to make me cry. "And congratulations to your brother on getting married next year," I added.

"Thanks," James said, smiling.

"Is your brother's fiancée Asian?" I asked.

Actually, I meant to ask if she was also Japanese, but didn't know if James would be offended if I was too specific.

"My brother's fiancée is Singaporean. She's pretty good-looking and petite like you," James said.

I smiled, not knowing if he only meant petite like me, or if he meant pretty good-looking and petite like me. That was my ego talking, fishing for a little bit of a compliment from a race track superstar who had made me feel extremely unattractive that morning at the car show.

"I see. But when did you come into the picture?" I asked, my lips quivering.

I looked at my plate, contemplating whether to eat my leftover pancakes or not, wondering if I could still save a piece underneath a mound of gooey strawberries covered in maple syrup.

"Good question. I thought you'd never ask," James said, smiling, looking at me as if he could read my mind. I dropped my fork on top of my plate and tried to look at James's pretty eyes instead, hoping against hope he didn't notice my flushed face.

"When Patrick left, I hung out with Will, and we have been best friends ever since, despite our age difference. Will is five years older than me but he's so cool, I can't even tell the difference. When my brother left, I was barely getting out of my teenage phase, and I missed Pat really bad. Will has become my older brother since. I studied harder in college because of him. He inspired me to become an architect. My parents treat Will like he's part of the family, and I look up to your uncle and aunt like they're my own parents. So there. End of story. The end." James smiled as he finished narrating his story.

"That's sweet. Losing someone really close to you, then gaining another one in such a short time," I said softly, suddenly remembering my predicament.

I lost Anthony, I thought, *but unlike James, I don't have anyone who could easily replace my fiancé. The wound Anthony left is so deep, I don't know if I'm capable of trusting anyone, ever again.*

James seemed to realize the reason behind my comment. He suddenly became thoughtful, seemingly awkward, not sure what to say next. Luckily, our waitress came back to our table to save the day. She brought the heavenly plate of dessert with two scoops of ice cream covered with caramel syrup, sitting on top of a slice of apple pie smothered with golden pecan nuts.

"Perfect timing," James said.

James and I both reached for the small plates set on the table for us by the lovely waitress. We then took our spoons and dug in, one scoop of vanilla ice cream and half a slice of apple pie each.

The dessert was perfect. In fact, it was so good, we didn't even bother to talk while eating.

Halfway through his plate, James put his spoon down and drank his water from the huge goblet next to him.

He grinned after putting the goblet down.

"Yikes. Too sweet," he said.

I laughed, trying my best not to swallow the pecan nuts in my mouth without chewing them first.

"But why would you order dessert after eating pancakes, anyway?" I asked, amused.

"So you could taste this restaurant's special. You'll only be here for a few more weeks. You have to get the best of what Houston has to offer at every place you visit," he said, smiling.

I smiled back, grateful for his thoughtfulness.

"By the way," he said, "I meant to ask before I forget. Have you thought about our offer to you the other night? Did you have a decision yet? Today's Sunday. Would you like to start working with us at the office tomorrow?" James asked.

I looked at him, trying not to look flustered. I secretly panicked within, and thoughtlessly took my time finishing my scoop of ice cream before responding to his questions, to which I didn't have an answer yet. I didn't know how to tell him I wasn't trying to be rude, but I couldn't find the right words to say. Slowly, my mind began to wander. I thought about the girl who sized me up at the car meet, my dream account that went down the drain back home, Jay Anne being thousands of miles away, Anthony and Camilla sharing one bed in their dark, gloomy apartment, and my wedding that would never see the light of day. I realized I did need a monumentally challenging diversion to make my last few weeks in Houston bearable.

"I've made my decision," I told James.

He looked at me casually, probably rolling his eyes in his head for having to wait that long for a simple answer.

"I'll see you tomorrow at your office, nine o'clock sharp," I said.

"Wait. On which time zone? Houston time or Filipino Time?" he asked, teasing.

"What do you mean?" I asked back, feigning ignorance.

But of course, I knew what he was talking about. After all, I was only one of the most notorious advocates of Filipino Time back home. I remembered those people who were victimized by my infamous habit of coming late to non-work-related appointments, making them wait until "their hair and eye sockets turned white" before finally showing up.

But that had already changed, and I planned to prove the good-looking architect wrong.

I'm in America. The so-called "Filipino Time" will be removed from my book. It will be cataloged as a myth—a misconception whose only purpose on earth is to fuel the jokes circulating about the Filipinos' terrible habit of showing up one to five hours later than scheduled. My poor time management will then miraculously spin around just like my picture-perfect little life had suddenly gone imperfect. "Turumpo," in Tagalog; a spinning top that could go both ways like a devil turning saint, darkness turning light, or the complete opposite.

I hoped James couldn't hear my thoughts as he was busy talking to our waitress, who was refilling his glass of water.

How else can America change my life? I silently wondered. *I guess I have four more weeks to find out.*

Chapter 23

It was exactly twenty-eight minutes past eight o'clock. I smoothed my clothes as I waited in the lobby of James and Wooly's architectural firm after being dropped off by my uncle.

I wore my tan A-line skirt and paired it with my light pink sweater. I also wore my beige tights and dark brown suede tall boots. I bought my outfit yesterday from a store called Dillard's, when I panic-shopped for some business attire I regretted not packing in my luggage when I left for Houston a week ago.

I checked my reflection in the glass doors, proud of myself for coming in half an hour early. Compared to my hectic mornings back home in the Philippines, dressing up in Houston to go anywhere was a breeze. Perhaps it had something to do with my limited closet. Not having a lot of choices could really make a big difference to someone like me who could never decide what to wear on a daily basis.

It may also have had to do with my brand-new environment and my state of helplessness as a tourist, not having my car with me, relying on other people to drive me to places, for which I was compelled to show my gratitude and appreciation by being extra courteous. Respect for other people's time was a huge example of courtesy, and that was what I intended to let James know.

"Hey. Looking sharp today," James said.

The young architect looked sophisticated and businesslike in his black dress pants and flint-colored Oxford shirt as he emerged from the glass doors to greet me. He was also wearing black-rimmed glasses, which made him look like a fashion model for GQ magazine.

"You are too," I said, smiling.

"So, are you ready?" James asked.

"Sure," I said, not knowing what to expect from what I'd gotten myself into as I followed him through the glass doors.

He was not kidding when he said their workplace was nice. It reminded me so much of our work space in the advertising agency in the Philippines.

James and Wooly's architectural firm—or studio, as my cousin liked to call it—looked picture-perfect. It had dark wooden floors enhanced by bright contemporary area rugs. The classy design of the furniture was a combination of chic and comfort. Wall décor accented the multi-colored walls. There were three rooms within the spacious studio, and half of the walls in each room were made of glass. Based on the name plates outside the doors, it looked like one room belonged to Wooly, another room belonged to James, and the biggest room in between was the conference room. In one corner of the studio was a small area filled with cubicles painted in white and orange. The built-in book shelves in the cubicles were lined with colorful binders. I could see three people sitting in their cubicles already, preoccupied, working on their laptops and desktop computers. At the far end of the studio was a water dispenser located next to a tiny room, which I assumed was the pantry.

James led me to the conference room. Inside was a long, white oval table with ten white swivel chairs around it. The chairs were held by shiny metallic legs. Underneath the table was a plush rug in bright orange.

"Have a seat," James offered.

I looked at the windows and saw a ray of sunlight come through, illuminating one of the chairs, the soft light trickling through the corner where a huge painting was situated. I felt instantly comfortable and a bit energized by the splash of colors in the room. The dark, polished wooden floor absorbed the brightness, creating balance in the beautiful symmetry.

"So, welcome to our studio. This is our conference room. In this room we do a lot of brainstorming to come up with concepts for our clients. We have two junior designers-slash-architects in-house. Will and I are the lead architects, and we represent the firm to our clients. We're currently independent, but a big architectural company has recently invited our little firm to merge with them, and we're looking into that as part of our growth in the near future.

"We'll bring them business and we'll help in some of their projects, and they'll pay our overhead. We intend to keep them happy, but we'll demand for them to pretty much leave us alone to function on our own. You're from advertising, I know, because your cousin told me about your job in the Philippines, so you must know the culture. You have to develop a thicker skin when it comes to the staff and also our clients, if you'd have the opportunity to meet them.

"I'm really glad you said yes to this offer, because I know you're a grade A worker, and we need a lot of help. Will isn't here today, unfortunately. He has a meeting the whole morning until mid-afternoon, so I'll stick around for you until noon. After that, you'll be on your own. I'd love to take you to lunch, but I have to run and meet with a client at one o'clock. But don't worry, I'll be back to pick you up at three o'clock and take you back to your aunt's house or the mall, or wherever you plan to spend the rest of your afternoon," James explained.

"Okay. Got it. So what do I do today? Are you my boss? Should I call you 'Sir James'?" I asked.

James smiled.

"I wish I were, but I'm really not. You won't have a boss. You're an interim person, and you're only here for a short time, so we won't need any of that formality. And you can call me James like everybody else around here. What you'll do today is totally beneath your qualifications, but I think you'll have fun," James said with a grin on his face.

"Like what?" I asked expectantly.

"You'll be ... filing," James said hesitantly, as if waiting for me to pull my hair, throw the swivel chair at him, and run out of the room like a crazy woman.

"That's ... good. When do I start?" I said, smiling.

"You'll start as soon as we're done with this brief orientation. And don't worry. You'll work on clean files, no crappy stuff. You just have to label the file drawers and stack them inside as organized as you can," James explained, justifying my new role.

"Oh, I can do that," I said, thinking of the hundreds of complex contracts and presentations I had had to muscle my way around in the corporate jungles of advertising in the Philippines, just to get business; a signed approval from some of my difficult clients, who felt they were entitled to make our lives miserable for every single centavo they dropped into the bucket.

"Cool. Now, wait here. I'll call the gang so I can introduce you to them," James said.

I sat in one of the swivel chairs, amazed at my new surroundings, waiting for James and his so-called gang to come back to the room.

I was actually looking forward to having my first taste of corporate life in America. Being a file girl who has friends in high places would be the perfect opportunity for me to get immersed in this brand-new work environment as I interacted with different people in different levels, from the bottom all the way to the top.

The door of the conference room slowly opened and a handful of people walked in. I stood up from my chair.

"Everyone, this is Janelle. She'll be here in the office for a few weeks just to help out. I want everyone to be familiar with her. Memorize her features so you don't freak out when you see her walking around in the studio," James teased.

"Just kidding. Janelle, these are the wonderful people that work with me and Will. They're awesome and very helpful. I'm sure they'll make you feel welcome here," James added, looking at me as if he was expecting a spiel or a pompom dance or something.

I took the cue and spoke timidly in front of everybody. "Hello, everyone! My name is Janelle. I'm visiting from the Philippines. As James said, Will is my cousin. James and Will asked if I could help out with filing for just a few weeks until I go back home to the Philippines. It's nice to meet all of you. If you need me to assist you, please don't hesitate to let James or I know, and I'll be more than glad to help," I said.

One female employee with dark curly hair and a button nose whispered to the person next to her. Because I was born with semi-bionic ears, I overheard what she said.

"Did you hear that?" the female employee whispered. "She can speak English."

Chapter 24

I walked behind James, careful not to fall down the long flight of stairs leading to the lobby-*cum*-reception area of one of the most beautiful golf courses I had ever seen in my life. Being a rowdy fan of professional basketball, playing the glamorous sport of golf was not my cup of tea, but I did appreciate the calming beauty of a golf course.

The country club James took me to looked elegant and huge, with a breathtaking view of the vast golf course, the perfectly trimmed grass sprawled like green satin sheets under the powder-blue-colored skies.

Just an hour ago, James picked me up at the office—three o'clock, to be exact—like he promised. He found me in the conference room next to his own private office, where I was busy stacking the folders I'd meticulously labeled and sorted into a big file bin.

"I'm back. How was your first day at the office?" James asked, smiling, as he stood by the door, holding his briefcase and jacket.

He had just come back from his meeting looking exhausted—quite the opposite of the bubbly person who had greeted me at the reception area when I first came in that morning.

"It's great," I responded. "It wasn't that easy in the beginning, but I think I've developed a system. I only have a few left to label and file," I added.

"Cool. I knew you'd be awesome," he said.

I checked my watch and gasped. "Oh wow. It's way past three o'clock already. I'm sorry. Let me get my purse and then we can head out, unless you still have some stuff to do in your office. In that case, I'll wait because I really don't have a choice, do I? I don't have a car, and I don't know how to get out of here. You're driving," I blabbered.

James laughed, walking towards me, parking his jacket and briefcase in one of the swivel chairs.

"Did you have lunch yet?" James asked.

I looked at him and nodded, remembering my interaction with one of the office staff in the tiny break room by the water dispenser. I could still vividly recall what had happened.

"Hi, Sharmadelle!" the petite Caucasian girl warming her lunch in the microwave said to me.

"Hey. How are you? It's Janelle with a 'J.' My name is Janelle," I said, smiling. I noticed the girl had green eyes and looked quite stunning. She was wearing a dark-green-and-white knee-length wrap-around dress with a classy print, and matching nude high heels.

"Oh. Your name sounds so American. So, what is your Asian name?" she said while carefully taking out her ceramic bowl from the microwave. I looked at her with a puzzled expression on my face, not quite understanding what she said.

"Like, you know. We have a Vietnamese employee here. Her name is Tram. That's her Vietnamese name, but her American name is Tammy. So, what's yours?" she added.

I felt I had to say something but hadn't a clue what to tell her. I remembered my brother back home. His name was Michael but we all called him Miko, but that was not his Filipino name. That was actually his favorite expression when he was a child, when he wanted my mom to give him his milk bottle already.

"I want my milk," was what he had meant to say but couldn't pronounce the words right. His toddler tongue kept saying "miko" as in "milk *ko*," which meant "my milk" in English.

In the Philippines, we call that *Tag-Lish*, as in combining Tagalog and English.

Miko eventually became my brother's nickname.

Filipinos were colonized by many countries, which enriched our culture, making us a little more diverse and fortunately or unfortunately, a bit more westernized than we probably should be; our names reflected such a cultural attribute. Only a few Filipinos now, especially of the new generation, had native sounding names.

If I had a Filipino name, it would not have been *Maganda* or *Marikit* for beauty. Instead, I would have been named *Maarte* by my parents as punishment for being vain and a slave to trends. Instead of Maria Janelle, I would have been baptized in our church and registered in our municipality as Janelle Maarte Marquez, to my utter horror.

"I'm sorry. Did you say something?" the pretty girl looked at me funny. I didn't realize I'd been staring at her.

"Oh. I'm sorry. I didn't say anything," I apologized. "I don't have a Filipino name. It's simply Janelle. What's your name again?" I asked.

"Kathy. But people call me Kate around here. You can call me whatever you want. I'm sorry if I was being weird. I was just curious. Your cousin, our boss, grew up here in the States. I was just wondering how Filipinos who didn't grow up here are like. You know what I mean?" Kate said, looking genuinely uncomfortable.

"Oh. Not a problem at all. I completely understand. It's nice to meet you. I guess I'll see you later," I said as I started to leave the pantry, completely forgetting what I went in there for.

***

I snapped out of my musing. I didn't realize I'd been looking at James's tired eyes while my mind wandered.

"Oh. No. I didn't eat. I haven't yet. I forgot to eat lunch. But I'm fine. I'm not really hungry," I said quickly.

James shook his head. "Janelle. You can't do that. Your uncle will go ballistic when he finds out we're starving you. You know what? I haven't had lunch yet either. Our meeting took too long, and I had to beat the traffic to get here on time. Tell you what. Why don't you stop what you're doing and continue tomorrow? Grab your purse. Let's go get something to eat," James said.

James took me to the country club for lunch. Apparently, he and Wooly were VIP members and it served as their haven, their big escape from the toxic world of designing and marketing.

As we found our spot in the restaurant by the driving range, I sat in one of the comfortable chairs while James ordered dinner. He ordered extra for my cousin, who promised to meet us later that evening.

"Do you know how to play golf?" James asked when the waiter left.

"No, I don't. I'm not that sophisticated," I said.

James grinned.

"Golf is not about glamour. It's a relaxing sport to take your mind off your daily stress. You condition your mind in a calm environment, and your body follows. It's a good workout, too, because you're using your body's strength to drive the ball to where you want it to go, as far as you will your mind and your body to," he said, speaking like a teacher training a novice.

"Very interesting," I said, impressed.

We were seated at an outdoor restaurant that resembled a huge covered patio. In front of us was our driving range area with green mats that looked like real trimmed grass.

"So what interests you?" James asked as he inspected the clubs behind our table. There were different ones, in various sizes, for both men and women.

"A lot. It depends on what you specifically want to know," I said, hoping I didn't come across as arrogant.

"Fair enough," James said, picking a club that looked long and heavy. "Do you like music? Do you listen to bands?" he added.

"Most definitely. Yes," I said enthusiastically.

I loved watching music videos at home on weekends and watching concerts with my friends after work. I had already watched big names perform in concert, like Alanis Morrissette, Phil Collins, Barry Manilow, Bush, Pearl Jam, The Corrs, Sting, and yes, MC Hammer.

"What kind of music do you listen to? Any favorite bands?" James asked.

"I like male rock bands like Pearl Jam, Live, and R.E.M., The Smashing Pumpkins, Toad the Wet Sprocket, and Third Eye Blind, and Mr. Big, and some local bands at home like Wolfgang, and The Eraserheads," I said brightly, not knowing where the conversation was leading to.

"Cool. Why do you like them? I don't mean to stereotype, but most girls like boy bands and all-girl bands that sing mushy, pop covers," James said, teasing.

"I don't know. I like some boy bands. I think they're cute," I said. "But I like bands mainly for their music, not for looks," I added.

James smiled.

"Why are you asking?"

"Nothing. Just curious. Come on, let's eat," James said as the waiter came back with our feast. I reached for my Diet Coke and picked at some french fries.

"The Smashing Pumpkins. Why do you like them? Is it because of the singer or the band's music?" James asked, going back to our previous topic.

"Honestly, I like their music, but I like the guitarist more. He's cute. I love his voice. He seems sensitive; his songs are the complete opposite of his image onstage," I said.

James looked at me, pondering in between bites. "You're talking about the guy with the long hair?" he asked.

"Yes. He dresses nicely, too. Fashionable. Although his looks, in my opinion, are just secondary to his character. He's Japanese-American. I love Japanese guys, especially Japanese anime cartoon characters. Like Prince Zardoz of *Voltes V*, if you're familiar with the character. Long-haired Japanese guys are cute," I said.

Regretting what I said almost immediately, I looked down at my food in utmost embarrassment, wanting to reach out for my imaginary "invisibility cloak," and hoping against hope James didn't think I was hitting on him.

Always eat on time, Janelle. Skipping a meal makes you delirious, I thought.

"So, you like the long-haired, fashion-conscious Asian guitarist because you think he's good-looking and lots of female fans scream when he's onstage," James analyzed as if he didn't think what I'd just said was weird.

"No. I like him because he looks like a person of substance, despite his pretty boy image. I'm not ... shallow. I'd scream at concerts, but for a better reason than good looks," I said shyly.

James was quiet for a few minutes, making me curious on why he was so interested in the topic. "Substance. I like that word," he said, smiling.

"Something my ex-fiancé is lacking," I said out of the blue.

It took me a few seconds to realize what had just come out of my mouth, and I could feel my face turning red. I wondered if that was what Americans called a "double whammy," as in being in two awkward situations in less than five minutes. I knew Jay Anne wouldn't forgive me for my tactlessness.

James already knew about my sob story. Wooly told me earlier my aunt accidentally talked about it when he and James picked her up at the hospital last night.

I looked at James, who seemed frozen in front of me. "I'm sorry. I wasn't even thinking about that. I apologize if I asked too many questions," he said.

"Oh no. I should be the one apologizing. It's my fault. I didn't mean to bring it up," I said quickly.

We ate silently for a few minutes, feeling awkward, unsure of what to talk about. Suddenly, we heard someone scream behind us. James and I quickly turned around.

"James!" shouted the little boy in his cute Spider Man ensemble. James stood up from his chair and smiled at the boy as soon as he recognized him. On the other hand, I stared in disbelief, not at the little boy, but at the young woman standing behind him. The woman looked shocked upon seeing me as well, but she didn't say anything. James then turned to the woman and asked, "Camilla, what are you doing here?"

Chapter 25

Back in Anthony's apartment, Camilla had looked ferocious—like a wild animal, proud of her fangs, ready to shred anyone that would get in her way.

Back home in the Philippines, we describe that kind of demeanor as *bangis* or *astig*; Tagalog terms referring to the strong, remarkable, sometimes annoying character of someone who fears nothing and no one.

That fateful night when I broke into Anthony's apartment—the home that she stole from me—I was the subject of her loathing, the thorn in her side, the fire that she could never put out. Although she was not able to physically hurt me during our brief confrontation, her vicious, territorial body language almost broke me. But as she stood next to James at the picturesque country club, she looked surprisingly meek, uncomfortable, and jittery, holding the child in the Spider Man costume in front of her like a shield.

As much as I wanted to wring her neck and pull her hair out, I restrained myself for the sake of the child who was looking up at James like the latter was Prince of Marvel Comics. At the same time, my mind was swirling with questions.

How in the world did James know Camilla? How small could our world really be? Did my aunt not mention Camilla when she told James about my story?

Camilla was the woman I hated so much—the unremorseful person responsible for my sleepless nights, the one who killed my dreams of having a happily-ever-after, yet James spoke to her like she couldn't harm a fly.

"I'm babysitting," Camilla told James flatly. She then turned around slowly without looking at me, barely waiting for the child to give

James a high five, before heading back to the restaurant behind the driving range.

I looked at James with my eyebrow raised when he came back to his dinner. He sat down casually and resumed digging into his plate as if nothing significant had happened.

"Was she a friend? Family?" I asked nonchalantly, trying not to sound too interested.

"Who? Camilla?" James asked. "She's a friend of a friend, and the little boy is her nephew. We used to hang out a couple of years ago with a group of other friends. But we've drifted apart since. I haven't seen her in months, too. I just found it strange that she's babysitting her nephew. I've always thought she didn't want to be around kids, especially not Lance. He used to drive her nuts," he smiled while explaining.

"She didn't seem very fond of you, either," I said, smiling back.

"Is that right?" James said, laughing. "Go finish your dinner. It's getting cold," he added.

***

"Earth to Janelle."

I looked up from the folder I was labeling—while daydreaming, apparently—and saw Tameka's face right in front of me. Her mouth was moving as if saying something in slow motion.

"Little Bit. Are you okay, girl?" Tameka asked, concerned.

I abruptly stood up, almost knocking over the swivel chair next to me. I'd been busy working in the conference room at the office, absorbed in my own thoughts about what had happened at the golf course where James and I had lunch-*cum*-dinner four nights ago on my first day at work. I didn't notice Tameka, one of the office staff, had come into the conference room to check on me.

I looked at the clock on the wall. It was way past my lunch break. I could see Tameka looking at me, waiting for me to say something.

"I'm fine. Thanks for asking. Is everything okay?" I asked.

"So far, yes. The building is still standing, and the office is still running, except you've been holed up in this room since you came in, and we were worried about you. Have you eaten lunch yet? You can take a break, you know," Tameka said, her kind face looking worried.

Tameka was an African-American lady in her mid-forties, who was always bubbly. She was trendy, talkative, and very friendly, especially to me.

I looked at her closely and gasped.

"Why? What's wrong, baby girl?" Tameka asked, her brows arched.

"How did that happen? Yesterday, you had short hair like a pixie cut. But today ... how come your hair is way past your shoulders today?" I asked, genuinely shocked.

"Are you serious, or are you kidding me?" Tameka said, laughing.

I didn't say anything, curious about how her hair grew longer overnight. I knew nothing was impossible, but that was way pushing it. When Tameka calmed down, she looked at me kindly and said, "That's a wig, baby girl. Everybody wears that. Ooh, I can't wait to tell my husband about this," she said, laughing out loud. "But anyhow, please come out of this room and take a break. If you don't, I'll call Mr. Pretty-Asian-Boy to pick you up and take you somewhere fancy. Again. You know you've stolen the ladies' handsome Baby Daddy. You're in big trouble, girl," she continued, still giggling.

I looked at Tameka, clueless about what she meant.

"Come on. Go to the pantry. William brought cake, pasta, and donuts from his meeting this morning. Go have some. I'll see you later, Little Bit. By the way, Mr. James Ren is still single, but lots of women are lined up right now taking a number. Just a heads up," Tameka said, winking.

"Thanks, Tameka," I said, smiling back, not understanding what she said about James.

131

I carefully walked out of the conference room, trying my best to be invisible. After embarrassing myself for being shocked at Tameka's magical hair growth, I didn't want to draw any kind of attention to myself.

James and Wooly had been so busy with their meetings off-site, I hadn't seen them in the office for days since I started working for them.

I slipped into the pantry. In there was Tram, one of the office staff who Kate was talking about the other day. She was stacking salad and pasta on her paper plate. She smiled when she saw me.

"Finally, you come out of your cave. Here, have some food courtesy of the boss, your cousin. The vegetables are really crunch. Just like what I grow in my garden. Very healthy. I don't eat vegetables that are not crunch and fresh. I don't like soggy, but it's depend on the kind. This one. Okay," she said.

Tram was a young Vietnamese mother with two kids. She spoke English with a heavy accent, but it was pleasant to my ears. I heard she was brilliant in math, and no one else at the office could figure out complex mathematical problems better than she did. On top of that, she was a very diligent worker. She looked like she was in her early thirties and taller than me by a few inches. She had long, straight, dark hair, fair skin, and a slim frame. She moved somewhat boyish, at ease in her faded jeans and button-down shirt. Her voice sounded soft and high-pitched.

I remembered the other Vietnamese lady in the office.

Her name was Anh, one of the designers. Unlike Tram who dressed casually, Anh dressed more fashionably. She looked sophisticated with all of the high-end brand-name purses, clothes, and shoes you could think of. Unlike Tram, she spoke English flawlessly without an Asian accent, but impressively, she could speak her native tongue, too, and fluently at that.

Tram and Anh were both friendly to me.

"Janelle, you have a phone call, my dear. It's James. You can take it in the conference room." Miss Mench, Wooly's executive assistant, stuck her head in the door and motioned for me to get out of the pantry and head out to the conference room to take the call.

Miss Mench was Mama Mench to everyone at the office. I chose to call her Miss Mench because I didn't want her to think I was already getting too comfortable. I personally felt I had to earn the privilege to call her Mama Mench. Given that I would only be in the office for a few weeks, that might never happen.

Miss Mench was an older Filipina in her early sixties who handled the operational side of the firm's business. She was disciplined and strict like an iron lady, yet everyone at the architectural firm treated her lovingly as if she was their second mother. She was a tiny lady who always dressed professionally, wearing dark suits, high heels, and flawless makeup. Her short, trimmed hair was stylish, and matched her light-rimmed glasses. She could speak English well, but her Filipino accent remained intact.

I was told her three children were already grown and successful in their chosen professions—an engineer, a nurse, and a pharmacist—and she had been hinting of retiring soon so she and her husband could go back to California. The couple planned to move back to the Philippines, purchase property, and settle there soon.

I thanked Miss Mench as I rushed back to the conference room. As soon as I stepped inside and closed the door behind me, I picked up the phone that sat in the middle of the long table.

"Hello?" I asked hesitantly.

"Janelle? Hey, it's James. I'll pick you up at your aunt's house at six tonight so we can still have good parking. It's a car meet party, but I suggest you dress comfortably because we'll be walking and standing a lot. Is everything okay at the office?" James asked.

"Oh. I almost forgot. Okay. I'll be ready at six. Everything's okay at the office. Who else is coming? I mean, is anyone else going with us to the party?" I asked.

"My friends will be there. You'll meet them," James said.

"Is Camilla going to be there?" I asked.

"Camilla? Not sure about that. But I know her boyfriend always shows up. That is if they're still together. It's been two years since I last hung out with them," James said.

"Really? What's the boyfriend's name? Just curious," I said, trying my best to sound nonchalant. I could feel my face slowly getting flushed, but I kept my composure.

"Let me think. Was it Jomari? Shoot. I don't remember.

"She called him Cupcake or something. It's been a long time ... Wait ... If I'm not mistaken, the guy's real name is Anthony," James replied.

Chapter 26

I wiped the lip gloss off my lips and reapplied my matte lipstick. The nude lip color complemented my sun-kissed cheeks and my outfit for the night—a short, black trapeze dress with one kimono sleeve, matched with my nude wedge ankle booties. James told me to dress comfortably, but knowing that my ex-fiancé and his "mistress" may show up at the party, I opted to be just a tad dressed up. I planned to deal with my sore toes when the night was over.

I sprayed my neck lightly with my favorite scents—a combination of Chanel No. 5 and Issey Miyake. I put on my white-gold heart necklace, small hoop earrings, and my Tag Heuer watch. I slung my black shoulder bag over my shoulders, wearing it like a messenger bag, and brushed my hair several times until I felt satisfied with the way it looked. I gave myself a mental thumbs-up as I inspected my reflection in the mirror.

Not bad for a girl in misery, I thought.

I remembered my phone conversation with James in the conference room at the office a few hours ago. According to him, Anthony was already Camilla's boyfriend when they started hanging out as a group two years ago.

What a coincidence. Anthony and I officially became a couple two years ago, too, after exclusively dating for more than five months. I wondered if he'd been lying to me since the day he met me. If he did, I missed the telltale signs. I was either too trusting or too blinded by my love to doubt his intentions or even mind the truth.

"Tita Janelle, your date is here!"

I heard Sophia's voice as she knocked on my bedroom door. I quickly turned off the lights in my room and hurried to open the door. Outside, my niece waited for me. She gushed at my "new" look.

"Ooh. You look beautiful, Tita Janelle. Are you and Uncle James boyfriend and girlfriend?" Sophia was giggling as she asked her question.

"No, sweetie. Uncle James is taking me to a party to meet his friends. That's all. We're just friends," I assured my niece as I kissed her chubby cheek. She then gave me a hug before running back to her bedroom.

I found James in the living room having a conversation with my uncle who was sitting by the bar area. The fine-looking architect stood up from the couch and smiled shyly when he saw me. My uncle, on the other hand, got up from his chair and started walking towards me. He handed me a cell phone.

"Janelle, *iha*, here, you take my cell phone with you. If you need me, call the land phone. Okay? Don't stay out too late," he told me. He then turned around to address James.

"And James, I trust you, *iho*. You must bring our *dalaga* back tonight, safe and sound, in one piece, okay?" Tito Boy said firmly.

Dalaga means young, unmarried lady in Tagalog.

My uncle was acting like my father—a demeanor that was new to me, way far from his comedic character. I nudged his elbow in appreciation, and he nodded in acknowledgment.

"Yes, sir. We'll give you a call on our way back, and please call us if you need us," James said, taking my uncle's hand, bowing slightly and pressing my uncle's hand gently on his forehead.

It was impressive and delightful to watch. I couldn't believe James knew about our Filipino tradition, a gesture called *mano,* one of the Filipinos' traditional ways of expressing respect to our elders. I wondered how much the architect knew about our culture. He seemed well-versed in our values and traditions.

James and I left my uncle's house in a hurry to avoid the rush hour traffic, but it still took us more than an hour to reach the venue.

I noticed that Houston was a flat city without mountains or hills. All I saw as we drove for miles to the party were highways, bridges, and flyovers. James referred to the eight-lane highway we were driving on as a freeway—a huge, wide highway that was amazingly congested at six o'clock in the evening. Interestingly, I didn't hear much honking from the cars on the roads compared to what I was used to on the major highways, and even the narrow streets in the Philippines. When I asked James about it, he said it was normal practice for commuters in the States not to blow their horns at other drivers, either as a sign of courtesy or for self-preservation. Apparently, many people got into fights—which could turn deadly for some—just for blowing their horns while on the road.

I also noticed the average speed limit on the freeway and realized the speed limit on major roads back home were nothing compared to those in Houston, and probably the entire United States.

In the Philippines, speed was commonly measured in kilometers. In America, speed is measured in miles, and if you were driving below the speed limit—seventy miles was the average speed on freeways—you might have received more than a happy wave from the impatient drivers around you.

I held on tightly to my seatbelt, making sure James didn't notice. I cringed as I witnessed how fast the other cars around us were going. They seemed to be flying. I felt relieved when James finally took one of the exits from the busy freeway and turned right towards a less congested street.

As we crossed a wide, deserted intersection, I wondered what kind of party we were about to go to, as my designated date and driver looked a bit dressed down compared to me. James was wearing dark cargo shorts, a light gray T-shirt, black socks, and black high-top Air Jordans with dark-pink highlights. He accessorized his grungy-sporty outfit with a silver ID bracelet on his left wrist and a dark brown silicone rubber band on his right.

"My phone number is on your cell phone. I don't know what the crowd will look like, but just in case we get separated or you lose sight of me, you have to stay put. Call me, and I'll find you." James glanced at me quickly to make sure I got the message right.

I played with my uncle's phone for a little bit until I figured out how to work it. When I found James's number on the contact list, I showed it to my unbelievably strict companion for his stamp of approval.

When we finally reached our destination, James parked his car meticulously in the open parking lot, making sure nobody was close enough to ding his beloved Evo.

"There'll be a small concert at the party. I may have to leave you in one spot for a few minutes to take care of stuff. I won't be far, and I'll keep an eye on you, but you have to promise me you can handle being by yourself for a few minutes," James said as we got out of his car.

"I'm twenty-five years old, I have a cell phone, and I took some karate lessons," I said, smiling as I stood next to him.

"Not funny," James said shaking his head. "Listen. I don't know if I need to tell you this, but just in case you forget, you're a pretty girl and you look great tonight. I've been to parties like this a million times. There'll be aggressive men in that cave. Because I made a promise to your uncle, I've no choice but to be overprotective," he added, folding his side view mirror in before arming his Evo.

"Thanks. I'll be fine," I said nonchalantly.

What James didn't know was there was a hysterical woman inside me secretly jumping up and down with her ears flapping, doing her crude version of the *Perfect Strangers'* "Dance of Joy." I soaked in his compliment. *He said I was pretty,* I thought.

"Janelle."

I snapped out of my musing. James was looking at me, his arms crossed over his chest.

"Yes?" I asked, disoriented.

"Uhmm. We've been standing here for, like, five minutes already. Do you still want to go the party?" James asked.

"Oh. I'm sorry," I said quickly.

James smiled as if amused. We walked in silence as we headed to a huge warehouse-like venue with big glass doors left wide open. The light inside was dim, and the music was loud. It looked like a modern bar or club crowded with young people hanging out. There was plenty of liquor, dancing, and a few people outside in groups, smoking.

As soon as we went in the door, women in their skimpy clothing came flocking to James. They gushed at the young architect in every fashion conceivable, almost throwing themselves at him without a care.

Despite the attention, James tried to politely ease his way inside, holding my elbow, making sure the aggressive groupies didn't pull me away from him. When we reached the bar area right in front of the small stage, James led me to a small table where a group of young men and a couple of young women were sitting. The group looked at us as we approached their table, as if paying special attention to me.

James introduced me to the group, who turned out to be his friends from racing. There were five guys in the group in total, whose names I could barely remember. There were two girls. One was named Haley, a Caucasian brunette who was friendly, and then there was Anh, the fashionable designer who worked at James and Wooly's architectural firm. She appeared to be dating one of the guys in the group.

I chatted with the two girls after breaking the ice over some nachos and iced tea. After half an hour of pleasantries, an older guy— probably in his early thirties, and holding a glass of wine—took the stage.

"Yo. Are y'all having a good time?" the man said after taking a sip from his glass.

The crowd unanimously said, "Yeah!"

"A'ight. We're here to rock you tonight. We want you to have fun. Have a drink. Have a chat. And while you're at it, let's hear it from one of the most exciting rock bands in the car scene tonight. Ladies and gents, they don't need a lengthy introduction. You know who they are. Let's give it up for Blue Fin!" the man shouted excitedly through the microphone. He raised his glass, leaving the stage amidst the deafening screaming from the band's female fans in the audience.

I heard James talking into my ear over the loud noise. I could also hear musical instruments being sound-checked onstage. "I have to leave you for a few minutes. Stay with the girls. I'll come back," he told me before disappearing behind the stage.

A few minutes later, the venue turned pitch black and the stage in front of us lit up. The sound of violins streamed in the background. Slowly, the music progressed into a symphony of melodies from the sound of electric guitars, keyboards, and percussion. Suddenly, I saw James emerging from the back of the stage. He was wearing a dark beanie. To my utter surprise, he took the microphone and began singing. The female shrieks and screams around me almost broke my eardrums.

James's voice was soft and raspy, yet powerful. He sang with passion, crooning with his eyes closed, oblivious to the frenzy. I recognized the song instantly. It was a cover of the song by the British rock band The Verve, called "Bittersweet Symphony."

I was picky when it came to singers, but James's vocals were spot on. His voice seemed to suck me in like a vacuum, taking me into a tunnel where everything was peaceful and I was content, oblivious to the raging storm around me.

Suddenly, my mind began to unravel what our conversation at the golf course a few nights ago was all about. When James quizzed me about my musical preferences and how I chose who to scream for when watching a band play onstage, he was picking my brain, probably wanting to know why girls would be screaming like loonies when he was singing onstage.

I could tell James was popular in the Houston car scene. Well, for one, he had groupies. I couldn't believe the nerdy-looking, rigid, intelligent, charming architect at the office—and the awesome chef who cooked dinner for us last week—was a local celebrity, in that exclusive circle of car enthusiasts at least. He was the pretty boy with the pretty car with the pretty voice, and those women screaming their lungs out to express their admiration for him would take a chance. After all, they may just get lucky.

"Are you really here, or am I just seeing double? What the hell are you doing here?" said an angry voice behind me.

Chapter 27

I turned around.

I saw a man standing a foot behind me, apparently drunk, holding a shot glass and a bottle of beer, mouthing invectives. He was wearing jeans, a hooded sweat shirt, and a baseball hat. I couldn't see his face clearly because of the dim lights in the venue. I couldn't even tell where his mouth was while he spoke. The shadows from the hazy lighting seemed to be playing tricks on my vision. I didn't know how long he'd been standing there. No one seemed to notice what he was saying, as the entire club was buzzing with all kinds of noise.

I felt scared. The drunken guy was rude and seemed to be talking directly at me. I looked back at the stage to look for James, but it was already empty, the next batch of performers already preparing for their turn.

I felt someone gently hold my arm. "Come with me back to the car," a male voice whispered in my ear.

It was James. I recognized his outfit and the silver bracelet on his wrist. I looked at him closely just to make sure my eyes were not playing tricks on me. When I was certain, I nodded, clinging to his shirt sleeve before walking with him slowly back to the parking lot.

James seemed confused but didn't say anything. I was confused myself, not having an idea why we were heading back to the parking lot, but I didn't care. The creepy man cursing behind me was more alarming.

As we reached James's car, I thought I heard the voice of the angry man screaming behind us, but James didn't seem to notice. I didn't look back, too scared to see what the angry man looked like.

As I settled inside James's car, I looked out my window. James took the driver's seat and started his car. The Evo made a roaring sound that made me jump.

"Are you okay?" James asked.

I kept quiet, debating whether or not to tell him about the angry man at the party. I looked at my side view mirror again. I saw a white car emerging from behind. I almost whimpered in fear when I saw the man behind the wheel. It was the same angry man who was screaming behind me at the party.

***

"Blue Fin. Does that have anything to do with *sushi* and *sashimi?*" I asked James, trying to shake off my fears as I kept an eye on the white car behind us.

James seemed distracted. He looked at me for a few seconds before my question clicked in his head.

"The band's name?" he asked.

I remained quiet, hoping James didn't think I was being offensive. For some reason, his band's name reminded me of fish, which was a staple on the menu of all the Japanese restaurants I'd been to.

"Yes and no," James said. "The band likes the word 'blue,' for some reason. We were in a *sushi* place when we were brainstorming for a name. We agreed on choosing Blue Train as our band's name, but then one of the guys pointed out 'fin' sounded better than 'train.' So we were, like, all enlightened and agreed. Plus, we didn't want to be branded a train wreck when we messed up. To me, Blue Fin sounds like a seafood restaurant, not really Japanese. But I get your point. I mean, I think I do." James was smiling as he explained.

"Okay, I don't mean to sound like I'm back-scratching, but I seriously like Blue Fin. I like the way it sounds. I like the way your band sounds. And your voice, it was beautiful. I didn't know you could sing

144

like that. Now I know why those women were doing what they were doing when they're around you," I said.

I gave James a compliment not because I was trying to undo my stupid question from a few minutes ago, but because I was genuinely awed by his voice and the way their band played. I loved alternative music, and their cover of that favorite song of mine would make any Richard Ashcroft fan proud.

"Thanks. That means a lot," James said, looking at me briefly and smiling before looking back at the road.

He's probably used to being complimented by everyone he meets, and I am no exception, I thought, feeling awkward.

I almost jumped when James's cell phone rang. When he picked up, he sounded as if he was expecting the call.

"Hey. Are you at the house? Everything okay? ... Yeah, we just left ... Really? That's good ... That was my plan, man, but now I'm not sure I want to do that. ... I don't know, bro. She's with me. I don't think that's a good idea ... Right. It's been tailing us since we left. It's a white Beemer. Never seen it before ... Oh. You're right. Who's working tonight? ... Okay, I'll give him a call ... Don't worry. I got this. I'll call you ... No problem, man." James's voice sounded cool as he hung up, but his face looked worried.

"Is everything okay?" I asked.

"Yes," James said reassuringly as he glanced at me, looking as if he didn't want to continue the conversation. But I had to pound a little harder.

"There's a white car behind us that's been following us since we left the parking lot. What's going on?" I asked coolly.

James didn't look at me but kept driving. When we reached a stop light, he heaved a sigh and talked to me. "This wasn't the plan. We were supposed to stay at the car meet, chat with my friends, and listen to some bands play music. And then I'd take you to this nice little restaurant so we can have dinner. But then something unexpected happened. Your

145

uncle called me after our band played. He said there was someone at their house who kept on knocking on the door and ringing the doorbell. There was also someone drunk who kept calling him on the phone, asking if I just left their house. Your uncle was worried about the kids, so I told him we were leaving the party and coming back to their house. That's the reason we left so soon."

James paused before speaking, his voice low. "So I texted Will while we were at the party. He texted back saying he was on his way to your uncle's house. He's the one who just called my cell. He said he's already at your uncle's house, and everything's okay, so far. He said there's no one outside, and there were no more weird phone calls, either. When we left the party, my plan was to drop you off at your uncle's house. But because this strange car has been tailing us since we left the parking lot, I don't think that's a good idea. If something were to happen, I don't want it to happen anywhere close to Sophia and Kenneth," he explained.

"I see. So do we have a new plan?" I asked, concerned.

"We're going to the office because we have security there. Whatever happens, they'll be there to help us. I'm going to park in front of the building. Now, I want you to stay in the car while I take care of business. Don't argue. Remember what your uncle said: I have to bring you back in one piece, safe and sound," James said, managing to smile despite his concerns.

"I remember what my uncle said. But I'm not staying in the car. We're in this together." I smiled back. "And don't argue," I added.

"Janelle ..."

"Shhh. Look, he's cutting you," I said, suddenly scared as I saw the white car swerve to the left towards our lane, almost hitting James's car in the process.

James seemed unfazed. Instead, he reached for his phone and speed-dialed a number. "Hello? TJ. Hey, man, it's James. Is everyone gone at the office? ... Are you working tonight? ... Cool. Hey, man, do me a favor. I'm on my way to the office. I need to park in front of the building. There's someone tailing me. Looks like an angry dude. Would you and Carlos come down to the front in, like, ten minutes? I have a lady in the car with me. I just want to make sure there's no trouble … A'ight. Cool. Thanks, man," James said before hanging up.

The white car, what appeared to be a new BMW, swerved to the right, slowed down, then cut several cars to fall behind us again.

"It's taunting me," James almost whispered.

"Are you okay?" I asked.

"Yeah. This is pretty normal, I should say, in the racing world. Some people's egos get bruised and they want to take it on the track. But this one's pretty aggressive. Almost personal. That's fine. We're close to the office. Let's see what he wants," James said as he made a left turn at an intersection. As we entered the front of the office building, the white car slowly followed behind. It made a roaring sound a few times, as if revving to prepare for a race. It reminded me of a hot-headed bull facing the *matador* in a bull fight. James parked his car in front of the building, which was deserted but well-lit, as I looked at my watch. It was already past nine o'clock. I heard a car door slam from behind. I saw the driver of the white BMW getting out of the car through my side view mirror. I heard him shouting and cussing passionately, his words slurred as if he were drunk. I also saw a woman come out of another car, which had just parked behind the white BMW. The woman came running to the driver, restraining him.

"James Ren! You prick! You think you can get everything you want? What the hell are you doing with my fiancée? Poisoning her mind, you stupid Jap?" the driver of the BMW shouted, his American accent flawless.

Wait a second. I've heard that voice before, I thought. I looked at the man screaming. He wasn't wearing his hat anymore, and I could see his face clearly in the bright light from the lamp post by the building.

"Anthony," I said under my breath. I wanted to kick myself for not recognizing him sooner.

James looked at me in disbelief, his eyes squinting, as we both sat frozen in the car.

He cleared his throat as if he was having difficulty spewing the words out. "Anthony, Camilla's boyfriend, was your fiancé?"

Chapter 28

I pinched myself.

My nails dug deep into my skin. Once, twice, three times. I felt pain and fear as I realized I wasn't dreaming. Confused and disoriented, I found myself in the middle of a dramatic confrontation I once thought was only possible in cheesy romantic films. But worse, I felt guilty for dragging James into my own personal conflict.

Why is the world so small for all of us, anyway? I thought. I jumped when I heard James take off his seat belt. I glanced at my side view mirror as I heard Anthony resume hurling invectives at James, screaming his lungs out.

I quickly made a decision. I didn't wait for James to get out of the car. I opened my door myself and headed out to confront my nearly demented ex-fiancé and the frantic woman next to him.

I already knew the woman who was helping Anthony get a grip on himself was Camilla, the only person in the world who would do anything ridiculous and dangerous for Anthony.

"Why are you doing this? What else do you want from me?" I asked Anthony coldly as I approached my "misery personified." His eyes were bloodshot, and he had difficulty focusing. He looked at me with loathing, as if I was the traitor who abandoned him at the altar and ran off to elope with his mortal enemy.

I almost laughed at the irony. I wanted to slap his face, but I restrained myself. I tried to keep my composure so I could analyze his body movements, looking for signs that would give away his real intentions.

If he's using reverse psychology on me, it won't work. I won't entertain anything ludicrous. He's not the victim here. I am, I thought.

"You didn't give me a chance to explain, baby. You disappeared for almost two weeks. Without a trace. And then I found out you'd been running around town with this fool. Really, Janelle? What were you trying to do? Getting even with me? Mocking me? Why, baby? Is it because this hot 'playa from the Himalayas' is better than me?" Anthony screamed without pausing, pointing his fingers at James who was already standing behind me.

"I don't know what you're talking about, and please, stop calling me baby," I said, half-mad, half-confused.

"Fine. I cheated on you. But I have valid reasons. I was lonely, and I have to admit, I couldn't handle a long-distance relationship. You're so freaking conservative, babe. With you, I've always felt like I was dating a nun. The most we could ever do was hold hands. I have needs, you know, like every friggin' warm-blooded man in this planet. So I found myself in the arms of Camilla, who is so much more giving and so much more nurturing. She understood my needs as a man.

"For a friggin' change.

"I was going to tell you about it, but I didn't have a chance. I didn't know you were coming and barging into my apartment unannounced, straight from the Philippines for crying out loud. Could you blame me? Could you blame us? I understand your anger and bitterness and your disappearance, but for you to replace me so quickly … come on … and with someone like James? What were you thinking, Janelle? Do you even know who this man is? Or was? I thought you were smart, baby. What the hell? Are ye sherr ya," Anthony slurred, almost falling on the grass by the sidewalk.

Camilla caught him swiftly without saying a word.

"Camilla, take him home," James spoke from behind me. His voice was low and controlled, yet brimming with contempt.

"Shut up, hotshot!" Anthony screamed. "Still not content with those skanky groupies screaming for you, you had to pick up my leftover here after your married girlfriend ditched you?" he continued.

I saw Anthony's body down on the ground, slumped on the grass as James lunged at him. Anthony somehow got ahold of James's shirt and pulled him to the ground, and tried to punch him. Anthony missed and was knocked back by James's balled-up fist instead. He tried to hit James on the face, but only managed to graze the architect's mouth.

I quickly ran to James's side when I saw him bleeding. He slowly got up and wiped his bleeding lips with his shirt sleeve. He looked at me briefly before turning to Camilla and Anthony, who were both trying to get up from the grass.

"Camilla, take your man home. Tell him the whole story before you forget the truth. Again," James said coldly. "And tell him to stay away from booze, because that's for grown men. Apparently, your boy can't handle it," he added.

In a flash, two tall young men wearing dark security uniforms came half-running towards James.

"TJ. We're okay, man. Can you take care of these two?" James asked, referring to Camilla and Anthony still struggling to get up from the grass.

"Make sure they don't do anything stupid, and send them home. The man is drunk, but his girlfriend is sober. She can drive. I have to go to the office to clean up," James told the security men.

"No problem, James. We'll be right there in a minute. Rhonda's down by the reception. She'll escort you to the office. See you later, bro," one of the men told James.

As much as I wanted to talk to Anthony and Camilla, I figured it wasn't the best time. Anthony was almost passed out, and Camilla stood there like a statue, unable to say a word. They'd be completely incapable of making sense of what I was about to say to them, anyway. There would be another time for talk.

It was strange how the wheels had turned for me and Anthony in just a matter of days. I had no more feelings for the man I was supposed to marry, the one who swept me off my feet two years ago; the same one who broke my heart into a million pieces when he betrayed me.

I followed James to the building. He was walking slowly, still dabbing his lips with the sleeve of his dirty shirt. I looked behind us before going into the building with him.

I saw the two security men assisting Anthony into the passenger side of Camilla's car, while Camilla dutifully took the driver's seat and prepared to leave.

Why did Camilla suddenly turn deaf and mute? Where did her fierceness go? What married girlfriend ditching James was Anthony talking about? Why did James turn livid when Anthony mentioned her? I asked myself quietly.

James turned around and looked at me to ask if I was okay. I touched his elbow lightly and nodded. There was so much I didn't know about him. Maybe later, when he was ready, he would tell me his story.

Chapter 29

I sat on the bright red couch in James's office, staring at a piece of contemporary art hanging on the wall behind his desk. I was mesmerized.

It was a modern sculpture of bright cherry blossoms in different hues of red and pink, suspended on invisible branches. The bright colors were refreshing, vibrant, and glowing, like radiant beauty emanated from within. I felt a strange sensation on my neck as if a mixture of warm and cold air were resting on my shoulders. I quickly tore myself from the alluring appeal of the sculpture on the wall and surveyed James's office.

The spacious room was stylish and masculine.

James's desk, which occupied almost half of the room, was a visual treat. It was made of clear glass and chrome metal, as if suspended in mid-air from where I was looking. It was cluttered with glossy magazines, pens, and colorful paper clips on one side, while the other half of the desk was neatly organized. A bright-red table lamp was sitting in one corner, illuminating a stack of CDs, comic books, hardback books, rulers, and rolled drafting paper. The desk sat on a taupe area rug with contemporary designs in cool hues of red and chocolate.

The dark wooden flooring was clean and polished. One wall of the room was made entirely of glass. Some loose furniture and drawers, made of chrome metal, glass, smoked plastic, and ebony wood, were neatly positioned in the spacious room. The windows were draped in cotton canvas blinds in neutral shades that complemented the walls. Hanging next to the window was a medium-sized canvas frame with three bold Japanese characters painted in black.

"Here you go. I made us hot tea. I'm sorry if it's freezing in here. Hopefully this will help until we get out of here to find something decent to eat," James said as he came back to his office from the pantry.

He set the mugs on his desk. I got up and took one before heading back to the couch. The mug felt good as it warmed my frozen fingers.

James handed me a small fleece throw blanket, which I used to cover my back and my arms.

I shouldn't have worn a short, sleeveless dress, I thought.

"The blanket's clean. My mom makes sure I keep an extra clean one in my office every week, in case I end up sleeping here during projects," James said, smiling while sipping from his cup.

"Thanks. I'm sorry I dragged you into this mess," I said apologetically.

He looked at me kindly after inspecting the stack of papers on his desk. "It's not your fault, Janelle. You don't have to apologize," he said.

"How's your lip?" I asked

"It's fine. The bleeding stopped. Just uncomfortable, but it'll go away. I put ice on it," he replied, smiling crookedly.

He sat next to me on the couch, maintaining a respectful distance, sipping his tea as if contemplating what to say next.

"Your mom will probably hate me when she finds out about tonight," I said, wondering if I should smile or look stoic, to show him I was really sorry for his swollen lips and what looked like a bruised jaw.

"Oh. I did that to myself," James said softly, feeling his lower lip with his index finger. "But anyway, we really should be talking about dinner. It's getting late, and we're running out of choices," he continued.

I noticed his eyes looked brighter, far from the gloomy look he sported when we were in the elevator on our way up to the office.

"By the way, who's ..."

"Just wondering. How did you ..."

We looked at each other and laughed. Maybe it was the hot tea, the freezing temperature in the office, the drama we just went through, or all of the above; laughing cheerfully felt like it was almost a yearning.

"Everything okay in there?" Rhonda, the security lady, knocked on the wall next to James's open door and checked in on us.

"Yes ma'am," James assured the security lady before she went back to her post.

"All right, ladies first," James said when we resumed talking.

He was sitting about a foot away from me, but I could still smell his minty breath from the tea he was drinking, and probably the toothpaste he used when he had brushed his teeth in the bathroom. I also noticed he had changed into a clean white shirt and gray sweats, looking and smelling like he just took a shower. I felt uncomfortable and self-conscious, not having the luxury to brush my teeth and change my clothes like he did.

I quietly moved a few inches away from him when he wasn't looking.

"Janelle?" I heard James's voice as I smoothed my wrinkled dress.

"Are you okay?" he asked, looking worried.

"Yes. I feel so much better. Thanks again," I said timidly.

James seemed thoughtful as he hesitantly set his mug down on the small coffee table in front of the couch

"Okay. Well, back to what you were saying before we got interrupted," he said, smiling.

"Oh. That. I ... I was just wondering. Not sure if you wanted to talk about it. You don't have to, you know. I'll understand. I was just curious. I thought it's ... It just surprised me. When you heard Anthony," I stammered, looking at James and my mug alternately.

I felt the strange sensation on my neck again. James looked charming, just like when I first met him at Bubbly Tea House with his regal-looking shoulder-length, blond-streaked hair and captivating almond-shaped eyes.

Maybe I'm only dreaming and I'm just having a conversation with Prince Zardoz of the Boazanian Empire, planning his next attack against the Voltes V team, I thought.

James looked at me, puzzled.

I quickly set my mug down on the coffee table next to his, afraid he could read my mind. After gathering enough courage, I looked at him and tried my best to get the words out of my mouth.

"First question; how did you know my ex-fiancé screaming behind us was Camilla's boyfriend?" I asked.

"Hmmm. I guess I just put the pieces together quicker than I would've done in normal circumstances. I recognized Camilla when she got out of her car, which I found really strange, at first. And then it got even weirder when your ex screamed behind us, addressing me, talking about his fiancée being with me and getting her mind poisoned by me. I figured you were his fiancée, because you were the only one in the car with me. And then, of course, I heard you say his name before we got out of the car, which validated my suspicion. I remembered our phone conversation this afternoon. You were curious about Camilla's boyfriend and asked what his name was. Everything just clicked together in my head like a puzzle, I guess," James explained.

Either my aunt didn't know about Camilla's involvement, or she chose not to tell James about her, I thought.

"Next question?" James asked, smiling self-consciously.

"Oh. Uhm. Your ex-girlfriend, the one Anthony was talking about; the one that made you upset and, well, got you guys fist fighting each other on the grass. She's married," I said.

So there, I thought.

I dragged the words out of my mouth, speaking slowly like a two-year-old learning to talk for the first time. James looked at me as if he knew what was coming before I even opened my mouth.

"Daniella," he said.

I looked at him with curious eyes.

"Daniella is my ex-girlfriend, and she's Camilla's best friend. She was married, yes, but ... Anyway, it's a long story.

"Your ex-fiancé painted a nasty picture of it, but it's really not all that. We broke up a year ago. But she's not the reason why I got upset," James said as he looked at my arm.

"What do you mean?" I asked.

He looked at me as if confused, waiting for me to say something, but I didn't know what else to tell him.

"Janelle, do you remember what Anthony did to you back there ... before your ex and I almost killed each other?" he asked, concerned.

I shook my head slowly.

"Look at your left arm," he said quietly.

I took the blanket off my back and hesitantly looked at my left arm. I was appalled when I saw a big red bruise and some scratch marks, right by my elbow. I looked at James as I rubbed the red, tender patch on my skin.

All of a sudden, my memory came back. I felt a sharp pain in my arm as my mind replayed the images I seemed to have already chosen to forget.

I saw flashes of myself being dragged by a strong force, the sleeve of my dress ripping as I resisted. I felt a sharp pain on my skin as if it was getting separated from my bone. Suddenly, the grip loosened. I saw Anthony and James scrambling on the grass while Camilla tried to break them apart.

Tears formed in my eyes as James spoke softly to me, but I held them back. I promised myself I wouldn't cry.

"Anthony grabbed you. When you resisted, he dragged you by your arm until the sleeve of your dress ripped. You screamed while restraining him, but he didn't let go. I had to do something. I couldn't just stand around and watch while that was happening to you," he explained.

Chapter 30

Puto Pie.

That's what the name said on the gray-colored paper box sitting on the breakfast table in my aunt's kitchen. I wondered if what was inside the box was the fluffy rice cake smothered with melted cheese and bits of red salted eggs, sliced like a pie, being sold in pastry stores in the Philippines.

My aunt's house was unusually quiet. Everyone was still asleep, except for me, of course—the "Energizer bunny" who woke up too early in the morning and couldn't go back to sleep. Wide-eyed and restless, I decided to take a shower, dress up in my most comfortable sweats, and catch up on my reading in the kitchen by the window, where I could see the first ray of sunlight kiss the moist grass outside.

I looked in my aunt's humongous two-door fridge to get some orange juice to perk me up but changed my mind. I went to the kitchen counter instead to make a cup of hot tea.

I smiled when I realized my aunt and uncle's house, despite being modern, had the humongous spoon and fork, normally displayed in Filipino homes' kitchens or dining areas, hanging on the wall by the breakfast table. The only thing missing was *The Last Supper* painting that most Filipinos are also fond of decorating their kitchen walls with.

My aunt, being tasteful and meticulous, however, was able to make the wooden spoon and fork décor blend perfectly with the modern stainless appliances, wall art, and furniture in her kitchen. Maybe Wooly had a hand in making the gigantic wooden utensils disappear into the background. Wooly was an architect, after all. He could easily make everything look perfect, like a magician.

I opened my aunt's pantry. I saw she had chamomile tea, so I started making a cup for myself. I then sat by the window to enjoy my soothing drink, watching the early joggers trotting by the *cul de sac*.

My aunt and uncle's house was located in the suburbs in a nice, quiet subdivision. It was built right in front of a manmade lake with a manmade fountain in the middle. Their subdivision was newly built with its own school for kids in the elementary level where Sophia and Kenneth, who stayed with my uncle during the day, were conveniently enrolled.

My aunt told me their subdivision was just an average neighborhood in Houston for middle class residents, not really as expensive as people thought, but I suspected she was trying to be modest about it. The gated neighborhood where they lived had its own community pool, a bike trail, a huge tennis court, a gym, a park, a social hall, and other amenities exclusive to residents and their guests.

I looked at my half-empty cup and glanced at the clock in the kitchen. I wondered if James was already awake. He'd dropped me off at my aunt's house after midnight last night, chatting with my uncle and Wooly first, in private, before heading to his apartment.

Before he took me home though, we had a quiet yet strange dinner together.

After recuperating from our ugly confrontation with Anthony and Camilla—freshening up and having tea at the office—James and I decided to head to the drive-thru of a burger joint across the street to grab some burgers and fries for dinner, which we took back to the office with us.

I set up the small wooden table by the pantry in the office, carefully using James's extra drafting paper as placemats, while James warmed our food in the microwave.

When everything was set up, we quietly ate.

I tried not to think about the strangeness of having fast-food dinner with my cousin's architect-partner in the deserted office right before midnight.

"Do you still love Daniella?" I asked James while nibbling on my french fries. It was so quiet in the office, I could hear my heart beating.

James looked at me as if he didn't understand English.

"You know what they say, right? Breaking up doesn't always mean you stop loving the person you said goodbye to," I said carefully in between bites.

James was quiet, as if contemplating what to say to me. "True ... but it depends on the reason why you broke up. Most of the time, the love a couple shared is too special to forget, throw away, or let go of, even from a distance. But there are times when what they had together is like poison. It has to be completely removed from their system so they can move on with their lives without each other," he said thoughtfully.

I looked at him for a minute, pondering what he said.

"To answer your question, I did love Daniella when we were together. But what happened between us—the circumstances, the reason for our breakup ... they all destroyed what we had. It's a long story, and really boring, if you ask me," he continued.

"I'm sorry. I didn't mean to dig into your past," I said apologetically.

"After what your ex said about me and Daniella, I understand why you're curious." He smiled, his hazel eyes looking as enthralling as ever.

He set down his cup of soda and sighed. "Janelle, I know I'm a guy, and probably the last person you want to open up to after what happened to all of us tonight, especially between you and your ex, but if you feel you want to talk about anything that's bothering you, or anything at all, I'm just here, okay?" he continued.

I smiled at him, forcing myself not to cry, making sure I didn't spoil our dinner with my life's little tragedies.

There'd be time for curling up and crying later on, perhaps when I talk to Jay Anne, bothering my best friend with my new sob story, I thought.

James looked at me as if reading my mind.

"Remember what you told me back in my car? You said you weren't back-scratching when you said our band was good," he said.

I nodded.

"Well, I'm not back-scratching either when I tell you I was pretty impressed with the way you handled yourself tonight. After everything you went through, I think you held your fort really well. You didn't even cry. You're a pretty strong person," he said. I looked at him, smiling timidly.

"Thanks. I'm not strong. I'm just holding my head above water. I don't want to cry. I can't. If I do, I'll drown," I said, biting my lips, my voice cracking.

James looked at me kindly.

"Crying isn't bad. It's just a process." He smiled before continuing. "Crying doesn't mean you're weak or you've lost your battle. Sometimes, it's a sign of acceptance, of acknowledgment, and you're just taking a moment to recharge and heal yourself," he said softly.

I looked at him, caressing his face in my mind, enjoying his seductively low, hoarse, raspy voice. All of a sudden, I couldn't concentrate. My mind was swirling with a million ideas forming in my head.

Maybe this is what going through a roller coaster of emotions feels like, I thought.

James and I resumed eating, not saying a word, the silence around us deafening, broken only once in a while by a humming computer.

"Do you still love Anthony?" James asked before sipping on his drink.

I stared at him, taken aback.

"I was kidding," James said, smiling crookedly. "I was just trying to lighten things up. You look really tired. I need to take you back to your uncle's house already, so you can rest. We need to get going. If you're ready, we can start cleaning up here and head out. I don't want your uncle to worry," he added.

I nodded in acknowledgment.

When we finished eating I started tidying up, carefully putting all our leftover food in the middle of the drafting paper. James folded the corners of the drafting paper one at a time on top of each other until it resembled a ball before throwing it in the trash can in one swift motion. I quietly put the chairs back in place as James wiped the table with paper towel doused with some disinfectant cleaning liquid.

I sighed in relief, glad James was only kidding when he asked me if I still loved Anthony. I wouldn't have been able to explain my tremendous loathing for my ex-fiancé.

I quickly walked up towards the sink so I could wash my hands in the faucet. I tried not to be distracted as I stood next to James while he was busy refilling the wooden rack by the sink with a new roll of paper towel. I could smell the citrusy scent of his cologne, seemingly trapped in the fibers of his shirt. It was pleasantly invigorating. I glanced at his striking profile, his perfect nose, his alluring neck, his blond streaks catching the light of the moon streaming through the window. Strangely, I found myself relishing the moment, standing next to him, taking pleasure in the warmth of his body.

With my four-inch heels, he didn't seem that tall. I could actually wrap my arms around his waist, look up at his beautiful face so I could swim inside the softness of his eyes. His lips looked soft and inviting.

I saw the image of my conservative grandmother in the Philippines with a shocked expression on her face, staring back at me in my head.

I jumped as I realized the faucet in front of me was spewing hot water directly over my hands, and I didn't feel the burning pain until it was already too late. James instinctively turned off the faucet and dried my hands quickly and carefully with sheets of paper towel drenched in cold water. I looked at him as he bent down to take care of my burning skin, yet the pain didn't seem to bother me.

And then it hit me.

I realized I was having a post-traumatic episode, and every cell and nerve in my body wanted to fight back by making James, the person who momentarily stood as a friend and "savior" to me, the object of my recovery. The scalding water was my punishment, reinforced by the scowling image in my mind of my grandmother, for having allowed my weak, ungrateful, and selfish coping system to have power over me, even for just a few seconds.

"James," I said quietly, my voice sounding exhausted as he carefully dabbed my hands with paper towel. "Thanks for everything, and thanks for being there for me," I added, determined not to cry and make a fool of myself in front of the very person who didn't need any more drama than I had already doused him with.

James looked at me and smiled kindly.

"You'll be fine, Janelle. You'll get over this, I promise," he said.

Chapter 31

I took a deep breath. It was the Saturday morning of my "surprise" party.

I was never good at lying, but my aunt and uncle, just for the duration of my vacation, didn't have to know my secret—that I already knew about the surprise party they had surreptitiously planned and meticulously organized for me for months ago, long before I even came to Houston. I felt guilty for making Wooly and James keep secrets from my uncle and aunt for me, but we were in our fabricated plot too deep already; there was no turning back. I stepped out of my bedroom to join Wooly, my aunt, and my uncle for brunch in the kitchen, ready to play actress.

My aunt was just taking out her baked chicken spaghetti from the oven as I sat at the breakfast table right across from my cousin.

"Wooly, why don't you take Janelle to the mall today, at the Galleria, so she can go shopping and unwind? She needs some fresh scenery instead of just being in the house." My aunt addressed my cousin while serving her crispy delicious *Lumpiang Shanghai*, which were egg rolls in English.

Wooly looked at me, discreetly raising his brow to remind me I was not supposed to know anything about the party.

"Sure, Mom," Wooly said.

After the quick brunch, as if nothing special was about to happen that night, we all headed out to mind our own businesses. Wooly and I went to the mall, while my uncle and aunt, who said they were going to the grocery store with the kids, actually went with Kenneth and Sophia to the venue of my party.

"Okay. Go to your stores quickly and then we'll head back home. I'll drop you off at my parents' house so you can get dressed. Don't overdo it. Remember, you're not supposed to know you're going anywhere special tonight. I'll pick you up in two hours so we can head out to the party. Cool?" Wooly told me on our way to the Galleria Mall.

"Thanks for doing this for me. Sorry we had to lie to your parents," I told him, feeling guilty.

"No prob. We're not doing anything bad, really. You can't help it if you're vain for wanting to look your best in the company of strangers. I get that. I'm married to Charm, remember? She'd do the exact same thing. Plus, you've had way too many bad surprises already. I don't think you deserve any more traumatic encounters than what you've already gone through," Wooly said, sighing. "Every dark cloud has a silver lining, Jan. One day you'll be grateful all of these things happened, because if they didn't, you wouldn't have met the better person or experienced the better relationship in the future," he continued.

I nodded in agreement, looking out my window. I saw retail establishments and bus stops along the road. I also saw a man in the middle of the street, on an island, holding a cardboard sign with scribbles in bold letters. His sign said, "NEED JOB. 4 KIDS. TNX FOR YOUR HELP. GOD BLESS."

Compared to the beggars in the Philippines, the man panhandling on the street with the cardboard sign looked relatively decent, well-groomed, and able bodied. He had a limp, but he could stand on his feet with no problem. He was also clad in comfortable running shoes, jeans, and a bomber jacket to ward off the cold wind.

In the Philippines, beggars looked haggard, bony, disoriented, dirty, frail, and sickly, with almost nothing on. They didn't bear signs. They held small tin cans or sacks, hoping generous people would drop coins in their buckets.

I frowned at the contrast, suddenly feeling guilty for sulking at my less debilitating misery. I didn't realize I'd only been in Houston for two weeks. It seemed like ages since I caught Anthony in bed with Camilla, the ugly truth that had turned my life around in ways I'd never imagined. But despite my previous fixation for what I once believed was an unbreakable relationship, I was moving on. Even after my dream of marrying the perfect man on the other side of the world had disappeared like a bubble.

And Wooly was right. Once in a while, since the incident at the office, I found myself thankful for the ugly turn of events, because if that hadn't happened, I wouldn't have realized what was on the other side of the fence. I never knew the grass could be greener somewhere else, the scenery so much lovelier.

I thought about James. I didn't know why I was constantly thinking about him. After what happened last night, the image of his face wouldn't leave my mind. Maybe it was because he was there when I needed someone to keep my emotions in check—that crucial time when I had to confront the demons nesting in the deepest corners of my sanity.

He made sense when everything else didn't. He made me feel better, even when I believed I shouldn't.

I was sure he was one of those "greener grass on the other side of the fence." But then again, he was too put together for me—sophisticated, balanced, beautiful, and intelligent. At the same time, he seemed arrogant, bossy, and, well, someone my grandmother back home wouldn't want for me, simply because he had a relationship with a married woman in the past—a truly immoral, socially unacceptable, and irresponsible choice in life that my religious grandmother would be surely shocked about.

He probably just looked at me as a task, a mere obligation—that weird, helpless chick from the Philippines who he had to take around the city out of courtesy.

I looked at my healed hands and recalled how he took the time to carefully apply a soothing ointment on them after dabbing them with cold paper towel last night at the office.

"How's James? Is he okay?" I heard myself saying like my lips had a mind of their own.

My cousin looked at me, puzzled. "James is fine," he replied.

"Is he coming to the party?" I asked casually.

"Not sure. Maybe not. He called me this morning. One of his friends is moving to a new apartment and asked for his help. I doubt if he'll be able to come to the party," Wooly stated.

"Which friend?" I asked, trying to sound uninterested so Wooly wouldn't be suspicious.

But my cousin didn't say anything. He seemed preoccupied until we reached the street going towards the mall's parking garage. He drove with care, slowing down as he went farther down the dark basement parking of the mall. When we got to what I thought was the lower level of the basement, Wooly carefully parked his car in an empty spot by the wall. He took off his seatbelt before gathering his wallet, car keys, and cell phone.

"James is helping someone he knew from a couple of years ago. I haven't seen her in a long time, but I know she still makes contact with him once in a while. She and her husband recently divorced, so she's moving out of their apartment to a new one and she asked James to help her. That's all I know," Wooly told me while getting ready to get out of the car.

"I see. Which friend is it?" I asked.

"Her name's Daniella," Wooly replied.

Chapter 32

I stepped out of Wooly's car, clutching my Louis Vuitton pochette like a security blanket. I was never into expensive purses, but my sister, *Ate* Bianca—*ate* is the Tagalog term for older sister—gifted me with the lovely white Damier Ebene accessory just a couple of weeks ago, before I left for Houston.

Ate Bianca bought the purse for me when she traveled to France last year with her friends, after impressively passing the bar exam on her first try just like my mother did when she first entered the law profession.

Ate Bianca meant to give the purse to me as my birthday gift, but decided to let me have it sooner, anyway. My birthday was not for another two months.

My sister is two years older than me, and definitely smarter, prettier, taller, and more curvaceous—well-endowed, as she claimed. I used to be quite jealous of her when we were teenagers, especially when more boys started paying attention to her. But when we started working after college in different fields—I was in advertising, and she was at a legal firm—I outgrew my insecurities. We became closer and more supportive of each other as we grew older.

Ate Bianca made sure I brought the purse with me to Houston so I could sport what she called "LV," during parties or if I had to go out on a date with Anthony. She said Louis Vuitton, Gucci, and Chanel were the more preferred brands among fashionable Asian women in America, and I shouldn't be caught dead not toting one.

Had my trendy sister found out I almost forgot about the fancy purse, she would have gone nuts. Thank goodness for my missing lip gloss—I had accidentally found the purse in its brown protective sack while rummaging through my luggage.

***

Wooly had dropped me off at his parents' house as planned, two hours before he picked me up to go to the party. For the first time in the history of my two-hour ritual of prepping up, I didn't have more than one outfit change while deciding what to wear for the party. I wasn't supposed to dress up like I was going anywhere fancy, anyway, so I quickly grabbed an outfit hanging in my temporary closet without much thought.

I settled for a pair of white denim pants. They made me look taller, hugging my slim legs and tiny hips. I paired them with my white Via Spiga platform heels, which showed off my pretty pedicure. I had on dark-magenta nail polish, which complemented the baby-pink chiffon sleeveless blouse I chose to pair with my pants. I found it hanging by its lonesome on the rack when I was shopping at Banana Republic two weeks ago. The romantic hue matched my pale make up, adding more glow to just a hint of pink blush, white eye shadow, and nude lip gloss. Without much energy to accessorize, I traded my Tag Heuer watch for a slim Tous white-gold bracelet. I also wore my daintiest pearl earrings.

James won't be at the party, anyway. Who cares if I look like a cupcake? I thought.

I coughed the word "cupcake" out of my system quickly, remembering what James had said to me on the phone the other day. Cupcake was Camilla's term of endearment for Anthony.

I looked in the mirror one last time before running out the door to my cousin's car, its quiet motor humming patiently in the driveway.

"So that's what you call dressing down; not going anywhere special. How many long gowns do you have in your closet, waiting to be worn for special occasions?" Wooly shook his head, amused.

"It's a girl thing. Ask your wife. She knows," I teased back.

We arrived at the venue half an hour later.

"Let's get inside. You ready?" Wooly asked me as we finally stood by the reception hall's big wooden entrance.

"I'm scared," I said.

"Don't be. It'll be fun," Wooly assured me.

We quietly stepped into the big social hall. The lights were dim, casting shadows in the corners, creating a festive, romantic mood. My tension eased a little bit. I realized I may enjoy the party after all. The bustling activity inside seemed more exciting than I had anticipated. We walked to a big round table in the middle of the spacious hall where my uncle and aunt sat with Sophia and Kenneth. We took our seats while waiters in their handsome black and white suits served us our preferred appetizers, entrees, dessert, and drinks from the menu.

For the guests, there were two long buffet tables on both sides of the hall, teeming with Filipino, American, and Italian dishes. Aside from serving iced tea, water, and soda, the waiters walked around offering glasses of champagne to guests. In one corner, by the dessert table, was a tempting chocolate fondue.

I noticed the guests at the party were from many different cultures, running around, socializing in their pretty outfits while classic instrumental music was playing in the background. It almost looked like a wedding reception, except the bridal party was missing.

Half an hour later, the tiny stage with a simple wooden elevated platform by the bar area lit up. Almost instantly, the background music came to a stop. I saw my aunt standing on the stage with the microphone.

"Good evening everyone. Are you all having fun?" she asked excitedly.

The rowdier guests shouted "Yes!" mixed with some wolf whistling from a table of young men, probably in their early twenties.

"Very good. Thank you. My family would like to say thank you to all of you for joining us tonight in celebrating an important occasion for us. As some of you may already know, one of our family members from the Philippines recently came to Houston to visit us, and we wanted to introduce you to her. Of course, what's the best way to do that than by hosting a *Pinoy* party? Yeah?" my aunt giggled as the guests cheered.

"We are having this party to celebrate her birthday in advance, and also to congratulate her. But first, let's call her onstage. Ladies and gentlemen, let's give it up for my beautiful niece, Janelle Marquez," my aunt continued.

Wooly then looked at me and motioned for me to get up onto the stage.

I was dumbfounded. I sat frozen in my seat as I tried to wrap my brain around what my Tita Girlie had just said.

Congratulate me for what? Didn't she know I broke off my engagement with Anthony already? I thought.

I felt someone tapping my shoulder. I realized my Tito Boy was standing next to me, asking if he could escort me to the stage. I hesitated for a second before getting up from my seat to oblige out of respect. At the back of my head, I was fuming at my cousin for pulling his little trick on me without giving me a warning.

I thought he was on my team, I told myself quietly. As I walked slowly to the stage with my uncle, I heard some teenage boys in a corner whispering behind me.

"She doesn't look like a fob," one of them said.

Wait. Fob? Did he mean fab? I thought.

When I finally reached the stage, I smiled sweetly at Wooly, secretly plotting his downfall when the night was over. I then mentally exhaled, waiting for yet another tragic surprise.

Suddenly, a familiar face caught my attention.

Standing in the far corner by the entrance door with a bunch of young men, smiling casually and looking at me, was James.

Chapter 33

Sisiw.

I was talking in my head, saying my slogan over and over, shaking off the edginess and the nerves that threatened to eat me alive if the tiny platform in the social hall didn't swallow me first.

I was having the worst stage fright of my life, just like the time I did my first interactive, animated Powerpoint presentation for our ad agency in the Philippines, in front of about a hundred critical, unforgiving clients who, I swore, were sizing me up.

I tried not to look at James who was standing at the back, behind the seated guests.

The mantra in my head was making me more anxious. I looked away and tried to concentrate.

"Janelle."

I heard Wooly's voice calling my name. I looked at him as he took over the microphone on the stage, as my aunt went back to the dinner table.

"Ladies and gentlemen, y'all still having fun?" he asked the audience enthusiastically.

The guests at the party responded eagerly, "Yes!"

"Awesome. Well, I'm about to tell you all a cool story, and I want you to pay close attention. Last year, our architectural company—WJ and Associates—was moved by an idea. It was so powerful that we were compelled to take action. We're about to show you what that idea is, and you be the judge. See if it will change your lives as much as it did ours," he said.

The lights grew dim, slowly at first, until all corners of the social hall turned pitch black. A sliver of light escaped from the projector

173

mounted on the stage behind me. A short movie clip began playing onscreen. I stood frozen as I saw the film begin to unravel its magical story that I was ever so familiar with.

It was the film clip Jay Anne and I had produced to solicit donations for a small non-profit organization in the Philippines called Love in the Bucket. It was a charitable organization, helping abused and neglected street children in Manila and neighboring areas.

Jay Anne and I decided to give not just our time, but our marketing expertise to the organization for free so we could raise money to support their mission—to give the underprivileged kids a chance to get off the streets and live better, safer, and more meaningful lives.

I felt awed by Jay Anne's creativity and the amount of passion he had invested in the short film, to encourage donors to contribute in helping the weakest among us and raising them, even from a distance, as if they were our own. When the film ended, my heart was crying in secret. Helping the street kids had always been an emotional journey for me.

I heard the guests clapping their hands and whispering among themselves. Slowly, the lights in the social hall came back on, one by one.

"Ladies and gentlemen, thank you for your patience. Without further ado, let me introduce you to the co-creator of that short film, and one of the forces behind the organization's campaign to help the street children of the Philippines. Let's give a round of applause for my awesome cousin, Janelle," Wooly said proudly.

I walked slowly towards him and stood by his side, my anxiety gone, replaced by a sense of understanding and gratitude. I smiled sweetly at my aunt and uncle, who were beaming at me from the audience.

"Janelle, when you sent the film to us, I knew it was going to be special. So I took it to the firm. When we saw your film, we were all moved. It's hard to explain, but to make a long story short, we all felt we had to do something. So James and I spearheaded soliciting donations from the generous people of Houston who were willing to help the organization that you're passionately supporting. In fact, they're here tonight to present you with their donations to help Love in the Bucket care for the street children of our beloved Philippines.

"I'd like to call my good friend James to the stage. Come up here, *pare*," Wooly said, smiling. He had used the word *pare*, which means buddy, or friend, in Tagalog. It originated from the Spanish word *compadre*.

Within a few minutes, James was walking towards the stage holding a gigantic check addressed to the street children advocates of Love in the Bucket. He presented the check to me onstage, followed by a few other people representing several organizations in Houston who had also made donations.

At that moment, I forgot all the bad surprises I'd been through since Anthony and Camilla ruined not just my vacation, not just my life, but my whole perspective of life. Two weeks before I was to say goodbye to Houston, I couldn't believe the nearly hostile city had given me the sweetest gift Jay Anne and I, and the entire organization helping the street kids, could ever wish for.

I didn't have a prepared speech, but when I took the microphone to speak to the audience, the words just flowed easily.

"Thank you.

"I would like to thank all of you for sharing your time and blessings in reaching out to an organization on the other side of the world that's been working tirelessly to make the lives of our unfortunate kids in the Philippines so much better than what they had in the streets.

"I'd like to thank my family here in Houston for hosting this get-together, and for keeping the purpose of this party a secret from me until just a few minutes ago. This is a wonderful surprise. Thank you, Tita Girlie, Tito Boy, and my cousin Will, my niece Sophia, my nephew Kenneth, and of course, James.

"On behalf of Jay Veneracion, my friend who conceptualized and created the short film shown just a few minutes ago, I thank you. Jay has tirelessly campaigned to solicit donations for the kids as well. On behalf of the rest of the volunteers and staff of Love in the Bucket, the organization responsible for using your generous donations to help the kids, I would also like to say thank you."

"Finally, I'd like to express my deepest gratitude on behalf of the street children in the Philippines—those little abandoned angels roaming the streets without food, protection, supervision, guidance, caring, shelter, clothing, education, and other basic needs that most of us are privileged to have at our disposal. Be assured that with the help of your donations, their lives tomorrow will be much better than what they had yesterday. God bless your hearts everyone," I said.

I could barely remember how the audience responded to my speech. I heard clapping, but I was too overwhelmed to observe what was going on around me. All I knew was I did my best not to cry.

After my speech, I saw James looking at me, his soft brown eyes probing. I left the stage quietly and went back to sit at the table with my family. I heard a slight commotion from some teenage girls forming a huddle in front of the stage, giggling among themselves.

I saw James walking onto the stage, his bright yellow electric guitar slung on his back. He went over to the front and adjusted the height of the microphone stand, momentarily calming the teenage girls swooning at the sight of the architect.

"Before we all call it a night, let's give our guest of honor one more reason to smile," James said on the microphone, smiling at me.

His band started playing as he began to sing the first lines of my favorite Smashing Pumpkins song, "Blew Away." James strummed his guitar slowly, rhythmically, singing the lyrics of the song with his soft, raspy voice.

It was surreal. Blue Fin played the notes perfectly, as if they owned the song. And before I could even wake up from my epic dream, James and his band went on to recreate "With a Smile," my all-time-favorite Eraserheads song. The teenage girls in the audience went nuts, screaming and jumping.

I looked at James as he sang the familiar lines of the song, his head bent down, oblivious to the wild reception in front of him, seemingly distant, perhaps in a different sphere, lost in his rhythmic strumming of his electric guitar. In the middle of the song, he looked at the audience, finding me a few seconds later. For a moment our gazes locked, giving me goosebumps all over my body like I'd never felt before.

I smiled at James, acknowledging the wonderful young man who I had only met two weeks ago—the same one who knew only half of my story, but chose to be on my side. I hoped I wasn't falling for him. Not another long-distance relationship that would hurt me in the end. Not another failure to struggle to get over with.

James stood in front of the microphone and sang the last lines of the song *a cappella*, still looking at me, his hazel eyes piercing, burning a hole in my skin. He smiled warmly when he finished singing, momentarily taking his gaze off me, raising his arm to thank his supportive audience.

When his teenage female fans calmed down, he looked at me again, smiled warmly, and bowed slightly with his palms touching, positioned perfectly right in front of his chest, the way Japanese people express their acknowledgment and respect.

I smiled at him warmly, trying to imitate his Japanese bow. He smiled back at me. I knew right then that leaving Houston wouldn't be easy.

Chapter 34

"Mom, can you get me the purple stuff?"

I looked at the teenage girl by the buffet table, talking to her mother.

"Ano'ng gusto mo?" The teenager's mother tried to clarify what her daughter wanted from the table.

"The purple stuff. The sticky thingies with the sugar and the shaved coconut," the teen replied.

I looked at the table and realized the teenage girl wanted the *puto bumbong.*

Puto bumbong were the traditional Filipino rice delicacy available in most restaurants in the Philippines. They were purple, shaped like soft pretzels, steamed, and sprinkled with sugar and coconut flakes.

When I was little, *puto bumbong* were only sold outside churches where people attended the traditional *Misa de Gallo,* during the Christmas season. They were the rock stars of the pastry lot in the Philippines, selling like hotcakes after the mass, shortly before sunrise.

The teenage girl at the buffet table called them sticky purple thingies. I found it strange and a bit funny how in Houston, some Filipino kids would love certain Filipino dishes, but wouldn't know what they were called. Back home in the Philippines, I couldn't imagine anyone not knowing what some popular American dishes were called.

We don't refer to the famous American sandwich the-beef-patty-in-a-bun-with-tomatoes-and-pickles-and-the-red-and-yellow-sauce thingy. We call it a hamburger, I thought a little too defensively.

"Hey. You okay?"

James's voice startled me. I was so engrossed in people-watching, I didn't realize he was standing next to me. I wondered how long he'd been waiting until I finally noticed I had company.

"Hey. I'm fine. Great performance, by the way. And thanks for singing those two songs. They're my ultra-favorites," I said, smiling.

"Thanks. We tried to learn the songs in time. Glad you liked the cover," James said.

We hung out by the buffet table feasting on appetizers until my cousin popped out of nowhere.

"Dude, I kinda knew you wouldn't flake out on me. Thanks for coming," Wooly told James, patting his Japanese-American friend on the back.

"My pleasure, bro," James said smiling.

"So how's Daniella? Did you see her new place? Did you guys finish hauling her stuff into her new apartment?" Wooly asked casually.

"We didn't," James said, looking at me and then at my cousin, as if confused.

"Oh. My bad," Wooly said slowly, looking at me, then back at James. He patted our backs and started heading back to attend to guests at a nearby table.

"What are those?" James asked, trying to shake off his confusion it seemed, referring to the plate I was holding.

"Cheese sticks, cheese cubes, and mini *puto* with cheese," I said casually.

"I can tell you hate cheese." He laughed softly.

"Haha," I said mockingly.

"What about those?" James asked, curious about the dessert on my other plate.

"*Pichi pichi,*" I said.

Pichi pichi was another Filipino pastry made from sweet sticky rice, steamed, and served with coconut flakes.

"Looks good. My mom makes something similar called *mochi balls*," he said, smiling.

"Japanese dessert?" I asked

"Yeah. They're good. Before you leave for the Philippines, I'll ask my mom to make some for you so you can taste some homemade Japanese cooking," he said.

"Does your dad cook too? Looks like everyone in the family loves to cook," I said.

"Nah. Pat hates being in the kitchen, and my dad relies on my mom for his daily sustenance," James said, laughing. "But my mom and I love hanging out in the kitchen. I like cooking. My mom loves it. I'll take you to her kitchen one time when she's not working at the hospital. She may even have time to teach us a new Japanese recipe if we're lucky," he added.

"Your mom works in the hospital?" I asked, wondering if his mother was also a nurse like my aunt.

"She's a cardiologist, but you can't ask anything about her work when you're in her kitchen. She doesn't like talking about her profession when she's at home unless, of course, there's a medical emergency," he said while spearing a couple of egg rolls and putting them on his plate.

James didn't like talking about his profession when we were together, either. He must have gotten that trait from his mother.

"Has your mom met Daniella yet?" I heard myself asking.

If it were only possible to push a button and turn into a stone after saying something embarrassing, I would have done so already, I thought.

James looked at me as if pondering how to respond.

Where was that turn-into-stone button again? I scolded myself in my head.

"No. I never introduced her to my parents. Not to be disrespectful to Daniella or anything. I just didn't think about it. And for the record, I didn't help her move into her new apartment, like Will thought. She asked for my help, so I called a moving service for her—the moving company that we use for the firm. They're trustworthy. The moving company called Daniella instead so they could make arrangements. I haven't seen her since we officially separated a year ago, and I'd like to keep it that way," he explained.

I looked at James, trying my best to hide my relief.

So he wasn't back with Daniella. Not yet, at least, I thought.

"James, we need help dismantling the audio-visual equipment on the stage." I heard Wooly's voice from behind.

James and I turned around to see my cousin half-running as he approached us.

"Jan, I need to borrow James for a few minutes. Think you can handle the appetizers all by yourself?" Wooly teased, smiling.

I smiled back and nodded, letting the two men dash to the front to help my uncle and his *compadres* with the heavy equipment on the stage.

I resumed eating, spearing a *pichi pichi* and popping it into my mouth.

"*Neng,* do you know how to speak Tagalog?"

I almost dropped my plate when I heard a man's deep voice coming out of nowhere.

Chapter 35

I looked behind me, wondering if the mysterious voice was talking to me.

A good-looking middle-aged man stood by the bar area, holding a drink. He was smiling kindly at me.

"I know you came from the Philippines, but I didn't know the local language you speak. Is it Tagalog, Ilongo, Cebuano?" the man said, smiling.

"*Tagalog po. Kumusta po?*" I said respectfully. I told him I spoke Tagalog.

He smiled and then slowly walked towards me.

The man was like an angel, appearing out of nowhere, telling me a beautiful, inspiring story. For what purpose, I didn't clearly know at that time.

He said he was an engineer, getting ready for retirement. He had ten years to go and was saving up for a wonderful and financially comfortable life back home in the Philippines with his beloved wife.

Twenty-five years ago, he and his wife set out to immigrate to California. He was an engineer back home, and his wife was a financial consultant in a prominent bank. They had a comfortable life as a newly married couple, but their aspirations were far loftier than the average yuppie in the Philippines.

They both thought about the future of their kids and the much better quality of life they wanted to live. So they decided to set out for their American dream.

At twenty-seven, they knew they had a promising future in the much-sought-after land of opportunities. But life was not that easy. When the couple arrived in the United States, they had extreme difficulty settling in a decent home, and even more difficulty landing the kind of jobs appropriate for their education, expertise, and professional fields. Bad luck struck many times, and their pride was whipped over and over and over.

Dreams then turned into desperation.

After a few months of trying, their savings going down the drain with no one but themselves to rely on, the man and his wife found themselves working as janitors in an apartment complex. His once-fashionable wife cleaned elevators, while he maintained the rest of the building. They often found themselves crying in private during their rare mid-afternoon breaks together.

But like old fairy tale stories, their storm clouds had a silver lining. It made them tougher and hungrier to get what they promised themselves they would achieve.

After years of hard work and sacrifices, between disdainful looks thrown by fellow Filipinos who scoffed at their plight, and a handful of kind *kababayan* who gave almost everything they had to help them overcome their difficulties, a ray of sunshine finally showed up.

He was finally accepted as a maintenance worker in a prominent engineering firm and almost instantly, his wife became an administrative assistant at a financial consulting firm. After ten years, he became one of the most recognized engineers of the firm, and his wife rose to become one of the most award-winning financial consultants in the company that took her in.

They moved to Houston five years ago to buy a new house in an exclusive subdivision with more amenities than they had had in their older California home, for almost the same amount. He was retired, and his wife was currently working as an executive assistant in a firm, just to fight off boredom.

And they lived happily ever after.

"The End?" I asked.

"Of course not," the man said.

"Life goes on. You don't know what it has in store for you, but you ride with it. Wherever it takes you, you flow with it until you mold yourself to sustain the bumps. You'll never go down, no matter what, because you've already learned to brace for the impact. Seeing the darkest days in the ugliest phase of your existence in this unpredictable world has its benefits. You fear nothing because you've already been there, you've seen it, and you've survived," he said philosophically.

"*Alam mo, hija*—you know what, young lady? That good-looking gentleman with you, James. I know his family. Good family. You may hear some young people here in Houston saying bad things about James, but that's all in the past. I know deep inside he's a good man. And I know, deep inside, you believe me too. If one day you two end up together and you decide to live here in the United States, you will encounter a lot of bumps. It's not a bed of roses like what most of the people back in the Philippines think. Life will be hard and great at the same time. Sometimes, you'll feel like going back. But you fight the urge. You focus on the great. You have to make sacrifices. And then, you'll have a good life," the man said, smiling kindly.

I had no clue why the man suddenly showed up to tell me his story and impart his words of wisdom that night. But later on, it served as my guiding light in making one of the most critical decisions I had ever made in my life.

***

"Are you kidding me?"

I heard James's flustered voice as he sat in his chair next to me, visibly shocked, looking at the young woman coming in through the big wooden doors of the social hall. She was a gorgeous-looking brunette, slim yet curvaceous. She had long, rich, wavy hair, a fair complexion, and prominent *mestiza* features. She was wearing a short black dress and red stilettos, which enhanced her long, beautiful legs.

Walking next to her was an older lady, seemingly in her late fifties. She also looked sophisticated, yet more conservative, wearing a nice beige suit and matching nude, pointy high heels. Her hair was tied in a classy bun, and her pearl jewelry glistened under the soft lights of the social hall.

"There's nothing fashionable about coming to the party this late. The caterers have already packed up. They're putting the person who coined 'Filipino Time' to shame," Wooly whispered, half-joking, half-serious.

"Dude, I don't freaking believe this. She had the nerve to show up here. Was she invited?" James addressed Wooly, also whispering, making sure none of the people around us could hear him.

"Mrs. Schultz is on the guest list, but Daniella is not," Wooly replied, sounding a little confused.

I looked at the young woman in the little black dress. "So that's Daniella," I said, talking to myself in a hushed tone.

James looked at me as if he had momentarily forgotten I was sitting there with him and my cousin, right in the middle of the social hall.

"She's very pretty," I whispered to James.

I thought I saw him flinch, but he quickly checked his demeanor and chose not to say anything.

"So there you are. Hiding from everybody. As usual."

James and I looked at the woman standing in front of us. Her voice was soft and melodic, yet catty, reminding me of my phone conversation with Camilla the day after I caught her in bed with Anthony. She made quite an entrance, making people's heads turn, especially those of the younger men, and their mothers and grandmothers glaring at them.

Daniella's right hand rested on her hip, standing proudly, her eyes caressing every inch of James's body. She looked very sensual, a bit inappropriate for my taste, which made me feel quite uncomfortable.

I tried my best to mask my unease. I sat next to James, poised, as if waiting patiently for what was going to happen next.

"Daniella. Of all places, I didn't expect you to be here," James said casually.

He sat on his chair for the next ten seconds, but the gentleman in him finally took over. He reluctantly stood up and offered his chair to the lovely party crasher.

"Thanks, babe. But I'd rather stand up. How have you been? You look great. As if you didn't miss me. I missed you," Daniella cooed.

Suddenly she slipped her arms around James, who was standing just a foot away from her, and gave him a tight hug.

"I missed you. You smell so good, baby," Daniella said in her sultry voice, putting her head on James's shoulder, sniffing his shirt like a hungry puppy.

I felt awkward, but I still didn't move from where I was sitting, trying to be the little Miss Goody Shock Absorber. I saw the guests around us looking wide-eyed, not knowing how to react to Daniella's bold behavior. My grandmother would have called her *malaswang kerengkeng,* meaning a woman who is both inappropriate and a flirt.

I heard some ladies whispering among themselves, telling their little kids to wrap up as they were getting ready to leave. James seemed embarrassed as he carefully removed himself from Daniella's grip. His soft brown eyes suddenly looked dark, shocked at how his ex-girlfriend was behaving in public.

"Daniella. Please," James said, his voice low as he untangled himself from her arms.

"Anyway, I'd like you to meet my friend." James looked at me, motioning for me to stand next to him, as if begging me to save him from Daniella's tentacles. I stood up obligingly, smiling sweetly at his ex-girlfriend.

"Daniella, this is Janelle. She's Will's younger cousin. She's visiting Houston," James said, holding my elbow lightly. I felt an electric shock zap through my bones and I almost jumped, but I pretended nothing had happened.

Daniella stared at James's hand resting on my elbow with enlarged eyes. Even with my high heels on, I was at least four inches shorter than her, but I didn't let that dampen my faked self-confidence. I smiled innocently, even though I secretly wanted to strangle her just for being the best friend of the woman who'd ruined my future. She reminded me so much of Camilla and every other woman who broke up happy homes, promising relationships and people's trust.

"Oh. It's you," Daniella said, her voice quivering, trying to hide her contempt.

"It's me what?" I asked her politely, feigning surprise yet fully aware that being Camilla's best friend, she knew exactly who I was.

"Nothing, dear." Daniella said it in her sweet voice, yet her eyes were glaring.

"Anyway. James, honey, I only came here because I wanted to see you, since you left me all alone today when I moved to my own apartment. I was wondering if you can take me home tonight so I can show you my new pad," she continued in her purring voice, pouting at James.

"No prob. And sorry I couldn't help you today. Been really busy," James apologized.

"No problem, baby. You can make it up to me tonight," Daniella almost purred in James's ear.

James looked at Daniella and smiled, his soft brown eyes drawing his ex-lover in like magnets.

"I can't. I'm sorry. I'm taking someone else home tonight," James said.

"And who could that be?" Daniella asked, smiling hesitantly.

"Janelle. I'm taking Janelle home tonight," James said casually.

I looked at James. He looked at ease, yet the expression in his eyes seemed cold. I looked at Daniella, whose smile seemed frozen on her lovely face; her eyes were fixed on James's eyes, as if she was struggling to contain a range of emotions exploding simultaneously inside her. I was left in the middle, trying my best to determine what was transpiring among the three of us.

Suddenly Daniella turned and looked at me, her smile perversely fixed on her face. She looked quite vampiric, her pouting lips quivering, ready to shred me into pieces with her sharp fangs concealed behind her voluptuous lips.

I looked into the dark pools of her eyes and could have sworn what I saw in there was frightening. It was boiling rage beneath the confidently cool façade of a beautiful woman who wasn't used to being denied what she wanted.

Chapter 36

I locked the door of the tiny cubicle behind me, careful not to stain its brightly painted walls with the melted chocolate still oozing from my chiffon blouse.

The small toilet stall in the rest room of the social hall was just big enough to accommodate my tiny body struggling to get out of my sticky top. With one eye on my precious purse and the gray cotton shirt hanging next to it on the wall, I meticulously took off my jewelry while holding onto the bottom part of my blouse with my teeth, making sure the chocolate stayed on the blouse where it was supposed to be.

I listened for any sounds inside the rest room, making doubly sure I was the only one in there. When I sensed no movement, I quickly wrapped my jewelry with toilet paper and stuck it in the deep pocket of my pants. I then began the difficult process of taking off my blouse without getting any sticky stuff on my hair.

When I finally set myself free from my chocolate-drenched top, I dashed out of the toilet stall, grabbed some paper towels by the sink and soaked them in warm water. Feeling self-conscious, almost half-naked with just my chemise on, I quickly ran back inside the toilet stall and locked the door behind me.

A few seconds later I heard the outer door of the restroom open and close. The sound of footsteps quickly followed.

"Don't let this consume you, *hija*. It's not worth it. She's not worth it," a female voice said. She sounded older, with a clipped, sophisticated Filipino accent.

"I don't get it, Tita. Why is that girl always in the way? It's annoying," another female voice said. She sounded young; her American twang and melodic voice were strangely pleasant to listen to.

I wiped my arms and neck with the damp towel in my hand slowly and silently, careful not to draw attention to my location. Fortunately, the toilet stall's door extended all the way to the floor—for more privacy, I guessed—which made it difficult for anyone outside to know whether there was anyone inside the stall or not.

The two voices outside didn't seem to care, anyway, as they continued their conversation.

"My daughter will definitely have a fit when she finds out you're having problems with the same girl who came all the way from the other side of the world to inject herself in her relationship with her boyfriend—the same night my daughter found out she was pregnant. What a terrible intruder. *Que horror!*" the older woman said dramatically.

"And now she's trying to steal my man. What a bitch. She doesn't know what I'm capable of. She better thank her lucky stars I only chose to drench her with melted chocolate. It could have been worse. I'm not done with her yet," the younger woman said angrily.

I stopped what I was doing.

First, the melted chocolate. Second, stealing her man. Third, a girl coming from the other side of the world. Fourth, and most shocking, her daughter is pregnant. What in the world? I thought.

My head pounded as if my nerves were swimming in all sorts of emotions. I held onto the door, making no sound, trying my best not to hyperventilate inside the stall. The connection between me and the women outside was getting clearer.

"Daniella, don't tell me you're threatened by that short F.O.B. who probably can't speak English. I don't think James would fall for someone like that," the older woman said while chuckling.

And with that, my suspicions were finally confirmed. The women inside the rest room with me, who talked freely without any reservations, were no other than the party crashers—Camilla's mother and Daniella, James's ex-girlfriend.

"You're right, Tita. Little Miss Fresh-Off-the-Boat has nothing on me. She's a joke. James is only using her to get even with me, and heaven knows it won't take long before James comes crawling back to me, begging me to take him back," Daniella said confidently.

"Right. But anyway, hush, hush. Make sure her aunt, my *comadre*, doesn't find out I know the story between that F.O.B. and Anthony, and the extent of Camilla's involvement. You know how news travels fast around here. I'll be the talk of the town. And you know what that means. I will lose my position as president of the biggest Fil-Am organization in Houston. That is never happening," Camilla's mom warned Daniella.

Perfect timing, I thought.

I bolted out of the toilet stall to surprise my scandalous detractors.

Camilla's mom and Daniella were shocked beyond belief, but being the smooth, cunning women they were, they were quick to recover. Their facial reactions changed in an instant, as if nothing was said. They both smiled sweetly at me.

Big mistake you mean women, I thought.

And just as I expected, the pretense did not last very long. Daniella's eyes were set ablaze, glaring at me when she saw the gray top I was wearing.

It was James's button-down shirt, the one he was wearing at the party. He took it off and handed it to me on my way to change in the restroom after he saw me dripping in melted chocolate—right after Daniella "accidentally" spilled the chocolate fondue on me as we all headed out of the social hall after the party. Fortunately, James was wearing a white T-shirt underneath.

I smiled sweetly at Daniella in the restroom, fully aware that I had just successfully "kicked" her in the teeth.

"Nice shirt, but it looks better on my babe, James," Daniella said coldly.

"Gee thanks. The same thing happened last night. James took me to a concert. We were out until midnight and I felt really cold, so he took off his shirt and told me to wear it instead … because I was wearing a pretty skimpy top. I don't know what the modern American term for that is. I'm not that good at speaking American English, but I thought someone at the party said I looked … uhm … smoking hot? Is that what it's called? But anyway, James took off his shirt inside his car while I tried to warm up next to him in the passenger's side. It was funny you mentioned that. James told me last night his shirt looked so much better on me," I said sweetly, smiling innocently, pretending I wasn't lying through my teeth.

"Is that right?" Daniella said, upset. I heard her voice reverberating inside the spacious rest room.

"Yeah. He's such a sweet guy. And super cute. I'm so glad I met him. I didn't know the grass could be so much greener on the other side," I said coldly, turning to look at Camilla's mom.

I instinctively grabbed my purse and my soiled blouse from the stall, washed my hands in the sink, and started to head out the door when I heard Daniella say something behind me.

"You know what, Tita? I really wonder how it feels to be second best," Daniella said, her voice cracking, full of contempt.

I slowly turned around to look at the two conniving women staring at me.

"I really don't know why you're wondering, Daniella. You shouldn't look very far. You can ask the woman next to you, oh I almost forgot. You may ask her pregnant daughter, too. Camilla—the one who's now living with my former fiancé. You must be acquainted with Anthony. You know, the man I came to Houston for—the same man who proposed marriage to me? I'm sure they'll tell you how it feels. Now, if you'll excuse me. James, your former babe, is waiting outside. Not for you, dear, but for me," I said icily. I opened the restroom door slowly, holding back my tears. I wanted to explode, but I held myself together.

I stepped outside and didn't look back.

Chapter 37

The cold water felt good.

I drank a full glass with my eyes closed, savoring every single ounce of sustenance my body could take.

I had had a long day. My body and mind were beaten up, exhausted beyond comprehension. I stood by the polished wooden breakfast table in my aunt's immaculately clean kitchen, lost in thought, wondering if I would make it to my bedroom across the hallway.

If I were at home in the Philippines, I would have just passed out as soon as I opened the big oak door in the living room, not giving a care how my shocked family and household help would be when they found me the morning after. My mother would have freaked out upon seeing me sprawled on her lovely rug, still clothed in my dressy outfit, and given me a stern lecture on maturity and responsibility while asking me on the side what I wanted for breakfast.

But I wasn't home.

Instead, I was thousands of miles away from my protective shell, in a finicky city—sometimes cold, sometimes warm—where strangers judged me.

F.O.B. for Fresh Off the Boat, or fob.

That's how they labeled me.

I didn't really know where the boat concept came from, because I did not travel by boat to come to the United States, and just thinking about floating in a small water vehicle for more than fourteen hours in the vast oceans to get to mighty America from Asia made me cringe.

But being a fob seemed more complex, derogatory, and reeking of negativity. I remembered Camilla's mom laughing in the restroom at the party when she was talking to Daniella about it, referring to me as the unworthy, short F.O.B. Even James looked uncomfortable when I asked him about it after the party.

James.

The silver lining in my stormy journey in America, the good-looking rock star who everyone wanted to have a piece of; one of the few significant people in Houston, outside of my family, who had never shown a single sign of negativity nor discrimination towards me.

I remembered how we ended up at Bubbly Tea House after the party.

We were one of the last people to leave the parking lot of the social hall. Daniella waited by James's car to wage her last battle to win her ex-boyfriend over, at least for the night, but James was firm on his decision not to take her home. He offered to drop her off at her apartment, though, but on one condition: I had to come along.

It was obvious what had happened next. Daniella threw a fit. Not the scandalous kind, but that which we imagine supermodels do when they get ditched by their lovers—the subdued, sophisticated, but brimming with hatred kind. After brushing off her loss, Daniella conceded, blowing a kiss to James and throwing a glaring "you're dead" look in my direction.

To make up for his ex-girlfriend's behavior, James offered to drive over to Bubbly Tea House so he could buy me a drink.

"And we're here again." James laughed softly while handing me my delicious cup of cappuccino bubble tea. It was our second time at the tea house since I met him that fateful night when I ran away from my terrible encounter with Anthony and Camilla.

"I love this stuff," I said enthusiastically as I sipped on my cold *boba*.

"Sweet," James said, looking half-concerned, half-relieved.

When we got settled in a small booth by the corner window, James spoke first.

"Janelle, I want to apologize for Daniella. She can be immature sometimes. If all that melted chocolate doesn't come off your top, we'll go get you a new one."

I smiled as I replied. "James, please don't feel like it's your fault. You have absolutely nothing to do with her behavior. I'm fine. I'm a shopaholic, and I can't believe I'm saying this, but I have a lot of tops like that. I don't need another one," I said reassuringly.

"Hmm. I can't believe you said that. Other girls wouldn't pass up the opportunity to go shopping," James said, laughing.

Other girls won't pass up the opportunity to go anywhere with you, I thought.

"Correct. What was I thinking?" I said, smiling. We sipped on our cold drinks, enjoying the rich flavors.

"James, do I look like an F.O.B.?" I asked, suddenly remembering how Camilla's mom mocked me in the restroom.

James looked at me, disoriented. A mixture of emotions invaded his face in one swift motion. They were there one second and gone the next.

"What do you mean?" he asked, his eyes squinting a bit.

"I don't know. I don't even know what it means. I think it's not nice from the way it was used to describe, well, me," I said.

"To describe you? Who did that? I'm … confused," he said.

"Camilla's mom, Mrs. Schultz, the lady who came with Daniella to the party. I found out who she was in the ladies' room when I was changing in one of the stalls. She was talking to Daniella—she didn't think I was in there, or that I could hear their conversation. I think Daniella thought I was out to steal you from her, and she was pretty upset. Mrs. Schultz told her not to worry about me, the short F.O.B.," I said timidly.

James sighed.

"Hmm. Unbelievable. But anyway, how do I explain?" he said, setting his drink aside before continuing. "F.O.B. is short for Fresh Off the Boat. I don't know where that came from, but it's a term used to label people—Asians mostly—who migrated to the United States as refugees, usually from a country that didn't allow their citizens to get out. So people escaped using boats to travel to America to flee from persecution, find better opportunities, and start over. They're usually made up of families and extended families traveling in groups. Some survived and others didn't. For those who were able to get to America, they settled in refugee camps or places that enabled them to start from the bottom, find opportunities or employment, and progress in life. Of course, since they came from an absolutely different culture and environment and lifestyle, they usually struggled to adapt to their new country. They had to learn the language and the way of life," James explained.

"And what's wrong with that?" I asked, interested in the information I was just learning about.

"There's nothing wrong. It's normal, really, and pretty basic. I mean, what did people expect, right? But of course, people will be people. So locals and other Americanized immigrants started noticing the way these refugees interacted with them, and how sort of comical their ways were—having an accent, dressing differently, eating differently. And so they started making fun of them, and they gave them a name.

"F.O.B., or fob. And these terms have evolved. Now, even tourists or anyone who came to the United States for the first time can be labeled a fob, depending on the standards of the person doing the labeling," James said.

"So, Camilla's mom called me a fob because this is my first time to come to America. She said I probably didn't know how to speak English," I told James as I recalled what had happened in the rest room.

James looked at me, his hazel eyes looking soft and bright in the dim light of the teahouse.

"Janelle, I have to tell you this. There's nothing negative or wrong about being a refugee or a person that has newly set foot in America. The people who come here with nothing but dreams and then progress to become successful in the end are admirable. If people call them F.O.B., so be it. But they are the strongest and most resilient people I know, and I have nothing but respect for them," he said. "I, personally, think you're far from being a fob, because of your circumstances and your personality. But who cares? I don't think it matters. If they start calling you an F.O.B. for the mere fact that you're new here and they want to make fun of you, don't worry about it. You can't control people. You can only ignore them. You shouldn't really be affected," he added.

"Of course, not," I said, smiling. James smiled back as if a heavy burden was taken off his back.

***

I snapped out of my musing.

I looked at the clock on the wall in my aunt's kitchen, shocked at the time. It was almost three in the morning. I hadn't realized I'd been sitting in the kitchen for almost two hours already, since James had dropped me off at the house. I could feel exhaustion taking over my body. I quickly tossed the remaining water from my glass into the sink and washed the glass, enjoying the warmth of the water caressing my hands like silk.

After turning off the lights in the kitchen, I headed to the hallway. Without even turning the lights on in my bedroom, I headed straight to the adjoining bathroom to take a warm shower.

After an hour of prepping for bed, I came out of the bathroom in my pink pajamas and matching fluffy Hello Kitty slippers. I sighed deeply, inhaling the aromatic scent of verbena shower gel and lotion.

Whoever said happiness couldn't be bought has never shopped at L'Occitane, I thought.

I turned on my bedroom lamp. I almost had a heart attack as I jumped at the sight of what was sitting on my bed. Next to it was a small note. The handwriting was printed in small letters, but I could still read the words.

Dear Janelle,

I thought you wanted these. Call me first thing when you wake up tomorrow morning.

James

Chapter 38

I heard the phone ringing.

Five, six, seven times. I was about to hang up when suddenly someone on the other end picked up.

"Hello?"

The masculine voice sounded raspy and low, as if recovering from a hefty dose of will-you-please-hang-up-and-let-me-sleep-all-day medicine.

"James?" I asked hesitantly.

"Yeah. Who's this?" James almost whispered. He sounded like he just woke up; his bedroom voice and throaty breathing gave me goosebumps all over. I quickly shook the feeling away, putting my focus instead on the fluffy yellow stuffed toy sitting on my bed.

"Hey, it's Janelle. I think I woke you up and I'm sorry. I didn't mean to disrupt your sleep. I'll just call you back later," I said quickly. I felt embarrassed for being too eager to get ahold of him first thing in the morning, just as he'd instructed in his handwritten note.

"Janelle? Hey. Wait. I'm good. I'm up. Not sleepy," James said in his remarkably sexy voice. I heard the rustling of what sounded like sheets in the background. I tried to focus on the purpose of my call and not imagine what he was wearing in bed.

I had to smile as the face of my shocked conservative grandmother flashed in my mind. I knew she wouldn't approve of my random unladylike thoughts.

"What time is it?" James asked.

"It's seven twenty," I said, glancing at the clock on the nightstand in my bedroom. I inspected my manicured nails absentmindedly, wondering what James was planning to tell me.

"James, you left a note for me last night. You told me to call you first thing in the morning," I continued, speaking slowly, suddenly doubting whether I had understood his note correctly.

"Yeah, I did. Sorry. When I wrote the note, I didn't think we'd be home past midnight after the party. I didn't realize you'd only get a few hours of sleep last night. Shouldn't have asked you to call this early," he apologized.

"Oh. That's fine. You're forgetting. I'm a tourist. I'm supposed to lose a lot of sleep," I said, smiling.

I glanced at the stuffed toy and the three bright pink balloons tied around its chubby wrist. They looked really cute, as if they didn't nearly give me a heart attack when I found them on top of my bed last night.

"James, I also meant to ask. There's a yellow stuffed toy with three balloons sitting on my bed right now. Somebody left them in my room last night next to your note," I said carefully.

"Oh yeah. Pikachu," James said in his bedroom voice. I wondered if he'd sound as cute when he spoke Japanese, if he even knew how to.

"Yes," I said.

I heard James laugh softly. "I asked Will to give the stuffed toy and the balloons to you when you got home last night, but I guess I didn't anticipate we'd go out for *boba* and get home late. He must've just left them in your room," he said, sounding amused.

"But from whom? What's the occasion? I'm confused," I said softly.

"Uhm ... Remember when Will and I came to your uncle's house from the office with the kids? You were home alone. Well, when I was standing by the door, I saw you looking at the Pikachu stuffed toy and balloons I was holding. I couldn't forget your facial reaction when the kids took them from me. I thought you were sort of disappointed? Not in a bad way. So I kind of made it my mission to get you your own Pikachu and balloons ... uhm ... before you leave Houston. I guess for

202

some odd reason, at that time, I had the impression you thought the stuff I was holding was for you," he explained a bit hesitantly.

Oh no. He could really read my mind. What else did he know about me? I'd better stop thinking about how sexy his voice is or what he's wearing in bed. Hay naku, I thought, cringing.

"Janelle? Are you still there?" James asked.

"Yes," I said, feeling small as I sat stiffly in my bed, holding the phone with my trembling hand. "Thank you … for thinking of me. You're very thoughtful. I love the Pikachu," I said shyly.

"You're welcome. Consider it my advanced birthday gift," James said, his voice sounding a bit melancholic.

I was quiet on the other end, uncertain on what to say, feeling a bit nostalgic myself, knowing James wouldn't be with me when I celebrated my birthday in the Philippines in two months.

"Janelle, are you doing anything today?" James asked.

"Me? Not really. I don't have any plans yet," I said.

"Cool. I don't either … uhm … I meant to ask," he said hesitantly.

I was silent on the other end, wondering what James was going to say. I had no idea what was happening, but my tummy started feeling queasy, and I could feel my heart beating faster than normal.

"I was wondering if you'd like to spend your Sunday with me," he continued.

I almost dropped the phone.

Maria Janelle Marquez, ano ka ba? What's going on with you? James only wants to hang out. Calm down, I scolded myself silently.

"Yes! … I mean, yes. Let's spend Sunday together. That would be fun," I said, my face turning red, my heart and mind confused with my strange reaction to James's invitation.

"Great," he said, sounding more upbeat. "You may want to start getting ready now. Traffic will be horrendous pretty soon. Dress casually. No high heels please," he said, teasing.

"I'll pick you up at your house in half an hour," he added.

"Two hours," I said. "I need two hours to get ready."

"Uhm … Is that a Filipino thing?" James asked, laughing softly.

"No. It's a Janelle thing," I said, smiling.

Chapter 39

Sunday morning at my aunt's house was pretty hectic. By eight o'clock, everyone was already out the door.

My uncle and aunt were meeting with friends from their local church, to attend the monthly bake sale right after hearing the first mass of the day, and Kenneth and Sophia were dropped off by Wooly at a sports facility nearby for their weekly swimming lessons. Wooly then headed out to the gym for his early morning workout.

When I asked Wooly why the kids didn't go to church with my uncle and aunt, my cousin said he and the kids only went to church when Charm wasn't traveling. I knew I had to go to church as well, but since I was on vacation and had very limited time, I figured God would understand and give me a pass until I went back to the Philippines to resume my normal life.

My family was Roman Catholic, and we hardly missed a Sunday mass. My parents would be disappointed when they found out I hadn't attended church for three consecutive Sundays already.

I offered to clean up in the kitchen after everybody left, while waiting for James to pick me up at the house.

I almost dropped the plate on the kitchen floor when I heard the doorbell ring. I stood frozen in front of the dishwasher, disoriented, until the cell phone my uncle gave me started ringing. It was James.

"Hey. It's me. I'm outside. Are you ready?" James asked.

"Yeah. I'll be there in a minute," I said.

I grabbed my purse from the living room and did a last-minute check, making sure the lights in the house were turned off and no water faucet was running. I carefully armed the house, opened the front door, and locked it securely just as my uncle had instructed.

Just leaving your house to go somewhere here in America is too much work already, I thought.

James got out of his car when he saw me by the front door. He had on khaki cargo shorts, a simple white shirt, Michael Jordan sneakers, a diver's watch, and a gray baseball cap.

I felt awkward walking towards him. I was wearing shorts and sneakers myself and felt insecure about my height.

James was probably a little over 5"10'.

He smiled at me.

"So, where to?" I asked shyly.

"To my parents' house," he said casually.

"Your parents' house?" I asked, confused.

James opened the passenger door of his car for me and said, "Yeah. They want to meet you."

***

Two curious pairs of eyes stared back at me as if wondering how the funny-looking stranger trembling in front of them could invade their home. I wanted to laugh but was too scared to even breathe.

I thought James's parents wanted to meet me. How presumptuous could I be? I scolded myself in secret, careful not to let them realize what was going on in my head.

When James picked me up at my aunt's house, he had clearly said, "They want to meet you," and not, "My parents want to meet you."

How did I miss that? To think I had spent the last twenty minutes worrying about how I'd manage to make a great first impression on his family, and for what? I continued rambling in my head.

I looked around me, mindful of the artistic décor inside James's parents' house. They were minimalists, just as I had expected. Theirs was a two-story house, just like my aunt and uncle's house, but it looked humongous, more spacious with higher ceilings and elegant French windows.

The living room area looked cozy with comfortable couches and wing chairs in white and mocha. A huge polished wooden coffee table was at the center of the room sitting on top of a contemporary area rug. The wooden floor, in dark espresso, was a pleasant contrast to the furniture. Black, red, and white were the dominant colors in the Japanese-inspired interior set on mocha tinted walls. An exotic Japanese lantern was hanging from the ceiling, hovering over the top of the breakfast table. Instead of chairs, the dark polished wooden table was flanked by two benches. A bright yellow bowl stood out, set on top of the table, sitting next to a black porcelain container holding a stack of chopsticks.

In the middle of the kitchen was a tiny island with two bar stools. The dining area, located behind the kitchen, was adorned with an area rug that complemented the beige carpet. On top of it was a low tea table surrounded by throw pillows. Dainty tea cups and a teapot in light pink and white, set in the middle of the table, lent charming character to the room.

"Are you okay?" James asked, amused.

His voice startled me, suddenly bringing me back to the two pairs of eyes observing me. I tried my best not to whimper. I thought, after everything we'd been through, I trusted James wouldn't let anything bad happen to me.

"Relax. They're not going to hurt you. I promise," James assured me, smiling. He then turned to the two pairs of eyes and spoke to them. "Guys, this is Janelle. She's my friend. She'll help me take you to your hotel today."

The two pairs of eyes looked at their master as if listening, taking note of everything he was saying. James got down on his knees and patted the head of the bigger dog. It was fluffy, playful, and husky. When it stuck its tongue out, I was surprised to see its tongue was purple.

James introduced the dog to me. "Janelle, this is Alvin. He's a chow chow. I got him from a farm when he was still a puppy. He's been with us for six years now. He lives here. He's my parents' guard dog," James explained. I instantly felt at ease, awed by the dog's intelligent demeanor.

The smaller dog next to Alvin started whimpering, trying to get James's attention. James turned around to ruffle its hair. "And this one is Jet. He's a Japanese spitz. This is my dad's pet. He just turned four the other day. He lives here, too," James said.

I wanted to touch Jet's white fur, but my dog trauma got in the way. I stood like a statue, careful not to get it too excited.

James noticed my strange behavior.

"You don't like dogs?" he asked.

"I had a bad experience with dogs when I was a child. I was chased by two dogs when I was very little," I explained.

"Oh. Really? I'm sorry," James said kindly. "I wish you could've hung out with these dogs. They would've cured your dog fears fast. They're pretty awesome once you get to know them, and they become familiar with you," he added.

"Did you say we're taking them to a hotel today?" I asked.

"Yeah. My parents left for Japan this morning, and I have to go to San Antonio tomorrow for a meeting. These guys will be in their hotel for almost a month until my parents come back. The hotel's pretty expensive, but it's the best choice we've got," James replied.

"I didn't know dog hotels exist. We have a dog at home, too, in the Philippines, but our household help takes care of it when we're not home," I said.

"You have maids?" James asked.

"Yes," I answered.

"Wow. You must be pretty rich folks to be able to afford maids," he said.

"Not really. In the Philippines, maids are not expensive. Almost everyone has extra help at home ... unlike here. I believe they're expensive in America," I explained.

"Yeah. But that's fine. We don't need maids. We do our own stuff here. We clean, cook, take care of pets, do our errands, laundry, everything else while maintaining a job, and if you're lucky, a social life. If you live here and you're single, it's easier. Married with kids, probably harder, but possible," James said.

"Our household help is like family to us. They raised me and my siblings. They were already with us when I was born. We're very lucky to have them," I said, feeling a bit defensive. James was thoughtful when he looked at me.

"I didn't mean to offend. I'm sure you're very lucky to have them," he apologized.

He read my mind again, I cringed in my head.

"But just curious, I wonder how you would have survived living here ... if you and your ex-fiancé had gotten married ... if you're used to having maids to do things for you back in the Philippines," he said, his eyes squinting, as if half-embarrassed for asking the question.

"I'm self-sufficient. I could handle the lifestyle here. I could live in the States without maids. I'd survive," I told James, trying not to sound arrogant and defensive.

James was quiet for a minute.

"Cool," he said. "So, shall we?" he added.

"Shall we what?" I asked, disoriented.

"Shall we take these gentle dogs to their hotel?" James asked, smiling.

"Oh. Of course," I said, embarrassed.

Chapter 40

We took Alvin and Jet to their new temporary home—a huge facility in a secluded area that looked like a farm. The animal hotel housed a lot of pets, mostly dogs. I noticed Alvin and Jet seemed comfortable in their surroundings, as if James and his family had taken them there a few times already.

After getting the dogs' paperwork completed, James and I headed out.

We drove to a lovely town called Clear Lake, where we stopped by the remarkable National Aeronautics and Space Administration (NASA) Space Center.

James bought tickets for the day tour. The shuttle ride on the vast NASA property was one of the most fascinating parts of the tour, which included a visit to the mock control center where sections of the classic Tom Hanks movie *Apollo 13* were filmed.

After the tour, I bought a dozen NASA T-shirts for myself, and my friends and family back home. I grinned as I read what was inscribed on the shirts.

It said, "Failure is not an option."

Well, too late for that, I thought, as I remembered my failed relationship that clearly did not give me an option. Evidently, failure just got shoved in my face without any kind of introduction.

I glanced at James, who was diligently stacking the shirts inside my shopping bags as I quickly banished the ugly thought from my mind.

After NASA, James took me to another tourist attraction located just a few miles away from the famous Space Center. We went to a huge entertainment complex that looked like a pier with novelty shops, restaurants, hotels, games, rides, and a marina. It was called Kemah

Boardwalk. According to James, it was built along the coasts of Clear Lake and Galveston Bay.

There was no entrance fee to the Kemah Boardwalk, but we had to buy tickets for the rides. We stood in the long line to purchase our tickets first, along with hundreds of people visiting the complex, enjoying the exquisite attractions on a sunny and breezy Sunday afternoon.

After surviving the long queue, James took me to a nice little restaurant by the bay. We enjoyed our feast of sumptuous seafood, steaks, pasta, salad, and crepes on the upper deck of the restaurant, overlooking the water.

I was startled by the loud honking of a huge boat bearing tourists enjoying a tour. Interestingly, the tourists on the boat waved at us and the other diners on the deck as they passed by the restaurant.

After dinner, James and I strolled around the boardwalk, enjoying the cool breeze as little children played in the middle of the complex where water fountains spewed out from the ground. We saw street performers on stilts entertaining the crowd of spectators gathered around them. We also passed men and women by barbecue pits on the sides of the streets, grilling, roasting and smoking turkey legs, beef, and sausages. The aroma of the cooked meat and spices attracted diners, some of whom were huddled close by, listening to a local band playing Old West music.

James and I reached the theme park before dusk, where we rode Ferris wheels and carousels like little children. When we got tired of the regular rides in the park, we braved the famous Pharaoh's Fury. I hung onto the sleeve of James's shirt the entire time we were suspended in mid-air, screaming my lungs out. James laughed when I promised to buy him a new shirt when the ride was over.

We saved the boardwalk train ride for last, resting our tired bodies in the wooden seats, fascinated as we went through tunnels and enjoyed the sweet scenery of the beautiful Texas landmark, while enjoying the refreshing night breeze.

In the middle of the train ride, we passed through a dark tunnel. A loud noise that sounded like gunshots startled me. I instinctively clung onto James with my eyes closed until our train got out of the tunnel. I felt his body stiffen, as if he didn't know how to react to my reflex. He seemed to have been put in an awkward position as I put my arms around his shoulders, holding onto him tightly.

When we got out of the tunnel, I quickly untangled myself and sat quietly next to him, crossing my arms and looking away to avoid his eyes.

We headed back to Houston shortly after that. I felt awkward after the train incident, but James seemed to have already recovered by the time we hit the freeway. We listened to the radio during the long drive, only having sporadic mundane conversations to break the silence, initiated mostly by my cordial companion.

We were beyond exhausted by the time we parked in my aunt and uncle's driveway an hour and a half of driving later. Despite feeling self-conscious because of the train ride, I felt strangely content and happy, grateful for the privilege to immensely and truly enjoy Houston even for just one day, in spite of my turbulent journey in America.

I looked at James and cleared my throat as I prepared to get out of the car. I was about to say my thank-you speech for our wonderful time together, but he caught me off guard. Before I could even open my mouth to speak, he touched my arm lightly. His action transmitted a zapping electric shock through my veins. I quietly stiffened in the passenger seat, speechless.

"Janelle, there's something I need to tell you. But first, I'd like to ask you a favor," he said. I raised my brow and shrugged my shoulders, not knowing what to say as he casually let go of my arm.

He cleared his throat before speaking.

"I'm leaving for Japan in a couple of days. Something came up. I haven't talked to my parents since they left for the airport this morning, so I'm not sure what's going to happen in the coming days. I'll let you and Will know as soon as I find out. In the meantime, I was just wondering … uhm … if you'd like to come with me to my client meeting in San Antonio tomorrow."

Chapter 41

A middle-aged lady came out of the convenience store holding a drink and a big bag of chips. She seemed wary, holding onto her shoulder bag tightly, looking around the gas station as if making sure no one was following or checking her out.

It was only a few minutes past six o'clock in the morning. The sun was still asleep, hiding behind the shadows of the evening past. The gas station was already busy, full of cars and people filling up before heading out to their destinations.

The lady opened the driver's side of her car as if in a hurry, squeezing her body inside. In a few seconds, her break lights lit up, the engine roared to life and the car rolled out.

I counted to five.

Just as I expected, the car suddenly stopped, and the lady got out in a hurry. A man pumping gas into his car ran to her side. Another man also left his vehicle by the gas pump to run into the convenience store to ask for assistance.

Apparently, the lady drove out of the gas station not knowing the gas pump was still attached to her car's gas tank. In a few seconds, a man and a woman from the convenience store came out and headed towards the group of people huddled around the lady's car.

We were only five gas pumps away from the commotion. I saw the whole episode while sitting inside James's car, waiting for him to finish filling up his tank. I was horrified. I looked at James as he got into the car.

"Are you okay?" he asked.

I didn't know what to say to him, still imagining all the possible scenarios that may have resulted from the broken gas pump. James seemed to understand what I was thinking.

"You saw the lady dragging the pump with her car?" he asked while putting on his seat belt. I nodded.

"When you get a chance to drive here one day, you must always pay attention to everything around you, including your car. Do you drive in the Philippines? I'm sure you already know not to do what she did," James said as he started his car.

"In the Philippines we have full service. We don't have to get out of the car. We drive to the gas station, park next to a gas pump, give our car keys to the gas attendant, and wait. When the attendant is done putting gas in our tank, we pay usually with cash," I explained.

"Sweet," James said. "You guys are spoiled. We actually do have full-service stations here too, but there's not a lot, and most people use the regular pump. I, personally, would rather fill up my tank myself."

"Has that ever happened to you?" I asked.

"What do you mean?" he asked back.

"Leaving the gas station with the pump still attached to your gas tank," I said.

"No ma'am. I'm a car person. I pay attention to my car more than anything else around me. So there. Sue me." He laughed softly.

I smiled timidly, wondering how I'd survive in the States if I didn't even have the guts to hold a gas pump.

That's why I'm going back to the Philippines in two weeks. Anthony has abandoned our future plans to get married, and I don't have to worry about living in the States anymore. No need to adapt to its culture and ways of living that I'm not familiar with and will never get accustomed to. Never mind if it means not seeing James ever again, I thought with a bit of sadness.

I sat quietly in the car, immersed in my own thoughts as James drove. The sun was beginning to peek out from behind the clouds.

James turned on the radio.

"Bye, Bye, Bye," a popular 'N Sync song, streamed from the speakers.

I smiled quietly while looking out the window as I caught James glancing at me, as if making sure I wasn't looking, before pushing the button on the radio to change the station.

I figured he couldn't stand boy bands.

He kept on pushing buttons, letting his hand search for a good song while maintaining his focus on the road. A few seconds later he found his song. He cranked the volume up, just loud enough not to annoy me.

Matchbox 20 crooned to their hit "Push."

I could have been wrong, but I personally thought the song was an angry ode about a guy trying to get over a toxic relationship. I wondered if James was paying attention to the lyrics, because that may very well have been his breakup song for Daniella.

"Did you know that's a breakup song?" I asked James.

"What's that?" he asked back, seemingly surprised.

"The song playing on the radio now. It's about an angry guy trying to get over a bad relationship," I explained.

"Oh really? I didn't know that," he said, still focused on the road.

"But didn't you like the song?"

"Yeah. Why?" he asked, glancing quickly at me.

"Nothing. I just thought if you really like something, you should know what it's about," I said.

"Do you always pay attention to the lyrics of a particular song that you like?" James asked.

"Of course," I said.

"I see. Then I guess we're different. When I hear a song, I don't pay attention to anything else except my reaction to it. If my ear says awesome, I'll listen to it more. I don't have the patience to sit down and listen to the lyrics word for word. I don't transcribe lyrics. I don't know.

Maybe it's a guy thing. Our minds are so much simpler than what you women think," he said, smiling.

"So you're saying that's not your Daniella breakup song," I said.

James squinted as if stung by my words.

"No ma'am," he said, laughing. "Geez, Janelle, stop making it complicated. It's only a song. You're overanalyzing," he continued.

"Fine. I'll be quiet now," I said, smiling, trying to hide my embarrassment.

I realized even though James looked cool and sophisticated, he seemed so much simpler than what I presumed him to be.

I looked at the green sign on the road as we cruised down a seemingly endless highway, going to San Antonio, Texas. I glanced at James in the driver's seat next to me, his face focused on the road as if deep in thought.

"What's this road called?" I asked, just to break the silence.

"It's called I-10. Interstate 10. It's a major highway in the States. This is, I think, the fourth-longest interstate highway in the US, and the longest part of the road is within the state of Texas," James said.

I looked out my window. The green fields and trees we passed looked beautiful.

I remembered Clear Lake and Kemah Boardwalk, and how exhausted I was yesterday. Had James not asked me for a big favor to go with him to San Antonio when we came back from our trip, I would've been curled up in my bed still, resting my tired limbs.

James was going to meet with one of their architectural firm's biggest prospects, and the client requested to hold the meeting in San Antonio. The young architect needed an assistant to help him set up his audio-visual presentation and take notes for him while he was talking to the client.

Anh was originally supposed to go with him, but the interior designer was on a tight deadline too, and needed to finish a project due for submission on the same day. I learned it was the firm's practice to always have at least two people—a presenter and an assistant, regardless of designation—during a pitch.

When James asked me to go with him to San Antonio, I said yes. I wanted to return the favor to the young architect, who had spent his entire Sunday driving more than a hundred miles for me, taking me to fascinating landmarks in Houston. At the same time, I wanted to experience what an architectural pitch was like, and compare it with our pitches in advertising. I was certain I'd learn a few things I could share with my team when I returned to the Philippines.

I also enjoyed long drives and visiting new places. According to my brief search on the Internet before I went to bed last night, the four-hour drive to San Antonio was worth it. The historic city promised to be charming, rustic in some parts, busy, and beautiful.

But there was one other reason why I agreed to travel with James to San Antonio, and just thinking about it made my stomach flutter in my state of gloom—I wanted to spend more time with him until we couldn't spend any more time together.

"I'm leaving for Japan on Thursday, in about five days," he told me last night when we came back to my aunt's house from our little excursion.

I was speechless, struggling to conceal my emotions.

How can our wonderful day together have such a dismal ending? I thought.

"Soba, our grandmother who lives in Japan, is very ill. Her health is deteriorating, and the doctor said she may be gone soon. The entire family made a decision to visit her and stay with her while she battles her illness," James explained.

According to James, his ninety-three-year-old grandmother lived in a small town with one of her widowed daughters and a stay-in nurse.

"I'm sorry to hear that. I hope she feels better," I said sadly. "How long will you be there?" I asked, trying my best to be objective, not letting my sadness mixed with disappointment take over my sensibility. Although I felt sad for James's grandmother, I felt worse for being guilty of feeling sadder for myself. I'd already grown accustomed to having James around, and I wondered how I'd spend my last two weeks in Houston without him.

I heard James sigh before speaking.

"Just less than a month probably. My parents are now on their way to Japan to take care of my grandmother. Patrick and his fiancée will arrive in Tokyo with me on the same day. We'll plan our next steps when we get together with the rest of the family, I guess," he explained.

"Is there anything I can do to help you with your trip?" I added.

"Maybe, but I haven't got that far yet. Why don't you help me win my prospect first, so I don't have to worry about leaving Will to manage the firm by himself while I'm in Japan for almost a month?" He looked at me, smiling timidly, his eyes tired.

"Of course," I said softly, smiling back at him. "James, I want to end the night with a positive vibe. Now that we only have a few days left to hang out with each other, we should banish anything negative. You'll win the pitch, your grandmother will recover from her illness, my cousin will hold the fort for you and manage the firm well while you're in Japan, and you and I will both have a great time in San Antonio tomorrow," I said, trying to sound enthusiastic.

James smiled.

"Cool jeans?" I said confidently.

James looked at me, amused.

"I meant cool beans," I quickly corrected myself.

We both burst out laughing.

Chapter 42

After an hour and a half of driving on I-10, it started drizzling.

It was my first taste of rain in America, but I could only watch the raindrops hammer down on the pavement from inside James's car.

I've always had a thing for firsts—my first job, my first car, my first relationship, my first kiss, my first taste of success, of failure, of betrayal, of being on a road trip in another country with a good-looking non-Filipino I only met three weeks ago.

For our trip to San Antonio, James brought his silver Lexus sports car, his birthday gift from his parents. He said it was his daily driver, so his Evo could rest in his garage.

I listened to the sound of the rain beating down on the windshield. I wanted to roll down my window and extend my arm outside to feel the cool, cascading water on my skin, but then I remembered how meticulous he was about his cars and quickly dismissed the thought. I concentrated on the side of the road instead, where I saw several cows grazing in the vast fields.

Those cows are getting wet. They're not moving, either. Won't their owners get them to a drier place for shelter? What about their kids? I don't know much about raising cows, but it looks like they're not bothered by the rain. Just another day in the life of a cow, I guess, I thought.

James glanced at me for a second, smiling.

I smiled back, hoping he wasn't smiling at me because he could hear my inner ramblings about the wet cows in the fields. I cringed at the thought and continued my road trip musing, straying away from my trivial thoughts.

A few hours later we reached the entrance to our destination.

I looked at the paved road leading to the resort where James and I were to meet the firm's clients. It was located on top of a hill, overlooking the scenic La Cantera district of San Antonio.

James carefully drove up the hill heading towards the huge gate, where the resort's security checked a few guests coming in. It was like entering a huge exclusive golf course in the richer part of the Philippines, where wealthy folks spent their weekends enjoying the amenities included in their expensive memberships. My parents didn't have memberships at such expensive exclusive resorts back home, but we'd been privileged, once in a blue moon, to get invited as guests by my mother's generous clients. I remembered how excellent the guest services, facilities, and restaurants inside those resorts had always been, and how I made sure to enjoy the momentary pampering whenever I could.

I wondered if I'd be able to enjoy the same luxury in the San Antonio resort, knowing James and I were only there for a business meeting.

After the security check, we continued to drive on paved roads, passing by lush, well-tended trees and carpets of green grass. I saw huge stones marking several areas in the resort with the landmarks' names engraved on them. I saw sections of what I imagined was a huge golf course within the beautiful, rich property.

When James and I reached the hotel, I had to hide my smile as my race-car-enthusiast-sports-car-loving companion hesitantly gave his car keys to the valet attendant.

We took our few belongings, luggage, and lap top bags inside the hotel, then headed to the reception area to check in. Miss Mench, Wooly's executive assistant, made prior reservations for us for our day trip. She booked us a room because we needed a place to put our belongings and presentation materials before heading to the client meeting.

I realized the firm had enough clout to have the privilege to enjoy an early check-in. I looked at my watch. It was only a little past noon.

James and I had a little over two hours to prepare for the meeting, scheduled to be held in one of the hotel's conference rooms at three o'clock in the afternoon.

"Ready?" James asked.

"Sure," I said as I followed him to the elevator going to the third floor of the hotel. I smiled as we passed by a quaint coffee shop that housed a Starbucks depot.

My coffee fix is not to be compromised, after all, I thought.

The hotel receptionist gave us two keys to our room. I took one and put it in my pocket, while James held on to his key as he prepared to unlock our temporary suite. I tried to keep my thoughts preoccupied with the client meeting ahead so I didn't feel awkward entering a hotel room with a man I'd only recently met.

I knew I could trust James, anyway. If Will and his parents allowed me to go with James unaccompanied to different places in Houston, I knew I was in good hands.

This is just a business meeting, anyway, I told myself.

I also knew my traditional grandmother back home would go ballistic if she found out her pure and innocent granddaughter allowed herself to be in such a shameful and disgraceful situation. Had she known I was going to share a hotel room with James, even for just a couple of hours and for business purposes, she wouldn't have been able to take, by her moral standards, such an incomprehensible and immoral transgression.

In the Philippines, our culture and my Christian upbringing would frown on my bold act of agreeing to be alone with a man in a hotel room, regardless of what I and my companion intended to accomplish. Filipino women were expected to be *mahinhin*, a Tagalog term for being ladylike. For the old-school Filipino, women must be meek, shy, modest, and unassertive at all times, and never should be seen in the company of men in certain situations.

Although I silently apologized to my loving grandmother just for the sake of giving her respect, I knew I wasn't doing anything wrong or immoral by being with James, so I brushed the thought away and quietly stepped into the room as my gracious companion held the door for me.

I was instantly impressed with our suite.

Inside were two queen-sized beds, the fluffy looking mattresses covered in white linens. The carpet was clean and comfortable, and the room décor was conservatively elegant. There were two chic lamps sitting on two polished cherry wood nightstands that matched the bed and the bigger desk by the window.

James put his luggage by the wall next to the desk and his presentation materials on one of the beds. He then walked to the window and parted the curtains. A sizable balcony was revealed outside the sliding glass doors of our room.

"Look, we have a nice view of the hillside," James said.

I put my things on the other bed and walked towards the balcony. I stood next to James on our tiny patio, holding onto the metal rails as we surveyed the magnificent view of the golf course and the scenic La Cantera, majestically spread out below the hills.

"That's the Six Flags Fiesta Texas. It's one of the biggest theme parks in Texas," James said, referring to an area located down the hills. I spotted a theme park with roller coasters.

"Nice," I said, admiring the scenery.

"It's always nice to travel here. Makes work a little bit more fun," James said before looking at his watch. "Since we have to prepare for the meeting, do you mind if we just order lunch from the hotel? Get room service? So we don't get pressed for time? I'll call in our order. The menu's on the desk. Let me know what you like," James added as he headed back inside the room.

His cell phone rang.

I walked silently to the desk and browsed through the menu as James took the call. I frowned at the prices on the menu list. Having been in Houston for not even a month yet, my mind was still converting American dollars to our local Philippine currency. I cringed as I calculated the grand total of what James and I could potentially spend for lunch. Room service with tax was a whopping ninety dollars, excluding tax and tip. That was potentially a shocking 4,000 in Philippine pesos—the cost of a month's rent for a small single-bedroom apartment in an average lower-middle-class neighborhood in Manila.

"Okay. Not a problem at all. I understand. I'll call the office in Houston so we can make arrangements. We'll meet the new meeting requirements and schedule. Call me if there are any more changes or concerns. Have a safe trip, and we'll see you when you get here."

I heard James talking on his cell phone, snapping me out of my math calculations and back to our hotel room.

"What's going on?" I asked him casually.

He looked at me after tapping his palm with his cell phone rhythmically, as if deep in thought.

"Janelle, we may have a problem," he said.

Chapter 43

The waiter handed the check to us.

James and I had just finished dinner at a steak and seafood restaurant by the famous River Walk, also known as Paseo del Rio, a strip of restaurants, bars, shops, and business establishments along the San Antonio river, just a level beneath downtown.

We sat by the restaurant's patio overlooking the waters to enjoy the cool breeze as dusk began to cover the historic landmark like a blanket. There was a lot of laughter around us from nearby restaurants and walkways filled with people taking pleasure in the bustling nightlife, amidst the festive atmosphere.

After dinner, James and I strolled on paved streets along the banks of the river, to head towards the dock where we tried to catch the River Walk Tour. Luckily, we got on board a barge just in time. We grabbed our seats along with other tourists eager to experience the celebrated attraction, waiting in anticipation for the narrated tour.

I took my place in the boat as I drank in the beautiful sights, taking pleasure in the cool wind caressing my face. The sky was clear, the stars were out, and the moon hung like a lamp, casting shadows on the river that captured the dramatic interplay of radiant lights and the vivid spirit of the strip.

James and I sat quietly next to each other, immersed in our own thoughts as we listened to the melodic voice of the tour guide.

I looked back at our day.

It started out fine until an unexpected phone call from the client disrupted our plans.

The son of the owner of the business establishment James was supposed to present his proposal to had called James early in the afternoon, just a few minutes after we arrived in our hotel room. The client's flight to Texas was delayed due to a storm in Seattle where they were coming from.

One of the clients opted to meet with us the following day instead.

"Bryan is the son of the owner. He'll represent their business instead of his mother, who originally arranged for the meeting. We have to present the proposal to him tomorrow," James told me as soon as he hung up with the client.

He looked more worried than usual, sitting on one of the beds in our hotel suite, staring at the lunch menu I was holding.

"What's wrong with Bryan?" I asked.

"Nothing really, except he's non-traditional, which means we're pretty much toast if we don't come up with something brilliant soon," James said, sounding a bit disheartened.

"What do you mean?" I asked, confused.

"We brought a traditional Powerpoint presentation and two hard copies with figures and savings, which, to me, is pretty cookie cutter. But then that was the original intention. Bryan's mom prefers that format. She likes traditional stuff, so we made a simple, straightforward proposal. But the problem is Bryan doesn't like that. He wants something more creative, less mass-produced. He doesn't like boring slides. I guess I never anticipated things would turn around. Dealing with this client has always been seamless until now, and I didn't prepare for that," James said.

I suddenly felt like I was back home, having a meeting with one of my colleagues in the advertising agency who was telling me, in not so many words, that our client had changed the campaign direction again— for the hundredth time.

James's predicament was nothing new to me, but I didn't say my thoughts out loud. I didn't want him to think I was being arrogant. After all, I wasn't on my turf. I was in his territory, and I had no clue how architects managed disruptions and changes in direction.

From out of nowhere, a light bulb lit up in my head.

"Are you familiar with Bryan's preferences?" I asked James thoughtfully.

"What do you mean?" he asked back.

"What does he find interesting? Would you know? Any particular sport, movie, hobby, food?" I asked.

James looked at me, seemingly sorting his memory.

"There's a certain film ... *Star Wars*. He loves *Star Wars*. He's kind of a geek. He talks about it like he wrote it," James said slowly. He looked confused yet hopeful, trying his best to go along with my thought process.

"Okay. We'll create a new Powerpoint presentation and tie your proposal with the movie's characters and plots. It won't be a hard sell. We'll subtly incorporate the movie in the proposal, just injecting bits and pieces, to stir his interest. We won't talk about *Star Wars* because Bryan knows that like the back of his hand. He owns it and we don't. We want him to have the impression that we're not there to lick his boots, but we're paying attention. We want to please him, but at the same time, we're running a business.

"Am I going in the right direction? I guess I'm coming from an advertising person's perspective. I'm not familiar with how you architects deal with clients, and how you temper your ego," I said, smiling.

My adrenaline was pumping, yet my mind was wondering if I had said too much already.

"Keep talking. I like the way you're thinking," James said, smiling.

"How do you sell an idea to your client?" I asked.

"Well, here's the thing. I'm a meticulous architect, and I always want to have it my way, but I know that doesn't work in the marketing world. So I always tell the client we're the best architects for this project. We'll give the client the latest and the greatest, the best design there is and ever will be, and it's pretty much carved in stone already. But you know what, we like the client, so we're willing to compromise, but only to a certain extent. I know that sounds a little harsh, so I'll need a lot of help in making sure the presentation doesn't sound stuck up. I'm a designer and I communicate through visuals, but I'm not great with words. I always tend to sound arrogant," James explained.

"We need to research," I said, my mind quickly traversing a hundred miles, it seemed, every second. "We need Internet access and time—lots of time."

James stood up and started jotting down bullet points on a notepad he found on the desk.

We brainstormed for another hour, discussing our strategy while munching on lunch catered by one of the hotel's restaurants. We chose to stick with our original plan to get room service, afraid to lose our momentum. We used the hotel's Internet service and created the presentation from scratch. James ran down the lobby twice to get us both Starbucks coffee to fuel our minds and waning energy. We worked diligently, only resting for fifteen minutes at a time to rejuvenate. When the clock struck six in the evening, we were done with the presentation. We then looked over the Powerpoint deck five more times before finally declaring our mutual satisfaction.

James looked at me intently, making me feel a little awkward.

"You saved my life," he said sincerely.

"No, I didn't. With the way this presentation turned out, it just tells us we're a great team. I'm impressed with your visuals and your designs. If you were in the Philippines, I would have suggested to my boss already that we pirate you. You'd be a great addition to our creative team in the ad agency. But then again, you're an architect, so you'll probably say no," I said, smiling.

James brushed off the compliment and turned the tables around.

"I'm actually more impressed with your ability to write great copy. How did you learn that? I thought you were an account executive, not a writer," James said, returning the compliment.

"Oh. That. I'm a frustrated creative. I try to play with words once in a while when I have an opportunity, which is rare, by the way," I said shyly.

James smiled thoughtfully and got up from his chair.

"Come on. Let's celebrate. I'll take you to dinner and go shopping with you, if you want. River Walk Tour. Anything. I'll head down to the lobby. I'll give you thirty minutes to get ready. Give me a call when you're done, and I'll come get you," he said.

In an instant, James was gone.

I stretched my arms and closed my eyes. I didn't bring any clothes except for a pair of sweats and sneakers, and my business attire for the meeting, which was hanging inside the closet. I wanted to panic but was too exhausted to even care. I went to the bathroom and freshened up, straightening the creases in my T-shirt and jeans.

My stomach began to flutter anew.

I was in a lovely town, with a good-looking man, in a beautiful resort, getting ready for a night out at the famous San Antonio landmark, the River Walk, but there was nothing romantic about any of it.

It was just a business trip.

James and I agreed to stay in the hotel room for the night, only because we didn't have a choice. We had to stay overnight so we could meet with the client early in the morning the following day. Strangely, the hotel was also fully booked because of a big double wedding taking place in a couple of days.

***

"Janelle, we're passing the bridge."

I snapped out of my musing as I heard James talking softly next to me, as if making sure the other tourists in the boat wouldn't hear.

"Make a wish," I said softly.

"Why?" he whispered.

"Because that's what people do when they're passing under a bridge," I said.

"Is that another one of your Janelle things?" he teased.

"I wish," I whispered. "No pun intended," I said smiling.

James laughed as our boat passed under the bridge, not minding the stares he received from the people around us. Suddenly, the boat shifted underneath—from the river's current, maybe—momentarily rocking it. I slid from my seat, almost falling sideways, but James caught my waist in one swift motion. I caught the sleeve of his shirt, crumpling the soft fabric, clinging onto it for dear life.

"Now that's a Janelle thing," James whispered, his soft brown eyes locked with mine.

Chapter 44

I tried to read my *Harry Potter* book as I settled under the covers.

I turned on the lamp next to my bed and forced myself to concentrate on the story. I blinked several times, adjusting my reading glasses, wondering why none of the words seemed to make sense to me.

I heard the door gently open and close.

I saw James, in the corner of my eye, walking quietly towards his luggage resting by the wall on the other side of the room. He glanced in my direction for a second but didn't say anything.

I looked at the clock on the night stand. James came back to our hotel room in exactly an hour, just as he'd promised.

After the boat cruise at the San Antonio River Walk, we headed back to the hotel. It was getting late, and we were worried about not getting enough rest in preparation for the big presentation to Bryan the following morning. We were both quiet in the car as we drove back. I felt awkward, not knowing how to start a conversation after what had happened to us during the thirty-minute boat tour, and I felt my face flushed in embarrassment.

I tried to recall what had happened.

Our boat must have hit a lump of water underneath, temporarily rocking on our way back to the dock. I almost fell. The boat's extra motion pushed me to the edge of my seat, but James caught me, avoiding the unthinkable. In my state of panic, I clung onto his shirt as the boat continued to shake. It was then that our faces touched, our lips almost connecting.

When our gazes locked, I peeked into the soft brown pools of his alluring eyes, almost drowning in their spell. It was only a brief moment, but it caused electric ripples through my veins. I looked away, hoping

James couldn't hear my heartbeat pounding in my chest like the fierce beating of drums in a tribal ritual.

As we drove back to the hotel, I focused on the majestic view of the resort on top of the hill, brightly lit like a guiding torch in the sea of darkness. When we reached the hotel lobby, James told me he would wait in the coffee shop inside the hotel for an hour so I could prepare for bed in our hotel room in private. He gave me one hour of solitude, for which I was grateful.

I didn't waste time. I quickly headed back to our room, took a shower, did my bathroom rituals, and changed into my sleeping clothes—the lone pair of sweats I fortunately brought from Houston—and settled in my bed under the sheets with my book in no time.

***

"Can I use the bathroom? Not sure if you're already done," James asked politely, almost making me jump, when he passed by my bed.

"Sure. I'm done. You may use the bathroom," I replied quickly before burying my face in my book, pretending I was absorbed in my reading. When James came out of the bathroom, I forced myself not to raise my head to look at him, and I continued to read.

So there's a beautiful man in the same room with me, and I don't know how to handle it, I thought.

I saw James from the corner of my eye when he got out of the bathroom. I noticed he was wearing a simple white T-shirt and sweats, yet he stood regally, looking tall and lean like a fashion model getting ready for a photo shoot. His long blond-streaked hair fell softly past his neck, barely touching his shoulders. And the citrusy scent of the shower gel emanating from his freshly showered body smelled heavenly.

He quietly retreated to his bed after checking the door by the hallway, and the other door by the balcony.

"Goodnight. Get some rest," he said before lying down in his bed and turning his night lamp off.

"Goodnight," I said before covering my entire body with my blanket and hiding my face with a pillow.

Half an hour later, we heard explosions outside the glass doors by the balcony. The sound was muffled, as if coming from a distance.

James got off the bed, quietly finding his way in the dark as he headed towards the balcony. He parted the drapes. Suddenly, a fascinating vision of dancing colors appeared in the darkness, lighting up the sky. Curious, I got up from the bed as well and stood next to him, awed by the spectacular display of lights.

"What's going on?" I whispered in the dark.

"Fireworks," James whispered back as he opened the door to the balcony.

We both stepped outside.

***

We braved the cold as we stood on the balcony, watching the display of lights until the last of the fireworks faded in the sky.

"This place is beautiful," I said, still looking at the sky, awed by the hundreds of stars ostensibly watching over us.

"Have you been here before?" I asked offhandedly.

James seemed to be caught off guard as he stood by the rails, looking at me.

"This place is one of the most charming resorts I've ever seen. If I were from Houston, this would be one of my favorite hideaways. And definitely, watching the fireworks at night will always be on my list," I continued.

"Hmm. I don't remember ever stepping out of my room to go to the terrace to admire fireworks, if that's what you meant. I've stayed in this hotel many times before, but I've never had the drive to do anything else except sleep and wait until it's time for me to check out," he explained.

I looked at James in the dark, trying to see his facial expression. I couldn't tell if he was serious or making fun of my quixotic chatter.

"I guess if you were a tourist like me, your perception would be different," I said. "Every time I travel to visit new places, there's always that silly romantic traveler in me, the one who wants to stop and smell the roses. I always make time, no matter what. I know I'm merely passing by and time is not on my side. And the roses … the roses won't wait," I continued, aware of the sappy, metaphoric words coming out of my mouth.

I realized the melancholic tone in my voice and was well aware of the reason behind it. I just wasn't sure if James had noticed the sudden shift in my disposition. The fireworks in the sky were like a time capsule to me, bringing me back to a once sweet memory gone sour, and my exhausted mind and body were forcing me to spit it out.

"One year ago, my ex … Anthony … proposed to me in a lovely restaurant, on a balcony just like this one, while we watched a breathtaking display of fireworks. It was our first-year anniversary. I took off from work that day, dared to skip a friend's wedding, just so we could go out of town and celebrate," I narrated.

I stood like a statue, suddenly feeling ridiculous. I could hear the sound of crickets oblivious to the tranquility, bashing the silence, piercing my senses.

James stood next to me for an agonizing five minutes, not saying a word. When he finally spoke, his voice was low, almost weary.

"Has Anthony reached out to you yet?" he asked.

"No. I haven't heard from him since … since the incident at the office," I said slowly.

"Is he aware that you're leaving in two weeks?" he asked again, glancing at me.

"I don't know," I said, sighing heavily. "I don't know if talking to each other will fix anything anymore, not with mere words of consolation and pathetic excuses. Maybe I'll have closure one day ... when I'm less angry," I said resolutely.

James was quiet, leaning on the rail, looking at me.

"Where did you meet Anthony?" he asked.

I searched my brain, trying to picture the quiet little neighborhood that Anthony and I grew up in.

"We were neighbors in a small subdivision in the Philippines. He was the guy next door that I never paid attention to. We grew up together, but from a distance. His name is Jose Mari Anthony De Vera. He's Filipino, but of Spanish descent. In the Philippines, they referred to him as *Tisoy,* the local vernacular for the Spanish term *mestizo,*" I recalled.

"What's a *mestize?*" James asked, struggling to pronounce the Spanish word.

"A *mestizo* is a male individual of mixed ancestry. Asian-European or Asian-American, someone mixed ... like you. If you were in the Philippines, they'd refer to you as *mestizo* as well," I explained.

"I see," James said.

"Anthony is a *mestizo.* He'd often catch the eye of a young girl or a grown-up woman because of his endearing facial features. In the Philippines, for some reason people generally find *mestizos* or *mestizas* attractive or appealing.

"Anthony is an only child. His mother would travel to the United States once in a while to visit his father, who worked at an engineering company in Houston. Anthony was left in the Philippines with his grandparents pretty much his whole adolescent life.

"We went to the same school. We rode the same bus to and from school since we were in first grade. We both graduated in the same year from the same high school, and played sports in the local community gym by our neighborhood. But we never really connected. We'd see each other almost every day in school, in our subdivision, in the gym, in local shops, and in our parish church, but we sort of ignored each other.

"Then one day, just one week after our high school graduation, I was told that he left the Philippines to live with his mother and father in Houston. We never saw each other again.

"I went to college, graduated, worked at a magazine company, then moved on to work in a TV station and finally, in advertising.

"One night, I went to dinner with my clients for the advertising agency that I worked for. I arrived at the restaurant ten minutes late because I was stuck in traffic. I ended up sitting with a guy I hadn't seen before. It turned out he was the North American brand manager for the product that we were meeting about, for which I was the account executive. The guy was nice but very reserved.

"The following week, to my utter surprise, he called me. He asked me out for dinner. I said yes … because he was a client, and I assumed it was going to be a business meeting. It turned out he was planning for a dinner date—not a romantic one, but a non-business-related date nonetheless.

"One week later, he asked me out for a lunch date, and then breakfast, and then coffee, and then ice cream, and then a chick flick movie, and then a stroll on the beach out of town. I said yes to all of them because I was beginning to like the guy. And then it became more interesting. We found out we were schoolmates in grade school and in high school, some years ago in a small town, just two hours away from the city.

"We traced back his roots, and we ended up in our neighborhood where we both spent our childhood. I found out he was Anthony De Vera, my neighbor, the one whose family moved to Houston years ago.

"He told me he was only on a business trip and would head back to the US in a little less than two weeks. He told me fate had reconnected our paths for a reason, and we had to continue what fate had already started for us.

"He left the Philippines to go back to Houston two weeks later, just as he said, but he came back to visit me five more times that year. On his fifth visit, he proposed to me. We got engaged after exclusively dating and being in a long-distance relationship for a year. He flew back three more times to the Philippines to help me prepare for the wedding.

"And then I decided to come to Houston to surprise him.

"And that's when I came face to face with the man I thought I knew but didn't; the one I chose to spend the rest of my life with, but who was already spending his time, and potentially his life, with somebody else," I said softly.

I saw intermittent flashes of light in the sky, causing a distraction, interrupting my thoughts.

"Did he ever mention anything about Camilla? Were you ever aware of her, or who she was in his life?" James asked, startling me with his voice.

"Yes. He told me she was his good friend. In fact, he traveled to the Philippines with her a few times," I recalled bitterly. "She was reserved, never talked much. I was too trusting. I didn't see the connection," I continued.

James turned to me, choosing his words meticulously. "Janelle, I know you haven't talked much about your relationship, and I don't intend to pry into your personal life or judge your ex-fiancé ... and it's also not my intention to sound self-righteous ... but speaking from an outsider's point of view, I strongly believe the least your ex-fiancé could do right now is own up to what he did and apologize to you. And I don't mean for him to show up drunk, cursing at everybody just to justify what he did. I'm talking about reaching out to you in the most respectful and responsible manner that a woman of your character deserves," he said.

I stood still as I processed his thoughts. I could feel his soft brown eyes probing, looking at my face in the dark, listening closely for any hint of disagreement in my voice. He had just tossed me a compliment, but my mind was too muddled to appreciate it.

"Was that how you broke up with Daniella?" I asked.

James was only a foot away from where I was standing, but I could sense the tension in his body when he took his hands off the rail and rested them both on his neck.

"No. It wasn't," he said softly.

Suddenly, strong flashes of lightning lit up the sky, followed by jolting claps of thunder. I stood on the balcony mesmerized, intrigued by the radiant light teasing the heavens, exposing its beauty inch by inch, hidden in the darkness of the night.

I felt James coming closer to me, holding my arm, trying to lead me back inside, but it was already too late. Rain poured from the sky like a vengeful sorceress unleashing her wrath. In just a matter of seconds, James and I were soaked, dripping from head to toe. I tried to apologize, but couldn't even open my mouth to speak as water dripped incessantly on my face.

James held my arm tighter as he led me back inside our hotel room. I followed closely behind, blinded by the rain, holding onto him, momentarily losing my sense of direction.

The rain was fierce, unrelenting, attacking us sideways.

I looked up at the sky. The mad torrent seemed to be plummeting from the darkness above us. And then it hit me. The rain was angry, setting its rage free, making itself known to everybody like a long-suffering being who's had enough. It was disturbing, beautiful, frightening, and invigorating. But in the end, I knew it would die down as if nothing had happened.

As if it didn't matter.

Chapter 45

As soon as we stepped inside the hotel room, James closed the doors to the balcony and pulled the drapes back in place. I turned on the desk lamp while he dashed into the bathroom to grab a bunch of fresh towels.

I saw the trail of water marks he left on the carpet and was horrified, running to the bathroom myself to save our room from getting drenched.

"Well, that was fun," James said, holding a pile of clean towels, looking at me with curious eyes when he saw me standing like a statue, dripping wet, by the bathroom door.

"What's wrong?" James asked. "I mean, aside from the obvious," he added, referring to our soaked, dripping selves.

I was on the brink of crying, holding back my tears. Frustration and the rest of what was going on in my brain was pushing me to the edge, and I tried to resist with what little control I had left, to keep myself from exploding.

I was mentally blabbering while shivering from the cold.

I didn't have extra clothes except for my business clothes safely tucked in the closet for tomorrow's meeting with Bryan, and two extra pairs of underwear; I thanked my ever-reliable gut feeling in the process. I thought of wearing the hotel's complimentary robe for the night, but when I had inspected it earlier, I noticed it came in the standard American size and was way too long for me. If I wore it, I'd look like Yoda buried inside his ill-fitting robe, its long sleeves majestically touching the floor. I had already got James into so much distress in one night, maybe I should do him a favor by wearing the robe tomorrow instead, playing the lovable *Star Wars* character when we pitched to Bryan, so I could be the larger-than-life prop. We'd win the pitch, and I'd be the honorary firm's mascot.

If I survive tonight, I thought.

"Janelle?" James asked.

"I don't have extra clothes," I said.

And then I cried, silently at first like a toddler whimpering in a corner, until it progressed into something short of uncontrollable. I could feel myself shaking and choking on my own sobs. I crossed my arms over my chest and hugged myself tightly, but the more I tried to keep myself together, the more I felt like breaking into pieces.

James quickly put the towels on the sink and walked over to my side. He stood next to me for a few seconds, bemused. Suddenly, I felt his arms around me as he held me gently. He patted my arm rhythmically, tenderly, until my muscles relaxed. I rested my head on his chest, my warm tears dripping down my face, my anxiety slowly leaving my body. We stood there for almost an eternity, not saying a word.

"Are you feeling better now?" James asked.

His voice was soft and raspy, and his body was warm against mine. I didn't want to let go. I wanted to be stuck in his embrace, feeling safe from the wrathful claws of my past.

The face of my grandmother back home showed up all of a sudden like a light bulb in my head, and I was jolted back to reality. I quickly untangled myself from James's arms.

"I'm sorry I got us both soaked in the rain because I wasn't thinking. I don't ... it's not going to happen again, I promise," I apologized as I tried to wipe my tears clumsily with my hands, avoiding James's eyes.

But he was looking at me, both amused and relieved, his soft brown eyes pulling me in like magnets.

"I'm glad you feel better. You must be cold. I don't want you to get sick. Go ahead and change in the bathroom. I'll just wait outside until you're done. And don't worry about not having extra clothes tonight," he said, smiling.

"What?" I asked, my brow arched, looking at him without blinking.

"I have an extra shirt," he said, laughing quietly. "It's clean, I promise. If you want to wear it, you can. It may not fit you well, but at least you'll be comfortable. I was going to wear it after the meeting with Bryan tomorrow for the long drive back to Houston, but that's fine. I can drive home in my *GQ* look," he said, still smiling.

He quickly went to his luggage and came back in less than a minute holding a piece of clothing.

"My shirts must really like you, 'cause they always seem to end up worn by you," he said, laughing softly, teasing me about his shirt that I'd had to wear after Daniella had soaked me in chocolate at my surprise party.

I frowned in my head, upset with my terrible conduct. It was bad enough that I had bored James with my love story, left him with no choice but to babysit a crybaby and even worse, robbed him of his comfort. It was like thoughtlessly getting on a bus filled with passengers, and prompting a man comfortably settled in his chair to give up his seat, only because I was a woman and he was trying to be a gentleman.

I knew my traditional grandmother in the Philippines would not approve of my thoughts, because she considered gentlemanly gestures as a woman's entitlement, not a privilege.

"James, I'm really sorry … for all the trouble. Thanks for your shirt. I think that would be more appropriate than … you know," I stammered.

James looked at me and smiled kindly.

"This is not about you not having extra clothes. This is more about Anthony and how you had to release all of your pent-up emotions when the fireworks reminded you of your past. But you don't need to say anything to me. I understand.

"Janelle, you may look at me as a stranger, just a friend of your cousin's, but after everything we've been through, even though we've only known each other for a very short time, I'm more than just a random person now. I want you to know if you need me, for as long as you let me be there for you, I will be," he said.

He took a towel from the sink, left the bathroom, and closed the door quietly, leaving me speechless.

Chapter 46

I heard a dull, constant buzzing noise reverberating from the other side of the hotel room next to James's bed.

I quickly glanced at the bathroom by the hallway. The door was closed. I could barely hear the muffled sound of running water from within, but I knew James was still in the shower and wouldn't be coming out anytime soon.

I got up from my bed and tiptoed to the other side of the room where the strange noise was coming from. I walked with extreme care, not making a sound, afraid that James would come out of the bathroom all of a sudden and see me walking around not just with only a T-shirt on, but invading his private space.

I saw James's cell phone on the nightstand, on vibrate mode, almost dancing to the rhythm of what seemed like endless ringing. The caller ID read "Unknown." When the ringing stopped, I was shocked to see the missed call notification displayed on the phone screen.

James had twenty-five missed calls from the unknown caller.

I wondered who would be calling him that many times at way past midnight. I thought of his parents and his ill grandmother in Japan. Maybe they were trying to call him because of a family emergency. I wondered if I should knock on the bathroom door to let James know about the mysterious phone calls, but then I stopped, afraid he'd think I was being nosy.

I decided to go back to my bed and just wait for him to come out of the bathroom instead. I figured if the calls were truly urgent, the caller would and should have the good sense to send him a text message as well.

As I was about to head to my bed, I heard another vibrating sound. I turned around to look at James's cell phone screen on the night stand. It had just received a text message.

James. On a break from work. Let me know your flight itinerary. Will pick u up at the airport when you get to Tokyo. Tell William I'll call him l8r. I just got his new cell#. TC.—Charm

I felt overly relieved when I found out Charm, Wooly's lovely wife, was James's unknown caller. I smiled as I realized we had nothing to worry about, after all.

I stretched my arms to relax my muscles and began to head back to my bed. Just a few steps later, though, for some weird reason, my intuition told me to go back and take a second look at the text message.

Since my intuition was responsible for my good judgment to bring an extra pair of underwear to San Antonio with me, which saved me from further embarrassment and discomfort after getting soaked in the rain just a few minutes ago, I turned back and heeded its call. I went back to the night stand and re-examined Charm's text message. I was shocked, as the discrepancy stared squarely at me.

The sender of the text message was Charm Gomez, Charm's full name as entered on James's contact list. On the other hand, the caller with twenty-five missed calls was an unidentified number, registering on the phone as "Unknown."

My heart started beating faster again. I quickly put the phone down and started heading for my bed.

I almost screamed when I saw James standing by the foot of his bed looking at me.

You've got twenty-five missed calls. The calls may have started coming in approximately half an hour ago when we both stepped out to the balcony to watch the fireworks and continued all the way 'til you stepped out of the shower for the second time tonight, because my stupid romantic inconsiderate self was mesmerized by the storm clouds and that special stupidity was responsible for getting us unnecessarily soaked from head to toe. You either have an urgent emergency situation somewhere out there that needs your immediate attention, or you have got yourself a stalker who would rather break your phone calling like a psycho instead of just leaving a text message or a voice-mail with a callback number. It's the new millennium. You would think these people are much smarter now with technology. Clearly, I was trying to do you a favor. I'm not being nosy. I promise.

I was mentally blabbering in my head in my state of panic, but in reality, I was just standing rigidly across from James, staring at him, incapable of saying a single word.

"Are you okay?" James asked, sounding concerned.

"No. I mean, yes. Your phone ... it's been ringing ... off the hook, so I had to check if it was urgent while you're in the bathroom. I'm sorry. I didn't mean to look as if ... as in ... like I'm doing something suspicious," I stammered.

James seemed amused but tried not to show it. He stepped closer to check his cell phone on the nightstand.

"Did it say who was calling?" he asked.

I stepped aside to give him space while he inspected his phone.

"Its name is unknown. I mean, it's someone ... without a name or ... a number on your contact list. Could be someone calling from out of the country or a ... secret admirer or ... stalker," I stammered, trying my best to spit the words out of my mouth.

James looked at his phone and was quiet for a moment.

"Weird," he said quietly.

"I'm sorry?" I asked, taken aback by his bluntness.

Did he just call me weird to my face? I thought.

James was still looking at his phone when he replied, deep in thought.

"It's weird. Only two people know this phone number, and I have their names on my contact list. This caller surprisingly knows this confidential number but is not on my contacts," he said, puzzled.

"If it's your parents and they're in Japan, their number may register as unknown," I said helpfully.

"Here's the thing. My parents don't even know this number," James said.

"Really?" I asked, confused, wondering what the private number was for.

"Only your cousin, Will, and his wife, Charm, know about this number. It's a private number we use for business and other important matters. We only use it when we're traveling and need to communicate," he explained.

"I see. But what's wrong with your personal cell phone? It's not good enough?" I asked

"It's a long story," James said.

I started heading back to my bed, feeling self-conscious wearing just a shirt that went all the way down to just a couple of inches above my knees.

"It was initially conceptualized for the Save James Project," he said wryly.

"The James what project?" I asked, stopping dead in my tracks, looking back at James.

"The Save James from Being a Jerk or Something Worse Project," he said casually, turning off the lamp on his bedside table, fixing his pillows as if getting ready to go to bed.

I sat in my bed, covering myself with my blanket, propping myself up with my pillows, observing James's every move.

"Please continue," I said.

James sat in his bed, facing me.

"Janelle, do you trust me?" he asked.

"Of course, or I wouldn't be here with you at all," I said, not knowing where our conversation was headed.

"Thanks. I really appreciate that. Now go to sleep. Let's call it a night and rest for tomorrow's big meeting," he said, glancing at me, trying his best to smile nonchalantly.

"So you don't want to talk about it," I said.

"Talk about what?" he asked.

"The James Project," I said.

"I can tell you feel so much better now than when we were rained on. That's really cool," he said sincerely, smiling kindly.

"Thanks for helping me out there. I really appreciate it," I said, smiling back at him. "But you're getting me sidetracked.

"Back to the topic," I said, sounding like a spoiled, unrelenting brat.

"No ma'am. There's no need to talk about it," he said.

"But if you didn't want to talk about it, why did you even mention it? You should know me by now. You knew I would ask you about it and won't stop until I get an answer," I said defiantly.

"My mistake. I apologize," he said, covering his mouth to yawn.

"And I know you just didn't fake that yawn," I said.

"Let it go, Janelle. Go to sleep," he said, checking his lamp and covering his head and body with his blanket.

"Not until you tell me about the James Project," I said.

"Look, I made it up. I'm sorry. Are you happy now?" James said under his blanket.

"No sir," I said. "If I'm sleeping in this room with you, I want to know everything about you, especially about anything that says, 'Save James from Being a Jerk or Something Worse.' Does that make sense?" I continued.

"Man. Are all Filipino women this stubborn? How did your cousin not give me a heads up?" he said, emerging from his blanket, his soft brown eyes exposed, looking at me as if he was both amused and resigned.

"So what is the Save James Project all about, and why did you need a private number?" I asked back, smiling sweetly at him.

"It's a long story and very boring if you ask me, but since you're insistent, I'll tell you the story. But don't say I didn't warn you," he said, sitting up in his bed, pulling his blanket down to his waist, putting his pillow on his chest, and looking at me like a grown-up getting ready to tell an inquisitive child a story.

I sat on my bed, looking at James expectantly, eager to listen to his story so I could put another piece of his puzzle in place in my memory.

Chapter 47

"Growing up with my brother Patrick was my greatest blessing in life, but it was also a challenge," James began his story.

"He was an overachiever. Everything he set out to do was a success story in the making. He never failed—not to my knowledge, at least. He was intelligent, charming, and hardworking. Everyone was fond of him—his teachers, our relatives, our peers, even strangers. Our parents didn't believe in favoritism, but Patrick's achievements alone could have potentially started a sibling war between us at any point in time, should we have chosen competition and envy to stand in our way as brothers. But that never happened. As much as I wanted to compete with Patrick or feel sour because he was always in the limelight, I couldn't. He was my best friend; the older brother who loved, protected, and took care of me when we were growing up. I then realized he wasn't my enemy. I found out, after much thought and reflection, that my real enemy was myself, the weaker minded person who didn't have the ability to believe in my own individual gifts and accomplishments. While Patrick was everyone's poster boy for a bright future, I took the consolation prize as the one most likely to succeed because of luck. I wasn't bright, but I was beautiful. That's what everyone said. They would often gather around me because they thought I had the most beautiful eyes and the rosiest cheeks and the fairest complexion. They said my hair, for reasons I didn't understand, would give Rapunzel a run for her money. And that stuck in my head. I grew up believing I was only worth my looks and nothing else. It was cool for a little bit, didn't hurt at all, especially for a teenager who was just beginning to discover that good looks could get you into a lot of things without even trying. But then Patrick became a doctor, and he eventually left Houston to live in another country. I was devastated. My pillar of wisdom and inspiration took away with him every single positive attribute and self-belief that I had in myself. I was lost and no one, not even my parents, knew about it. I became known as the bad boy with the pretty face in our local circles. I was drinking and smoking a lot and partying like there was no tomorrow. I'd skip class in high school when I couldn't find parking in the school's parking lot in the morning, and go somewhere else with my other misguided friends without our parents' knowledge. I was dating young girls left and right but never committed myself to a relationship. Doing drugs was the only thing I didn't try, only because I was scared of needles, and I had heard it made people look physically hideous. My parents bought me a nice car on my twenty-first birthday, and I used that as my ticket to get into the most snobbish, exclusive circles within the Houston car scene. I also got interested in rock bands and by accident, discovered I could sing. I became the vocalist of an infamous rowdy bunch of musicians in the car scene. The band was called Spoilers, if I remember correctly." James paused, laughing softly.

I smiled at him as I continued to listen.

"I was instantly famous, invited to every event I wanted to get into. Girls and women came flocking to our gigs and followed me wherever I went. It got so crazy, that those women created a schedule for who would be hanging out with me on a daily basis. They were willing to share me among themselves. I felt like a commodity," James continued. "I hardly slept because I couldn't keep up with the demands of my popularity. One day, I got sick. I was coughing out black stuff and throwing up on the side. I had to be hospitalized. Patrick came back from London to take care of me until I was released from the hospital. When I got better a few weeks later, Patrick had to go back to London to attend to his other patients. That was when Will, your cousin, slowly took over as my older brother, so to speak, in place of my brother. He promised Patrick he'd take care of me. It was awkward at first, but Will and I got along so well that we ended up more than what my brother had

252

asked and expected Will to be for me. Will became both my brother and my best friend, and at some point, my father. He's only five years older than me, but he's as wise as Patrick. Will, with the help of his wife, Charm, slowly brought me back to the right path. I started taking college seriously and eventually graduated. I realized I had brains after all and decided to pursue a career in architecture in honor of Will and everything that he did for me. I graduated sooner than expected and started the architectural firm that Will and I grew from the ground up. Life was great. And then, I met Daniella. Two years ago, in February. She was a kindergarten teacher in a local private school. I met her online through a friend who encouraged me to chat with her. After a few months we met in person, and I fell in love with her as soon as I laid my eyes on her. Daniella is half-Italian, half-Filipino. She was beautiful inside and out. She was kind, conservative, intelligent, and practical. She made me laugh, and we talked about many things—trivial, controversial, deep, and important—you name it. Stuff that I didn't even ponder on in my previous life as a mental bum." James paused and sighed.

I looked at him without saying a word. I felt a pang of jealousy for some strange reason, as he described his ex-girlfriend and their past relationship with tenderness. I quickly dismissed the feeling, hoping James didn't notice.

"I thought Daniella was the one," James continued. "The person that would keep me on the right track, encourage me to love myself as much as appreciate being loved, not for my looks, but for who I was to her—just an average man who loved her back. But I was wrong. Deeper into the relationship, as she found out about my past, she became fascinated with who and what I was to other people before we met. She became obsessed with my popularity in certain circles and was proud to flaunt who she was in my life. All of a sudden, I felt like a trophy—the person responsible for spicing up her life and her image to a much different set of people than the so-called boring folks she had in her kindergarten world. She drooled for the car scene and the band scene, craving the new world and lifestyle that she didn't even know existed before she became part of my life. I was back to square one, but I resisted the urge to break up with her because I didn't want to fail in my first-ever serious relationship. I fought for it day in and day out, hoping it would change for the better. But then it got worse. I found out, one year into the relationship, that she was married. One of her friends confessed to me one night while I was waiting for Daniella in the parking lot of the school she was teaching at. I was beyond shocked. I confronted Daniella after that, and we had a big fight. She told me she was married and was planning to leave her husband soon. I felt dirty when I found out, all along in the relationship that she had a husband, who she went home to at the end of the night after spending time with me."

James paused, thoughtful for a moment. I didn't say anything, absorbing his story like a sponge, freeing my mind from being judgmental.

James looked at me as he continued with his story.

"I was devastated. I blamed myself for my failed relationship. I blamed my face, my so-called magnetic personality for attracting superficial people, for turning good people into lying, selfish individuals. I began to hate myself, including my profession. Being an architect reminded me of aesthetics, symmetry, balance, external beauty, and perfection. I stopped showing up at the firm for days, drinking on the side, car racing in the streets, not being afraid to die, reverting back to my old ways. And that's when Charm stepped in.

"She insisted that I get a private number that only the three of us—Will, Charm, and I—knew so they could keep track of me. I resisted at first but then again, I wasn't young anymore at that time. I was almost twenty-five years old and was not as immature as I used to be when Patrick left. Will and Charm kept me on the right track. I don't know how they did it, but they did. The private line became my life line, my last resort when I couldn't handle a bad situation. I started facing myself in the mirror, slowly accepting my faults and shortcomings—even the face that I hated so much."

He looked at me self-consciously, as if clearing a lump in his throat. I looked at him kindly, not saying a word, silently encouraging him to continue sharing his story.

"I decided to turn my life around. I forgave myself. I started to change my outlook on life. I became more grateful for what I was given—my career, my job, my physical appearance—instead of fighting them. The only thing that I wasn't able to do was to reach out to Daniella and settle our separation in a more amicable manner. I tried but wasn't successful. She had changed a lot already. It's hard to reason with her. For a year now, that private line hasn't been used to save me from myself and my senseless inclinations. It has become just an extra number for confidential business communications we can't share with the rest of the staff in the firm. It became just a symbol. If Will or Charm called me or texted me on that private number, it meant it was really important.

"And that concludes the James Project story. The end." James concluded his story as he looked at me, smiling timidly.

"You're still awake?" he asked, smiling.

"Like I just drank a gallon of coffee." I smiled back.

"I hope you're not scared of me, but if you are, I'll understand. I have a turbulent past. I'm not perfect, Janelle. My life may look like a flawless template on a drafting table with straight lines connecting point A to point B, but it's not. I have a bunch of invisible metric, architectural scales in my system trying to straighten the lines, keeping me in the right direction. It's an ongoing battle inside of me, but it's getting better," he said.

When I didn't say anything, he continued.

"It's funny; I just realized, maybe your ex-fiancé is going through the same thing and just needs time to bounce back. He may not deserve another chance, but he deserves to be listened to if he's humble enough to accept his mistakes and ask for your understanding … if not forgiveness. I wasn't able to do that with Daniella, but you and Anthony still have a chance to fix your relationship, right the wrong, find closure, and move on," he said.

I looked at James without saying anything. For the first time in our friendship, or whatever kind of relationship that had developed between us, I was grateful to have come to know him despite the circumstances.

His honesty and humility in narrating his story put my feet back firmly on the ground as I realized I was not the only one swimming through the stinging tides of life. We all were. We just had different ways of keeping our heads up above the water in order to survive without having to draw attention to ourselves. I wished I could heal as fast as he had.

I felt suddenly miserable by the irony of our situation. It was funny how we were finally able to establish a legitimate connection through our life stories, our past, but I didn't understand why it had to happen just a few days before we said goodbye to each other.

I realized we may never see each other again.

"Janelle, is something wrong?" James asked.

I looked at him, trying my best to hold myself together.

"No. Nothing's wrong. Just thankful for your honesty and for trusting me with your story. I wish I had known you sooner, hung out with you longer. I wish you didn't have to leave yet so I can get to know you more. I'm fascinated by your life. You have a talent for telling stories. You brought me inside your past like I was there, a part of it but merely watching. You sounded almost like a … romantic novel writer," I said.

I was shocked at what I had said, but realized I couldn't take it back, so I just kept quiet and let everything sink in.

"I've never thought of myself that way. Maybe one day I could use that talent," James said, laughing quietly.

"You will and good luck," I said, smiling.

"Sure. I could use luck too," he said, smiling back.

A series of text messages suddenly went through James's cellphone, and he quickly spent a minute replying to them.

"Did you find out who your secret caller was?" I asked when he put his cellphone down.

"Nope. It's not Will. I texted his new number, and he just texted back saying he didn't call me. Charm texted. She said she didn't either," he said.

"Maybe tomorrow we'll find out."

"Maybe."

"Well, I guess, it's bedtime. Thanks. I enjoyed listening to your story," I said shyly.

"My pleasure. Good night, Janelle," James said, smiling.

"Goodnight, James," I said, turning my bedside lamp off.

James turned his bedside lamp off as well. "Don't dream of Yoda," he added, putting his blanket all the way to his chest and turning on his bed, facing the wall.

"What about Yoda?" I asked, wide-eyed, looking at his back.

Did he hear my thoughts when I was contemplating wearing the hotel bathrobe but was scared of looking like Yoda? I thought.

"It's a joke. It's about our *Star Wars* presentation tomorrow. Go to sleep. Night," James said without looking at me.

Maybe we're truly connected, after all, I thought, a bit disturbed by the notion that he could read my mind without even knowing. I closed my eyes, shocked at his mental perception.

I slowly drifted off to sleep.

Chapter 48

"Hola. Who's the new wifey today?"

An older-looking Caucasian man stood by the pool, wearing khaki shorts, sneakers, and a crisp red polo shirt. He had on an immaculately white sun visor, and a slightly baked complexion that made me think he just got back from a round of golf.

He looked like he was in his mid-forties, jolly, and moving with a younger man's agility. He smiled at James while stealing a look at the new face next to the well-dressed architect walking towards him.

"Bryan Teal. What's up, man?" James greeted the older man, offering to shake his hand.

So that's Bryan, I thought, smiling timidly next to James, not wanting to draw any kind of attention to myself.

"We meet again, Mister James Ren. Looking sharp as usual, bro," Bryan said enthusiastically while shaking James's right hand, his gold Rolex glistening in the sun.

Bryan turned to me as if waiting for a formal introduction.

"Bryan, I'd like you to meet Janelle Marquez. She's taking Anh's place today. Anh had an urgent onsite call to meet with construction people, so she can't be with us. She sends her regards and apologies. Janelle will be my teammate. She's William's cousin, by the way," James explained.

"I didn't know William had a cousin here. How're you doing Janelle?" Bryan said, smiling brightly at me.

"I'm doing well. Thank you," I said politely, smiling back at the gracious client.

"So what do you got for me today?" Bryan asked as he sat down in his lounge chair comfortably, motioning for James and me to do the same.

The poolside was almost deserted except for a group of young people at the far end, swimming in the pool.

James wasted no time.

He set his wireless laptop on the small table in front of us, opened the cover, and turned the device on. I sat poised next to him, putting each hard copy of the Powerpoint presentation in front of Bryan, James, and myself carefully. I took my pen and notepad out as I prepared to take notes.

I wore an Ann Taylor Loft suit, a gray and pink blazer with matching gray slacks for the meeting. James was dressed to the nines, showing up at the poolside in his gray suit. He removed his jacket when he started his audio-visual presentation.

James showed Bryan the animated slides on the laptop, going over his spiel just as we practiced yesterday. He looked relaxed and comfortable in his own skin, explaining his concepts to Bryan like an engineering teacher holding an interactive lecture on robotics.

Bryan's mother was opening up a new restaurant specializing in wines and tapas in downtown San Antonio. Construction was set to start next month, and James and Wooly's firm was asked to pitch for the business.

James was the architect representing the firm.

He laid out his designs to Bryan, explaining the logic behind every curve, every pillar, every tile, every color, and every little detail of his architectural vision for the classy, cutting-edge restaurant. Listening to him speak was like sitting in a class where art, science, and applied math were fused together.

James's proposed construction costs were reasonable, justified by his visually alluring designs.

Coming from an industry where I sat in meetings discussing advertisements—creative ideas used as marketing tools to help boost product sales—I was awed watching blueprints of shapeless facades transform into tangible works of art as visualized and built from the creative mind of a brilliant architect.

I silently cringed as my *Star Wars* visuals popped up intermittently during the presentation, hoping Bryan would not be turned off by our "mellifluous" sales tactic.

When James finished the last slide I glanced at Bryan, attempting to analyze his facial reaction. His face was blank, yielding no clues.

I looked in James's direction from the corner of my eye. I sensed he was fiddling too long with the keyboard on his laptop, probably trying his best to stall for time, not wanting to find out Bryan's final verdict too soon.

Bryan's cell phone rang.

The ring tone pierced the tension-filled silence among us, making the three of us flinch involuntarily.

Bryan grabbed his cell phone from his pocket and excused himself to take the call. He stood in a corner on the other side of the pool to talk to his caller.

James looked at me and smiled. I smiled back, patting his arm reassuringly, mouthing the words "Good job."

Both of us stiffened when Bryan came back a few minutes later, reclaiming his seat.

"Well. Going back to where we were at before we got rudely interrupted by my mother, by the way," Bryan said, smiling.

"How's Mrs. Teal?" James asked.

"Mrs. Teal, my loving mother, is very busy, but doing well. Thank you for asking," Bryan said.

"That's great," James said.

"Now let's get down to business," Bryan said, looking at James.

"So, what do you think?" James asked Bryan, smiling politely.

Bryan sighed, acknowledging my presence at the meeting by nodding at me, then looking back at James before speaking in his theatrical voice.

"James, you had me at Yoda."

James looked at Bryan, a bit confused. On the other hand, Bryan stood up from his chair and reached out to pat James on the back.

"You did it again, James Ren. Your future wife will be proud of you. The business is yours. Send us the contract soon so we can sign it ASAP. Construction of the restaurant will commence in three weeks, if not sooner. Let's talk about some changes on the color scheme on slides 5 and 6. Go ahead and schedule the briefing with the construction guys and our production people, and we'll see if Mom and I are available. Thanks for all your efforts on this. Appreciate the *Star Wars* interjections and your unparalleled visual concepts. You're a brilliant architect, bro, in case your mother forgot to tell you," Bryan said without pausing.

James stood up and shook hands with Bryan, thanking him for the business, and I did the same.

Bryan looked at me and winked.

"It was nice to meet you, Miss Janelle Marquez. I would love to take you out for coffee, but my schedule is super crazy today, so we'll have to do that some other time—without James, by the way, so I don't have any competition," he said, laughing. "You and Wonder Boy here take care on your way back to H-Town. I have to scram."

We said our pleasantries for another five minutes, shaking hands and patting backs and saying see-you-laters.

And just like that, Bryan was gone.

James and I were left by the poolside, ecstatic and wide-eyed, high fiving each other discreetly before clearing the table and putting our presentation materials back into our luggage.

James looked at me, his smile reaching his soft brown eyes that seemed to glisten under the sun.

"Let's celebrate, Miss Jedi Princess," James said.

"I'm not a princess. I'm more like a Jedi master," I said.

"Jedi mistress," he said.

"There's no such thing," I argued.

"There is now," he said, laughing.

"Fine," I said, smiling.

"Your place or mine?" James asked as we walked back in the hotel.

"What place?" I asked, confused.

"Japanese food or Filipino cuisine for lunch?" James asked back.

I looked at him thoughtfully.

"The day has just started for us, and Houston is still four hours away. Let's do both," I said.

"*Tara let's,*" James said.

We both burst out laughing, oblivious to the hotel's guests staring at us.

Chapter 49

"Jamesu."

I looked at James, not quite convinced he was telling the truth. I had asked him how his name was pronounced in Japanese, and he responded with what sounded like "Jee-mizu."

"But you just added 'zu' to your American name," I said, pouting.

James laughed while picking up a California roll with his chopsticks. "I swear, I'm not making that up."

"Do you even know how to speak Japanese?" I asked.

"Of course not, and I'm not proud of it, but I know how to pronounce and write my American name in Japanese. My parents taught me how to write it in *kanji*," he told me before popping the piece of *sushi* into his mouth.

We were having lunch in a trendy Japanese restaurant in downtown San Antonio after James's successful pitch to Bryan Teal, and were in the middle of quizzing each other about our cultures. I realized James's knowledge of Japanese was limited. I remembered Wooly telling me that was how it was for some, if not most, Japanese-Americans who were born in the States.

"What's your Japanese name … if you have one?" I asked, trying to imitate James's style with his chopsticks to pick up a piece of the inviting shrimp *tempura* intricately set on a black rectangular plate in front of us.

My shrimp *tempura* fell off, dangling from my chopsticks, landing on the tiny plate of *wasabi*, missing James's tall glass of raspberry iced tea by inches. James handed me a fork, laughing at my frustration.

I took the fork but set it aside.

I smiled at him, my matte VMV lipstick undaunted. With one swift motion, I picked up the fallen *tempura* from the plate with my bare hands, wiped off the *wasabi*, and put it in my mouth.

My tongue was on fire instantaneously, but it wasn't enough to embarrass me. I soldiered on, secretly regretting my silly stunt until the spicy zing went away.

"Akira Kenichi," James said, smiling, trying to hold his laughter.

"My full name is James Akira Kenichi Ren. My parents said they couldn't agree on what to name me, so they gave me both names. Mom and Dad wanted Kenichi, but my grandmother insisted on naming me Akira, a Japanese name that can be given to either a boy or a girl. I had long hair when I was a baby. I don't know. Maybe Soba wanted a baby girl in the family instead of me.

"My parents were Buddhists who converted to Christianity when they immigrated to the States before Patrick was born. My birth certificate has all my four names, but my baptismal certificate only bears James Kenichi Ren. I was baptized Catholic and had to have a biblical name," he explained.

I was surprised to find out James was also Catholic. I didn't think we had the same religious background.

"I didn't know you're Catholic," I said.

"I'm a Catholic only by affiliation, even though I attended a private Catholic school in grade school. My parents passed it on to me. I'm not religious. I hardly go to church, but I don't believe I'm a bad person either. Does that make sense?" he asked.

I nodded, absorbing his interesting revelations.

The waiter stopped by and put a platter of *yakitori* and a huge bowl of *ramen* on our table. Along with the dishes came two tiny white bowls and a pair of small plates. James and I thanked the waiter before enjoying our Japanese feast.

James put some ramen in my bowl before putting the rest of the soup in his.

"How about you? I've been revealing my life to you enough for you to write a book about me," he said, smiling, while digging into his bowl of ramen.

"I come from a religious family. We're Roman Catholic. We attend church and hear mass every Sunday as a family. I and my parents and siblings—I have two, an older sister and a younger brother—are all more open-minded when it comes to our faith and cultural values as compared to my eighty-five-year-old grandmother.

"My grandmother lives with us, by the way. We call her Lola. She's conservative and very traditional, aside from being loving and protective of us. She comes from the old—I'd say ancient—school of thought. For instance, if she found out we spent the night in one hotel room together, even if we didn't do anything but work on our project and sleep in separate beds, she would demand that we get married as soon as possible," I explained.

James smiled. "That's called a shotgun wedding. I learned that from Will," he said.

"Right," I said, smiling before continuing.

"I went to a Catholic private school from kindergarten to high school, but I went to a state university when I reached college. The campus didn't teach religion, but my Catholic-Christian beliefs remained intact. Yes, I am religious, but not very vocal about it, and I don't like to judge those that have different beliefs. I sort of like to coexist. I'm big on respect, if you know what I mean," I said softly.

James nodded.

"What about your Filipino traditions? Would your grandmother allow an interracial relationship? Do you base your decisions on what she believes in? Was Anthony accepted in your family?" he asked.

"Hmm. Interesting," I said, "My parents are okay with whoever I date. They trust that I know what I'm doing. I've been a good, responsible child all my life, and they just believe that I would make the right choices, especially when it comes to relationships.

"Well, we both now know that Anthony turned out to be a bad choice, but I couldn't control that," I said, laughing quietly, remembering the fireworks and the torrential rain last night.

"With regard to my grandmother, she's very territorial. She wants us to date only Filipinos. No other race. She adored Anthony, but I'm not quite sure how she's going to take what happened to us, especially the nature of our breakup, when she finds out. I love and respect my grandmother, but I don't always agree with her," I continued.

James looked at me as if carefully considering what to say next.

"What does your grandmother think of Japanese-Americans?" he asked.

"Let me see," I said, thinking hard before responding to James's question.

"She has experienced World War II when Japanese soldiers invaded the Philippines a long time ago. She's not very fond of Japanese people. She told us once that she'll never set foot in Japan, won't wear a *kimono*, and won't eat *sushi*, ever," I said, feeling awkward, hoping James was not offended.

"Ouch," he said, smiling.

"Please don't take it personally. You haven't met her yet. You just never know with my Lola. She could be a rock when it comes to her philosophies, but sometimes she changes her mind in a snap of a finger," I said.

"Ever since I met you, I've never heard you speak your native language. Except for '*Tara let's*' ... which doesn't count. Do you know how to speak *Tah-gah-log*?" he asked.

"*Oo naman*," I said, watching his facial reaction.

He looked puzzled, amused, and something else. I tried to read his eyes but couldn't.

"Fluently. I speak Tagalog fluently. I just didn't speak it because none of you would understand me," I said.

He smiled and was about to say something when his phone suddenly started vibrating.

It was his private line. He pressed a button to answer the call. After saying hello four times, he put the phone on the table and looked at the phone screen.

"Everything okay?" I asked, concerned.

"It's that mysterious caller again. I answered the phone, but all I could hear was breathing on the other end. And then the caller hung up," he said, not taking his eyes off the phone screen.

"That's weird," I said.

"Janelle, check this out. I have thirty missed calls from the same unknown caller since our meeting with Bryan," James said.

It was my first time to see him frown as if something was deeply troubling him.

"Maybe they'll stop calling when they realize you're not the person they meant to call," I said.

"I doubt it. This person knows me," James said.

Chapter 50

I sat quietly in the car, sipping coffee from my paper cup.

James and I were waiting outside a fast-food drive-thru window as the attendant behind the register took our orders. She was young and bubbly with a cute, spunky demeanor and a melodious voice—a little too attentive, in my opinion, asking more questions than needed—ogling my companion who seemed courteous yet oblivious to the extra attention.

"You should be in sales, or maybe politics," I told James as we inched our way out of the narrow lane inside the fast-food compound, heading towards the wide freeway on our way back to Houston.

"And why'd you say that?" James asked without glancing at me, his eyes focused on the road, making sure we hopped into our designated lane without getting hit by the throng of cars heading in the same direction.

"You may want to check that napkin wrapped around your coffee cup before throwing it away. That fast-food lady seemed smitten. I'm positive she wrote her phone number somewhere on your napkins," I said flatly as I looked out my window, sipping what was left of my coffee from a tiny straw.

"Well, don't be jealous, my dear. You're the one I'm taking home with me, not her," James said, laughing gently, his eyes still focused on the road.

I froze in my seat, embarrassed.

"No. I meant … I was just …" I stammered.

"I was kidding. Come on Janelle, loosen up. You're so serious," he said, smiling at me, his pretty eyes squinting from the sun.

I bit my lower lip as I realized I barely had a day left to enjoy his company, and it was making me cranky. I was certain that when we got

271

to Houston, he'd go back to his apartment soon after dropping me off at my aunt's house, pack his bags, prepare for his long trip to Japan, and head to the airport the following day.

"Hey, I heard people in the Philippines don't call McDonald's 'Mickey D's,' and I also heard you guys love the McDonald's competition in the Philippines, a Filipino burger place; its name sounds like a laughing bee, or something," James said in between sips from his coffee cup, startling me in the process.

"Oh," I said, half laughing, "We refer to McDonald's as 'McDo,'" I added.

"Mac Dough?" he asked hesitantly.

"No. McDo. You have to say it with a hard Filipino accent as in Mak Do." I repeated the words, stressing on the second syllable.

"Mak Duh," James said, laughing, "I'm sorry. I can't. Tongue twister. Just tell me about the happy bee."

"It's Jollibee. That's the name of the Filipino burger place. I'd take you there if I could, but they don't have a restaurant in Houston. I think they have one in California. I'm not sure. But, oh well. We're both leaving already. Tomorrow you're going to Japan, and next week I'm going back to Manila," I said, smiling, trying to mask my looming depression.

"Right," he said.

I could sense a tinge of sadness in his voice.

"Well, we had a great time at that little Filipino restaurant in San Antonio. I'm now a legit *curry-curry* and *hallow-hallow* fan," he said, laughing at his poor Tagalog.

I laughed softly, recalling our food adventure just a few hours ago.

James and I had stopped by a small Filipino restaurant located near the freeway after having lunch at a Japanese restaurant at La Cantera. The Filipino restaurant looked quaint and unassuming, with a small convenience store and a few wooden tables and chairs inside.

James and I stood in front of the small buffet table as I guided him through the limited selection of dishes. I didn't realize he was only familiar with our *adobo* dish and nothing else. He loved the *kare-kare* though, which was a beef stew made with peanut sauce that we smother with or dip in shrimp paste—*bagoong*, in Tagalog—for extra flavor. He called it *curry-curry* with *bug-aung*.

"Wow. This is awesome. I'll definitely marry the person who can cook this for me," James said in between bites, laughing. I sat in front of him, delighted to see his positive remarks about our popular dish, knowing he had meticulous taste buds, being a great cook himself.

"Oh yes. I will marry you. I'll cook for you every day," the older Filipina lady, who overheard James while manning the register, said loudly, coming over to our table to give him a high five.

I realized James and I were the only customers inside.

"Is she your girlfriend?" the lady asked James, winking at me. "Miss, you better start learning how to cook for this young handsome man, or else the other ladies will steal him from you," she added.

James was looking at me, smiling, when I glanced in his direction. I turned away, afraid he'd see my face red from embarrassment. I quietly scolded myself for feeling self-conscious over such harmless banter.

I found an opportunity to get the lady to go back to her post by ordering two humongous cups of *halo-halo*. She smiled at me knowingly before heading to the kitchen to get our dessert. When she came back, she carried a silver tray bearing two bowls.

James instantly fell in love with his *halo-halo*, the same Filipino dessert my aunt had prepared for me when I first arrived at their house more than three weeks ago. I felt nostalgic as I feasted on the sweet, icy concoction.

I wish the day didn't have to be over so soon. I wish James didn't have to leave so soon, I thought.

The loud honking from a car in front jolted me back to reality. I looked at James driving next to me in the car, busy maneuvering his Lexus in and out of the congested traffic as we headed back to Houston.

It was almost four o'clock in the afternoon.

James's cell phone started ringing.

I noticed he looked at the screen first to see who was calling before answering. He picked up as soon as he saw the caller ID.

"Hello? Yeah, it's me," he said. "Say that again? Are you serious?"

I held my breath, wondering if James was finally speaking to his mysterious unknown caller.

"Thanks, dude. There was too much going on; I didn't have a chance to call you. I figured you'd be home anyway when I drop off Janelle, so that's not a big deal. Yeah, she survived." James laughed casually. "Positive, dude. You taught me well ... Nah. It's all Janelle. She brought home the bacon ... Okay ... Right ... Cool. That's a better plan. We'll be in Houston in about four hours. Give us time to unload the car and you can swing by ... Tell your mom thanks for me. That's really thoughtful ... Okay, dude. A'ight. Later," James said before hanging up.

"Let me guess. That was my goofy cousin," I said.

"Yeah," James said, laughing.

I looked at him, waiting for him to tell me what they talked about.

"Oh," James said, "I won't drop you off at your aunt's house tonight. You have to come with me ... I have to take you with me," James said while looking at the road, trying to switch lanes. When he glanced at me, my arms were crossed and my brow arched as I waited for his explanation.

"I have to take you to my apartment," James said.

Chapter 51

Strangely, I had butterflies in my stomach.

Upon learning that I was going to stay in James's apartment for an hour or two before Wooly picked us up to go to my aunt's house so James could have a send-off dinner with the family before he headed for Japan, my insides went crazy—also known as topsy-turvy, in American lingo.

I had barely survived spending the night in a hotel room with James; I didn't think I'd be able to bear another episode of being alone with him in his apartment. After all, that was his personal space, his sanctuary, and I didn't want to invade it.

But I managed to maintain my composure, trying my best to act sophisticated so he wouldn't think I was being silly.

I realized young Asian-Americans like James and Wooly were more liberal and straightforward than my guy friends in the Philippines. There was no way I'd allow myself to step inside the apartment of a man I hardly knew if I were back at home. In the same way, only a few Filipino men of my acquaintance would be comfortable bringing a woman they were barely familiar with inside their living space.

Filipinos are generally conservative, and although we're quite hospitable as a people, opening our homes to strangers, bringing a person of the opposite sex into our homes, especially if we live alone, was a different story. It was considered improper and more often than not, immoral.

You've already shared a hotel room with James, what are you worried about? I told myself.

"So, going back to that lady at the fast-food drive-thru, why'd you think she was smitten again?" James asked out of the blue, breaking the silence.

"Well, aren't you the vain one," I said, teasing.

"Hey, we have three and a half hours to go before we reach Houston; you gotta keep me awake," he said, laughing.

"Fine. Let me see. Well, she kept asking you the same question over and over, and took time processing your transaction, smiling sweetly all the time, and staring at you, especially when you weren't looking. If I were your girlfriend, I'd be insulted," I said.

And there you go again, Janelle, I cringed quietly.

"Really ... You caught all that? You must have been paying that much attention," he said, laughing softly.

"I wasn't. I like watching people. I mean, I'm observant," I stammered.

"You're doing it again," James laughed. "You're too defensive. You gotta be more comfortable with me now. I lent you my last shirt last night, don't you forget that," he continued, still laughing.

"Okay, now you're making fun of me," I said, embarrassed.

"Wrong," he said, smiling. "Janelle, I'm going to Japan tomorrow. You must realize this may be our last time together. If it is, then I think we should at least enjoy a good, honest, fun conversation," he said.

I was speechless for a minute, letting his words sink in.

"Okay, let me start," James said, smiling, his eyes brighter than ever. "Let's turn the spotlight on you. If you can tell that lady at the fast-food drive-thru window was interested in me, how can I tell when you like a guy just by observing your actions?" James asked casually, his eyes on the road, glancing at me once in a while.

If I tell you, I'll only reveal how I feel about you. I think I'm beginning to like you ... Hay naku! Where did that come from? I cringed at my thoughts.

I looked at James as my hands strangely trembled, scared he could read my mind again.

"Janelle? Are you okay?" James asked as he glanced at me.

"Yeah. I'm fine," I said swiftly.

"Look. I was just trying to wake us both up. You don't have to answer my question if you're uncomfortable," he said, smiling kindly at me.

"It's fine. I can answer your question. Just give me a minute so I can think," I said, smiling back.

"Sure," he said.

I quietly heaved a sigh.

"Okay. When I like a guy, I don't forget his name, and I'm not talking about his nickname. I mean, I don't forget his full name—the one his parents put on his birth certificate," I explained.

James and I both laughed.

"Also, if you knew me, and you can confirm this with my friends and family if you get a chance, but I don't like relying on anyone for anything, for any reason. Not if I can help it. I'm very independent. Sometimes, too independent. My ex, several times in our relationship, even complained about it," I said, half-smiling, a little upset at myself for still allowing Anthony to be part of our conversation. "So, it's been a popular joke among my friends that whichever guy is able to convince me to let him carry me when I fall on my face for wearing my ultra-high-heeled shoes, that's a clear indication that I really like that person," I said, laughing timidly.

"Is that right?" James teased.

"Yes. And lastly, as a bonus, if the guy could make me cry out of my overwhelming feelings for him, openly and voluntarily, without any inhibitions, that means I've already fallen for that person. It means he's the one," I said softly.

James was quiet before speaking.

"I can believe that," James said, his voice sounding soft and raspy in my ears.

Suddenly a looming feeling of gloom seemed to fall over us as the silence in the car grew thicker. James continued to drive methodically, as if deep in thought, looking at the road ahead of us, changing lanes accordingly, without looking at me or saying another word.

Did I say anything wrong or offensive? I thought.

When James hadn't spoken for a good ten minutes, I had to break the awkward, almost maddening silence between us.

"How about you?" I asked quietly.

"What about me?" he asked back, disoriented.

"The same question. How can I tell you like a girl just by observing your actions, your body language?" I asked hesitantly.

James sighed.

"I'm really simple. I'm easy to read. Some people may think I'm hard to figure out, as if I'm wearing a thick armor when it comes to what I truly feel. And that's fine. But for those who know me, my actions are a dead giveaway. Like just for example, you're the person I've fallen in love with, you will definitely know," he said softly. "You'll be able to tell how I feel about you just by the way I act around you ... unless of course you're totally dense and unreceptive," he added, grinning.

"I see. But not all women are receptive," I said. "And even if we were, we'd never dare admit that the other person has feelings for us, unless we were told flatly how the other person feels about us. In the Philippines, we grow up in a culture where women are not encouraged to boldly admit their feelings for the opposite sex," I explained.

"Oh really?" James responded.

"Yeah. So just in case your special girl is really clueless on how you feel about her, is there anything that you'll symbolically do to express your feelings for her to let her know she's the one?" I asked, curious.

James was quiet for a second before replying to my question.

"Yes. There is one," he said.

"Really? What is it?" I asked, more interested than ever.

"I'll give her pink cherry blossoms," he answered.

"Wow. That's … so romantic." I smiled. "But how … I mean, what if you're in a place where there are no cherry blossoms, like here in Houston or even Texas, for example?" I asked.

James was thoughtful for a second.

"Janelle, when I love someone, I always find a way," he said softly.

Chapter 52

It was already dark by the time we reached the first exit in Houston.

We stopped by the nearest gas station to fill up and buy bottled water from the convenience store. When James got out of the car, I noticed my throat felt fine at the moment, as if nothing had happened, but then I also knew when I woke up the following day I'd have difficulty talking.

James and I had had a *karaoke*-fest in the car during the last two hours, listening to the radio, playing "Name That Tune" in between—guessing random songs that came on and singing the familiar ones as loud as we could.

It was the first time I'd "let my hair down" in America.

And even though I was aware that my croaking, froglike voice was terrible compared to James's rock star vocals, I belted the songs out loud anyway ... as if there was no tomorrow—a phrase I learned from James, which I kind of enjoyed saying.

I swore I'd never seen James laugh so hard during my entire stay in Houston, until I started singing the lyrics of "Dancing Queen" all wrong.

"Janelle, what you did should be against the law. You gotta make a public apology to all the drunken club hoppers all over the world. You've just messed the heck out of their universal anthem. That's the final song at the bar before closing; their signal to go home," James said, grinning, when I finished singing.

"I know but ... to each his own cherry blossoms," I said, smiling.

James looked at me for a couple of seconds, smiling back, completely understanding what I meant.

I remembered our conversation in the car on our way back to Houston.

His face lit up when I asked him why he'd give pink cherry blossoms to the girl he'd one day fall in love with. As far as I knew, men preferred to woo women with roses.

"My mom told me in Japanese culture, the cherry blossoms represent our polar views about life. One, that it's beautiful. Two, it's fleeting. To me the flowers symbolize the value of every opportunity that life presents to us, because it only comes but once. And because nothing lasts forever, we have to seize the moment before it fades away. No one knows what'll happen tomorrow. We don't know if what we have right now will be gone in a second," he explained.

He paused before continuing.

"Have you seen *Dead Poets Society*?" he asked.

I nodded.

"Remember when Robin Williams said '*carpe diem*'? It's funny, but ever since I saw that movie, I never really left his classroom. And to be honest, even though I care about the future, I'm more focused on the present. I don't want to lose sleep because I'm scared of what can happen beyond what's in front of me. I'd rather hold onto what I have right at the moment and enjoy it while I still can," he said.

I listened to James quietly, fascinated by his philosophy.

"Back at the hotel, you told me every time you visit a place for the first time, you always stop and smell the roses because you know time is limited and the roses won't wait. I feel exactly the same way, except I do it whenever and wherever," he continued, his voice low and contemplative.

I smiled to myself, both surprised and flattered that he was paying attention to my ramblings.

"That's the most beautiful thing I've ever heard from a guy. No offense to guys, but for a moment there, you sounded like my best friend at home," I said, suddenly missing Jay Anne.

"I bet the girl you'll give those cherry blossoms to is nothing but special," I added.

James smiled back.

I felt a strange pang of jealousy and a bit of sadness, but I dismissed the feeling quickly.

***

We reached Sugar Land a little past nine o'clock because of traffic.

I watched in awe as the black iron gates outside the apartment complex where James lived opened slowly, right after he entered his personal code by the entrance.

I noticed, even with just the lamp posts on, the place was huge, contemporary, and designed like a resort with lush pine trees surrounding the apartment buildings. James said they had a big outdoor swimming pool in the middle of the complex, complete with lounge chairs and a little gym in the corner.

I could sense that James was exhausted from the long drive, and wondered if he still had the energy to go to my aunt's house to have dinner with us. I told myself I'd offer to help him pack and tidy his apartment while we waited for Wooly to pick us up.

My cousin was supposed to be dropped off by Miss Mench at James's apartment complex anytime soon, so Wooly could get James's Lexus and park it in my aunt's garage until James came back from Japan. My aunt had a three-car garage and had extra space for it. I learned James's Evo was already parked safely in Wooly's garage.

I never realized that leaving for a long trip in America involved such meticulous planning, from cars to pets to jobs to any other concerns that needed to be settled. Back in the Philippines, when our family took long vacations, our trustworthy household help took care of our homes and belongings while we were gone.

James stood in front of his apartment unit, reaching for his key in his pocket. I offered to hold his luggage and binders as I waited next to him.

It was a bittersweet feeling.

It reminded me of that day when I unlocked Anthony's apartment door, not knowing what I'd discover inside. I bit my lower lip as the image of that ominous rooster came back to memory. I shook the negative vibe off and concentrated on the weight of the binders in my arms instead. I had twisted my ankle on our way up to James's unit, and it was painful to move around. I didn't want to say anything about it, because I didn't want James to think I was stupid, walking around in my high heels for more than ten hours already. I'd had a choice to wear my sneakers, but I was just too vain to do that.

I realized James's apartment was on the top floor of the building. It was quiet, as if his neighbors were already asleep.

"I don't have neighbors tonight. One went to Hawaii the other day, and that unit there to your right is currently empty. The couple moved to the lower level," James explained to me.

When his front door opened, James quickly walked inside to disarm his security system. He systematically turned on the light by the hallway, dropped his keys on the small wall table behind the door, and turned around to take the binders and his luggage from my hands.

When we were all settled in the hallway, he gently closed the door behind us, locked it, and re-enabled the alarm system.

I followed James as he led me to the living room.

A pretty, creamy leather couch was sitting in the middle of the room. In one corner was another set of couches in dark blue, and another one in a cool grayish hue. The different sofas were a mixture of leather and soft, comfortable fabric. In between the couches was a glass-topped coffee table, held by black metal chrome legs. It was adorned with architecture and interior design hardback books and secured by a pair of identical paperweights.

Mounted on the wall, facing the couches, was a flat-screen TV.

Next to the living room was a tiny kitchen and what I assumed was a bedroom behind it. There was also a small connecting patio right outside an elegant-looking pair of white French doors.

James's apartment was clean and tidy. Its prominent colors were white, cream, blue, and black, which lent a charming character—a breath of understated elegance—to the entire space. There was a calming sense of peace and tranquility about it.

"Janelle, if you need to freshen up, the bathroom is right there in that corner, and if you're thirsty or hungry, just grab anything from the fridge and the tiny pantry by the window," James said while checking his voice mails on the landline. I sat down on a couch when his cell phone started ringing.

I noticed he picked it up nonchalantly, without looking at the caller ID. I thought, as his mysterious caller hadn't called since we left the Japanese restaurant, it was just right that we stopped worrying about it.

"I'm sorry? For me? Can it wait? … Oh, okay. That's fine. I'll be right there. Thank you," he said before hanging up.

I looked at him, wondering what the call was about.

"Janelle, I'm going to run downstairs to the reception. They said my package came yesterday, and the delivery man left it in the office. Do you want to come with me downstairs? I guess you don't need to. I'll be quick. I'll lock the door and arm the apartment before I leave," he said.

"Is it okay if you don't arm your apartment? My cousin may show up before you get back. I don't want him to wait outside," I told James.

"Sure. Not a problem. Be right back. Will's on his way and should be here any minute now," he said before heading out the door, as if excited to get his package from the reception area.

I was a bit relieved when he left so he wouldn't see my almost violent reaction when I tried to massage my ankle to ease the soreness. Touching it was painful. I wanted to remove my shoes and prop my feet up on one of James's couches, but I didn't want the gracious architect to think I was disrespecting his place.

After relaxing my foot for at least twenty minutes, I took my uncle's cell phone and its charger from my purse and got up. I plugged in the charger on the lower wall of the hallway, connected the phone, and rested it under the wall table by the front door. I then walked over to the patio, my ankle throbbing with pain, just to see what the view looked like outside.

The loud chiming of James's doorbell startled me and nearly made me scream. I walked back inside the apartment, closing the French doors behind me in a hurry.

I hobbled to the front door.

I thought about calling James first, but then realized my cell phone's battery was almost drained. I started to panic when the doorbell continued to ring as if being pushed determinedly on the other side. I figured James was coming back any minute, so I made a decision. I slowly unlocked the door and opened it.

Must be Wooly trying to prank me again, I thought.

Standing in front of me by the door was Daniella, looking pretty in a creamy trench coat. Her face was fully made-up, but she looked a bit flushed. Next to her was Camilla, wearing a white baby-doll dress.

I was shocked beyond belief.

I tried to hide my reaction by focusing on their outfits. I thought it was odd that the best of friends were dressed as if they were going to attend two completely different events.

Daniella was wearing her signature red killer heels while Camilla, on the other hand, was wearing her baby-pink flats.

I also noticed Camilla wasn't wearing a sweater or any piece of clothing to cover her shoulders. It was chilly outside, and she looked pale. I suddenly remembered she was pregnant, and even though I was repulsed by her appearance and for having the nerve to show her face to me, I felt a little guilty for not inviting them inside.

286

"Hi there. We just saw James downstairs, and he told us you were here and that you'd let us in. If you don't mind," Daniella said sweetly.

Really? No nasty side remarks tonight from Miss Universe? There must be a full moon out there, I thought bitterly.

I opened the door wider and let the two women in.

I closed the door behind us gently, wondering why James wasn't back yet. Almost half an hour had already passed since he left. I turned around to lead the two women to the living room, but as soon as I did, the sight that greeted me was horrifying.

Daniella was smiling at me maniacally, like she'd gone mad. In the palm of her hand was a small gun, aimed at Camilla's back. Camilla started sobbing quietly. I could see she was trembling.

"Make the wrong move, and I'll kill both of you. I don't care which one goes first," Daniella said sweetly in her melodic voice.

I bit my lower lip as I tried to read her body language, but my mind had gone blank. My knees started shaking, and my hands trembled. I looked at Daniella as I tried to make sense of what was happening, silently coping with my fear.

She doesn't look mad-crazy. She looks bitter, though, and ... sad ... like she's about to cry ... This is not happening. I'm dreaming ... Ano ba? ... You need to think, Janelle. Stop shaking and think, I thought.

I glanced at the disturbing weapon in Daniella's hand. Her grip on the gun was strong, and her index finger was stable, perfectly positioned, as if determined to pull the trigger.

Chapter 53

I heard footsteps outside.

Daniella seemed restless, pacing back and forth in James's apartment, her heels creating cadenced echoes on the wooden floor. I looked at the clock on the wall. It had only been fifteen minutes since she left me and Camilla in James's bedroom, handcuffed side by side onto the metal legs of a stylish drafting table by the window.

I resisted rubbing my wrist on the metal cuff; my skin was already scraped from my numerous vain attempts to slip out of it. I looked around to see if there was a tiny pin that I could use to pick the lock. I didn't know how to do it, but I knew, oftentimes, desperation could make people do the impossible.

I surveyed James's bedroom, impressed with its stylish, minimalist appeal. It was tidy, and it smelled clean, yet it appeared to be lived in. His remote controls and phone chargers were scattered in different places, and a pair of T-shirts, CDs and headphones were casually strewn on the bed. He had a few picture frames on the walls with photos of his family and friends from the car scene. There was also one picture of him, taken when he was singing with his band onstage, smiling for the camera.

I suddenly missed James and wished he was next to me, protecting me from Daniella the way he protected me from Anthony during our confrontation. I was beginning to worry about him. He still hadn't come back. I tried not to think of the worst possible scenario. I focused instead on how I could get out of the handcuffs so I could look for him.

I sensed movement next to me.

Camilla was sitting on the floor, hugging her legs, rocking herself gently, and sobbing quietly. It was a moving image, a picture of a frightened woman comforting herself in the face of adversity. Tears welled up in my eyes, momentarily forgetting the amount of pain that she had caused me, and I reached out to pat her shoulder with my free hand.

She looked at me with sad eyes and mouthed the words, "I'm sorry." I didn't know what she meant, but I nodded, whispering, "We'll be fine."

I heard Daniella's voice in the living room, as if she was talking on the phone. Suddenly the doorbell rang.

I heard Daniella's heels trotting across the wooden floor. A door opened, and conversation ensued. I heard a masculine voice casually chatting with her, as if nothing was wrong.

"She's resting inside. Come on in," Daniella said sweetly, her heels approaching the bedroom.

The door opened slowly.

Suddenly, a man was forcefully shoved inside. He fell on the wooden floor, head first. He put his hands on his face, one arm on his chest as he instinctively braced for the fall, but the impact left him dazed and disoriented.

Daniella quickly put a handcuff on his wrist and fastened the cuff to one of the legs of James's contemporary bed.

Camilla screamed when she realized the man on the floor was Anthony.

"Well, well, well. One happy family," Daniella laughed.

Anthony was still in shock. He looked at me and Camilla, and the handcuffs that bound us. He turned to look at Daniella as he tried to break free from the metal cuff, but his efforts were futile.

"Daniella, what the hell? What's going on?" Anthony said, sitting up on the floor.

"Well, my dear. Ask these two ladies. If they had behaved, this wouldn't have happened," Daniella said as if she was chatting with a friend on a normal day. I was scared to talk, not knowing what her mental state was. I noticed her small gun was still in her hand, as if she was toting a cell phone.

Camilla sobbed uncontrollably. She was sweating profusely and seemed to be choking, unable to articulate.

"Please don't hurt us. Let us go. I want to go home," she cried.

Anthony's facial expression was that of frustration, anger, compassion, and fear upon seeing Camilla's outburst. For the first time, I had the chance to witness how much he cared for her. "Daniella, if anything happens to these two, I won't forgive you," Anthony said, his voice low, his anger controlled. I realized that he knew Daniella was not in her right state of mind, and she was dangerous with that gun in her hand.

"Oh. How sweet. Didn't you just cheat on these two women? You hypocrite. You all deserve this," Daniella laughed sarcastically, her eyes fixed on Anthony.

Do something, Janelle. Divert her attention before it all gets out of control, I told myself quietly.

"What is this all about Daniella? Do we need to do this? Can we just talk about it? I'm sure there's a way to resolve what you're worried about," I said timidly.

Daniella turned her attention to me.

"Shut up! You started all this. If you hadn't seduced James, none of this would have happened. Why did you have to come here and ruin everyone's lives?" Daniella screamed.

"Daniella, it's not her fault," Camilla cried.

Daniella stood up and beat the wall with her fist.

I quickly looked at Camilla, putting my index finger on my lips, shaking my head slowly, motioning for her to keep quiet. Camilla looked frightened, but she nodded her head in agreement.

Anthony was quiet, observing Daniella's actions, deep in thought.

Daniella turned around, her eyes ablaze.

"I know you spent the night with James in San Antonio. I called him a million times, and every time, I could hear your voice in the background. I don't know who you are, but you are not taking him away from me. I've ruined my life because of him, and you will not be in the way.

"You and Anthony will get back together, and I'll take care of Camilla. James will have no reason to want you anymore," she told me with unmistakable scorn.

"And just to let you know, I intercepted James's gift for you—the package that he thought he was going to pick up downstairs at the reception area. How absurd, he ordered a dozen pink flowers for you … because you probably offered your body to him, you bitch," Daniella said without pausing. "I want you to know, James doesn't give flowers to anyone. No one except me. He used to give me pink cherry blossoms … until the day we broke up. I'll make sure James won't give flowers to anyone else, especially not to a teeny-tiny-looking fob like you.

"I threw your pretty little flowers in the trash can and set them on fire, my dear." Daniella laughed. "And just in case you're wondering what kind of flowers he was going to send you … hint, hint. They're not pink cherry blossoms. They're plain ugly roses," she continued, sounding victorious.

It felt like a knife cut a sizable piece of my heart.

I knew I didn't have any reason to expect anything. I knew James didn't have any feelings for me, but still, finding out the bitter truth in such a fashion—when all I could think of was him being next to me at that very moment—did not make the pain any less bearable.

I remembered my conversation with him about the cherry blossoms on the drive back from San Antonio, and how he'd find a way to give them to the special girl who would steal his heart.

I guess Daniella shouldn't be upset, because even though her chances with James are close to nothing, at least she had experienced being loved by him. Out of all the women who pursued James, she was the only one he gave pink cherry blossoms to. I wonder how it feels to be loved by him, I thought, fighting back tears, scolding myself for feeling miserable when I didn't have any reason to. Maybe it was exhaustion and fear and all the emotions taking over my body, but I was breaking into a hundred million pieces inside.

I tried my best to control my emotions before speaking, making sure I didn't give my feelings away.

"James is not interested in me, Daniella. You said it yourself. He was sending me roses, not those special cherry blossoms. He only meant for the roses to be my going-away gift—a kind gesture. He knows I'm leaving next week to go back to the Philippines. You don't need to do this. I'll be gone before you all know it. Anthony, Camilla, and James are your friends. Don't let me break your friendship," I said, looking at the floor, afraid I'd break down.

There was silence in the room.

Daniella looked at me as if she had momentarily snapped out of her rage.

A man's voice came out of nowhere.

"Daniella."

We all looked towards the hallway outside the bedroom where the voice had come from. Suddenly, James emerged from the dark. Standing by the door, he looked exhausted. He glanced at me with his tired eyes, shifting his gaze to the handcuff that bound me to the table.

Daniella looked at James, a mixture of shock, fear, delight, and madness glimmering in her eyes as she walked excitedly towards him, her tiny gun safely tucked in her hand.

Chapter 54

The tension in the room was thick, but none of us dared speak.

Daniella's heels scurrying across the wooden floor broke the silence, every thud drilling a hole in my throbbing head.

James stood still, watching her movements carefully.

My heart began to beat faster as I watched in silence.

"Finally, you're here, baby. What took you so long?" Daniella spoke softly, her face ethereal. She wrapped her arms around James in a tight embrace, looking at him with a pained expression that was difficult to fathom.

"It's warm in here. Why don't you take off your coat?" James asked passively.

Daniella's eyes brightened as if she understood.

"Shouldn't we go somewhere else private, darling? Do you really want to see what's inside this coat?" She laughed softly, teasing James with her sultry voice, her demeanor alluring.

She looked at me in triumph, as if declaring her well fought victory, flaunting her acquisition, clinging onto James like a leech.

I looked back at her without flinching.

"Take it off, Daniella," James reiterated, his voice low and husky.

Daniella lowered her eyes and obliged, as if deliriously happy, undoing the buttons of her trench coat one by one. She looked like she was in a hurry, as if a massive amount of excitement had ignited the raging fire inside her.

Her creamy trench coat fell dramatically to the floor, revealing her scantily clad self in a traditional bright red Japanese *kimono*, hiked up all the way to her thighs, her cleavage proudly exposed.

Daniella looked like a stunning goddess, misplaced in the chaos.

She turned to James, wrapping her arms around his neck, squeezing her body against his, oblivious to the three pairs of eyes watching them.

"Let's get this thing out of the way," James said in his raspy voice, taking the gun away from Daniella's hand and resting it on a cloth hamper by the door. Daniella seemed to stiffen, faintly resisting James's action, but she was too drawn to his presence, her mental resolve melting as her carnal desires took over.

Daniella's hands roamed James's body as she kissed his neck like a hungry wolf preparing for a feast. When she was about to have a taste of his lips, James stepped back, disentangling himself gently from her grip.

"Daniella, I don't like an audience. Would you wait for me in the guest room? Freshen up and get settled. Let's do it right. Make it last longer. I'll be with you in five minutes," James assured her.

"My pleasure," Daniela whispered in his ear.

She turned around to look at me, laughing disdainfully.

She gave James a lingering look, as if having a serious discussion with her inner self, before slowly turning around to leave the room.

James didn't move from where he was standing until Daniella's footsteps faded in the silence. The sound of a door being opened and closed from outside could be distinctly heard in the room. Slowly, James walked over to the hamper and took the gun. He walked to his dresser and put the gun carefully into a drawer, closing it meticulously soon after. He then walked over to the door to pick up Daniella's trench coat from the floor.

He rummaged through its pockets as Anthony, Camilla, and I watched in utter puzzlement. I sat frozen on the floor, afraid to even breathe as I watched him uncover several metallic-looking items, which he secured in the palm of his hand.

James suddenly looked at us, putting his index finger on his lips.

He walked towards me, not making any sound.

"Janelle, let's try these keys on your handcuffs. Daniella will be back any minute now. I need you to stay focused, okay? I'll take care of this. I don't want anyone getting hurt from all this nonsense. But you need to help me," James whispered to me as he tried the different keys on my handcuff, one by one until something twisted perfectly inside, freeing my hand instantly.

"I need you to get a bottle of water from the little fridge by the window and give it to Camilla. She looks dehydrated. Try not to make a sound. I'll work on the rest of the handcuffs," James whispered before walking over to Camilla and Anthony.

I quietly limped over to the fridge to get water and crawled back, handing the bottle over to Camilla. She seemed extremely thirsty as she drank hurriedly with both hands, after James freed her from her handcuffs.

I saw James walking over to Anthony. To my surprise, my ex-fiancé appeared grateful, extending his hand to James without saying a word after his arm was freed from the metal cuff. James shook Anthony's hand in acknowledgment.

I heard a loud crash coming from the living room. I held onto James's arm as Anthony instinctively stood up and scooped Camilla up from where she was sitting.

"Head to my bathroom," James instructed, still whispering, as we all started walking to the small bathroom inside his bedroom. "I'll take care of Daniella when she comes back. The cops should be here soon. I called Will and asked him to call 911. I wanted to get inside the apartment as quickly as I could before anything got out of hand," he told me. I nodded in acknowledgment, fighting the painful throbbing in my sprained ankle that spread like fire into my lower leg.

Anthony carried Camilla to the bathroom. He came back quickly to get me, but I couldn't move from where I was standing. My foot felt like it was going to split apart as my ankle screamed in agony. Tears started to form in my eyes, but I was determined not to cry.

"I can't walk. It hurts. Give me a few minutes," I said, holding onto James's arm, closing my eyes to pacify the unbearable pain shooting up from my right foot.

"Janelle, do you want me to carry you?" James asked me softly.

I wanted to say yes, but then I remembered what I told him in the car about not letting any man carry me. It seemed interesting how that trivial conversation had played out too soon, testing my emotions and my ability to admit or lie about how I truly felt about him. I contemplated on revealing my strange longing for him, but the looming image of Daniella and the symbolic pink cherry blossoms he had no intention of giving me suddenly came to mind.

"No. Thank you. I can manage," I said, opening my eyes to look at James, trying my best to sound confident.

The look in his eyes was haunting, a reflection of sadness, regret, understanding, and acceptance combined. He stood there without moving, unable to say a word as I started to hobble my way to where Camilla was hiding.

"You liar! I knew you were out to ruin me again ... I love you, James. You will never be anyone else's babe. And I hate this little F.O.B. that has no business being with you. She needs to go to hell, and I will send her there where she belongs now!" Daniella screamed from behind, storming into the room like a lunatic, wielding a gleaming kitchen knife.

It happened so fast.

I was staring at Daniella's madness. She was rushing towards me so much faster than my body could respond. The anger on her face was intense, her mouth moving in slow motion as if she was screaming, yet I couldn't hear a thing, the silence in my head deafening. I numbly watched as Anthony grabbed her, holding her arms until she was overpowered, but she was fighting back with all her might until she was dragged into a corner and finally restrained by metal handcuffs that Anthony latched on the bed.

I saw James collapsing on me, holding his right shoulder with his left hand. I watched the blood on his white shirt become darker, more prominent, spreading faster and faster. I caught him swiftly, but his weight pushed me, pinning my frail body against the wall. My sprained ankle bore his and my combined weight, but I willed my mind to endure the pain silently. I concentrated on James, holding him tightly, using the wall to support us as I carefully and slowly slid down to the wooden floor. I heard him whimpering quietly until his eyes closed and his grip on my arm loosened.

I could see Daniella crying in her corner, as if screaming in anguish yet I couldn't seem to hear a single sound she was making until a familiar voice jolted me back to reality.

"Jan, listen. We can handle this. You're one of the strongest people I know, but I need you to focus right now, okay?" Anthony's voice was kind but firm. I looked at him as I trembled in fear. He put his hand on my head gently, ruffling my hair.

"Jan, I need you to stay with James. He's losing consciousness. Talk to him. Make him feel he's okay. I'll run to the bathroom to wash my hands. We'll get his bleeding to stop, okay? Everything will be fine, but I need you to focus right now. All right?" Anthony continued, looking at me with pained eyes, before running to the bathroom.

When Anthony came back, he had a handful of clean towels in his hands. Camilla was right behind him, talking on the phone with what I assumed was a call center for emergencies. She turned the speaker on as the voice instructed Anthony how to stabilize James and temporarily stop the bleeding before the actual paramedics took over.

I held James quietly as Anthony applied first aid, momentarily setting aside the excruciating pain in my ankle.

James's head was resting on my lap. I could feel his breathing, but he hadn't said a single word since Daniella stabbed him in the back. I felt him flinch a few times, but he never opened his eyes.

I could feel my tears forming a thick barrier in my eyes.

I saw blurred images of Wooly and men in uniform, paramedics and police officers perhaps, methodically stream into the room, assessing the situation. They talked to Anthony and Camilla while they tried to restrain the hysterical Daniella, who was cuffed to the bed.

I heard myself calling James's name softly as I brushed away a few strands of hair from his face.

Why did I say no to him when he offered to carry me? He seemed to have understood fully well what that meant. But then he still shielded me from harm—from death, perhaps—with his own body, risking his life for me, I thought bitterly.

A teardrop escaped from my eye, landing on his cheek.

I dried it carefully with my hand.

Amidst the chaos around me, I rocked myself gently in my head until all was quiet and peaceful and still and I was back home, thousands of miles away, sleeping soundly in my bed, oblivious to hurt, oblivious to pain, oblivious to love unreturned.

Chapter 55

"Janelle, it's time to go home." I heard Wooly's comforting voice, but I couldn't move from where I was sitting.

I knew it had nothing to do with my sprained ankle, which had just been treated in the emergency room at the big hospital my cousin and I were currently in. I was certain it had to do with my overwhelming fatigue and frustration, not being able to see James after he was rushed into the operating room by the ambulance crew and the team of nurses and doctors who had taken over his care.

It seemed like ages since we left his apartment and all the madness that had happened inside.

I remembered when the paramedics took him away from my arms, to rush him to the hospital. His eyes were closed and he wasn't moving.

I cried silently in the ambulance as I lay strapped on a bed, after the paramedics had treated the ugly swelling on my right foot. I thought I fell asleep after I started calling James relentlessly, like Daniella had back in his apartment. My whole body shivered as I contemplated the unthinkable while I dealt with my trauma, my guilt, my uselessness, and the excruciating pain on my leg.

I wondered what had happened to Anthony and Camilla, and Daniella who'd been inconsolable after she dropped the knife on the floor in James's bedroom, after stabbing him accidentally. I felt pity and sadness more than anger for her when I looked back to where she was slumped in a corner as James and I were slowly taken away from the chaos.

Everything was a big hazy blur to me after that.

"Janelle?"

I snapped back to the present as Wooly's soft voice seemingly glided over to where I was sitting, on a small bed in one of the recovery rooms in the same hospital where James was taken. I could see Wooly holding a wheelchair, standing next to a middle-aged nurse in a blue uniform, who was smiling kindly at me.

"How's James?" I asked instinctively.

Wooly looked at the nurse.

"Janelle, James is fine. He's recuperating in his room. You may visit him tomorrow, or when the doctors give the go-ahead that it's okay for him to see visitors. We just can't risk exposure right now, because of potential infection to the patient," the lady nurse told me.

"But is he okay? Safe?" I asked, worried, still a little groggy from the sedative that I had probably been given to calm my nerves while I was in the ambulance.

"James is okay now, Jan. The worst is over. He just needs to rest. We'll come back to visit him when we hear from the doctors. Mom's nurse friends working in this hospital are taking care of him, so he's in good hands. You have to rest, too. You've had a rough, long day, and I know you have a lot of questions. I'll tell you everything you want to know in the car on our way to the house ... but only if you promise to step into this state of the art, ultra-comfy, never-before seated, cute little sophisticated, sturdy-looking, thank-God-it's-not-pink wheelchair," Wooly said, mimicking a TV voice-over announcer, grinning at me.

I forced a smile onto my face, to show my cousin I appreciated everything he was doing for me.

"Sure," I said softly.

Wooly and the nurse helped me as I settled in the wheelchair, allowing them to push it all the way to the garage where Wooly's car was parked.

It took us only twenty minutes to get to my aunt's house, but my conversation with my cousin in the car as we drove seemed the longest I'd had, ever since I could remember.

"I don't recall what I told the police officer," I told Wooly absentmindedly, staring out my window as we drove on the deserted streets of Houston. I didn't realize it was almost four o'clock in the morning, eight long hours since James and I came back from San Antonio yesterday. I felt a burning sensation in my leg as I remembered James lay in the hospital by himself, probably in pain.

"You told them the truth, Jan. Don't worry too much. They just wanted to know what happened so if anyone files charges, they'll have a record," Wooly assured me.

"Daniella was right," I continued, "I shouldn't have come here. I shouldn't have disrupted everyone's lives. If I had stayed in the Philippines, none of this would have happened. I'm selfish. Always thinking everyone will accommodate me whenever I feel like barging in. James suffered because he was being nice to me, and what happened …"

"Janelle," Wooly interrupted.

I looked at him, fighting back tears.

He reached out to put his arm around my shoulders, patting my arm gently.

"It's not your fault. Don't blame yourself. Everything happens for a reason. And what happened to you and everyone else around you while you've been here, it's not random. I can't tell you right now, but I assure you, there's a purpose, a bigger reason why everything has taken place. It's just difficult to see it, and even more difficult to understand it right now," he said kindly.

My tears streamed down my cheeks.

I wished I could tell Wooly how I was feeling, but I didn't know how to start. I wished Jay Anne were there with me so he could talk sense into my head, even if what he'd tell me would hurt me even more.

"I can't believe I'm saying this, but I gotta tell you, love is complicated. It can make people do what they never thought they were capable of doing," I heard Wooly saying.

"You're talking about Daniella?" I asked, wiping my tears with the back of my hand. Wooly reached for the box of tissues in the seat behind us and handed it to me.

"Yes, and James, too," he responded.

I took the box from him, getting a handful of tissues as I looked in his direction, puzzled.

"Daniella was a kindergarten teacher; decent, with a good head on her shoulders. She was perfect until she met James. Her world turned upside down, including her values and principles. I never saw that one coming—what she did last night. The kind of love she had for him made her batshit crazy. But then again, I'm more puzzled with James's actions," Wooly said, sounding contemplative.

"What do you mean?" I asked as I put the tissue box back in its place.

"Well, when he called me yesterday on my way to his apartment, he was upset because the package that he was supposed to receive seemed to have been stolen. When I asked what it was for, he said it was for you—his gift before you went back to the Philippines. When I asked what the package contained, he said it was flowers," he explained.

"Yeah. Daniella told us she intercepted that package and burned the flowers," I said quickly, not meaning to interrupt Wooly.

"Strange. I've known James for a long time, and he has never given anyone flowers before, except when he was with Daniella. And for him to be really affected when he lost that package with just flowers in it was pretty new to me," my cousin said, glancing at me while driving as if waiting for me to do some kind of dance for joy.

"Cut to the chase, cuz. You're making me anxious," I told Wooly, smiling timidly, feeling less depressed.

"Okay. Take this. James doesn't like knives. The same way he doesn't like needles. Don't get me wrong. He's a pretty tough guy, but I know his weakness and that's seeing blood on him or anyone else. He can't stand the sight of it; just looking at blood can give him an asthmatic attack. Which, by the way, made his medical situation last night more critical.

"But for some strange reason, as Anthony told me, when Daniella ran towards you to attack you with her knife, James shielded you with his body. When I found that out, my mind was blown," Wooly explained, unsure if he was going to smile at me or not.

"Wools, I don't want to flatter myself. I think James just did the right thing, like most guys would do, for women and children especially. Don't get me wrong, I'm very grateful for what James did, and I know that's really, really special, but I can assure you, he only did that because he was being a gentleman ... because he has a good heart," I said, momentarily reminded of James's cherry blossoms, feeling a pinch in my heart.

"Janelle, I know you. If you're not dense, you're totally closed-minded, especially when you think it's not worth sweating for, but let me ask you this—what would you do if you found out James is in love with you? Would you even consider him?

"If you say yes, then you have my one-hundred-and-ten-percent approval and blessing," Wooly said, smiling.

I stiffened, feeling excited and sad at the same time.

"Wools, let me also say this. James is not interested in me," I said with a heavy heart, though I tried my best to hide my sentiment from my cousin. "Because he told me something in San Antonio that would confirm that. And even if, just for the sake of argument, he is, I don't think it would work. I don't think either of us could handle a long-distance relationship. I, personally, don't want to suffer twice from the same mistake, and frankly, living here in America is not my cup of tea. With all the bad things I've gone through in just four weeks, I don't think America is fond of me," I explained.

Wooly was quiet for a minute before speaking.

"Hmm. Two things. One, long-distance relationships do work. Charm and I are living testimony. Two, don't focus on the bad things that happened to you here. Focus on the lessons you learned, the adventures you experienced, the people you met, the stories you heard, the lives you witnessed, and the stronger person that emerged from all your frustrations and disappointments. And if there's something or someone here in America that's making it hard for you to leave, just accept that so you have a reason to come back," Wooly said.

I looked at my cousin, amazed at his wisdom.

"But you and Charm have always been perfect. You're a special couple. You're both successful. I don't see any reason for either of you to struggle, unlike others who came here with relatively less sophistication or guts to survive the bigger world that is America," I said smiling.

"Not really," Wooly said. "No one is special. Everyone who lives here has struggles, just like anywhere else in the world, but we have different ways of fighting our battles. Sometimes we win, sometimes we don't. The important thing is we've learned how to get up and move on. No one is immune to bullies. You just learn how to fight them.

"Charm and I have struggles. Just like you, she came from a well-off family with maids. She would whine to me about not having to do chores all her life until she came here to live with me. She complained every day that she was tired, not having any more time for herself, because she had to juggle her role as a mother, a housekeeper, and a career woman. She wanted to work because she didn't want to waste her talent and education. And guess who took the punches? Me, her Filipino-American husband who took her away from her good life in the Philippines.

"But it's not just my wife. I've had my own struggles, too. I've been tempted before to stray and have a better relationship with someone else ... someone who'd appreciate what I did for her so I could feel loved and needed again.

"But I didn't, because I held onto what was more important to me—my family, my kids, Charm, and of course, God. That's what my parents instilled in my mind.

"And if I get tempted again in the future, I'll deal with it the same way I dealt with my struggles in the past. I think Charm has been appreciative of that, because we started giving each other more of our time and attention despite the odds, only because we wanted our marriage to survive. Heck, maybe she's doing it for the kids. I don't know. All I know is I love her, and she's important to me.

"I want you to think of that, Jan. No matter how life sucks, no matter where you are, as long as you're with the person or people you love, you'll be fine," he concluded.

I smiled at Wooly, patting his arm to show my appreciation.

I never realized my ever-funny, carefree, happy-go-lucky, and dear, goofy cousin had his own problems to deal with. I contemplated telling him about my growing affection for James, my concerns and fears, but I thought it was pointless to talk about it anyway. James didn't want me enough for me to even create a reason to worry about the possibility of surviving a long-distance relationship, or living a totally different life in the States. I recognized that maybe I'd fare better if I just accepted it and moved on.

***

We reached my aunt's house in less than half an hour. Wooly helped me get to my bedroom.

I composed a letter to Jay Anne using my uncle's computer, sending it through my Hotmail account, narrating everything that had happened, from my confrontation with Anthony at the office, all the way to my conversation with Wooly in the car. I hoped he'd call me when he got home from work.

I tried to rest in my bed, but my mind was awake, perhaps excited to see James again when we went back to the hospital to visit him.

In a corner in my bedroom, sitting in a chair by my luggage looking at me was the bright-eyed Pikachu.

Chapter 56

I looked around for Room 417.

Strolling around the quiet hallway of the humongous hospital located at the Houston Medical Center, I was awed by the windows overlooking the colorful lobby downstairs, where an endless traffic of people, hospital staff in their blue and gray scrubs, and visitors waited and interacted by the elevators.

The way to the hospital wing where James was confined looked like the hallway of a hotel, with impressive paintings and big TV screens lining the walls, plush carpet, and colorful, comfortable-looking wing chairs and couches scattered around several waiting areas.

The hospital was bustling with people, some toting their luggage, others pushing metal carts with computer-like machines on top of them and some with bottles of medicine.

I walked carefully with Wooly, my aunt and my uncle, and Kenneth and Sophia, holding onto my little metal cane for support, making sure my bandaged foot didn't have to bear my entire weight as I moved. My ankle was still raw from the sprain it suffered a couple of nights ago, when James and I went through the frightening ordeal caused by Daniella. My aunt had cared for my sprain. She told me I had to rest my foot so it would heal appropriately, in order for me not to have any issues when I flew back to the Philippines in a few days.

I thought I'd see James the day after he was admitted to the hospital, but I was wrong. I hadn't realized the San Antonio trip and the traumatic episode I'd experienced in James's apartment had taken a toll on my body. When I went home from the hospital, my body seemed to have crashed and enforced its much-needed recovery on its own. I'd slept for more than twelve hours since I passed out in my bed that morning, and I was too sluggish to do anything else after that.

It had been two and a half days since I saw James last, and I was excited to see him again. At the same time I was nervous, not knowing how to act around him after he had saved me from Daniella, and after fighting with myself for stupidly being infatuated with him.

"Here's Room 417! I found it first!" Sophia said loudly, jumping up and down in the hallway, the blue balloons in her hands hitting my uncle's face in the process.

"Sophia, you have to be quiet, *iha*. You'll wake up the other patients ober deyr, *apo*," my uncle said to his grandchild, using Tagalog.

Kenneth laughed, using the Doraemon stuffed toy in his hand like his mini-puppet to make fun of his sister, which irked my niece instantly. Wooly scooped up Sophia before she started crying.

My aunt knocked on the door before turning the knob to open it. We all walked inside the room behind her.

I saw James sitting up on his bed wearing a hospital gown, the bandage on his shoulders peeking out from his loose collar. He was holding a magazine, and his cell phone rested next to him on the bed.

He glanced up from what he was reading and smiled when he saw us.

A middle-aged lady stood up from a couch by the hospital bed and walked towards my aunt to give her a hug. She then greeted my uncle, Wooly, and the kids. When she came to greet me, she paused and bowed her head with her palms on the sides of her thighs.

It was my first time to be greeted in the traditional Japanese way, and I almost panicked, not knowing how to react, knowing all eyes were on me, especially James's, who was smiling in his bed watching me.

I tried my best to imitate the lady's courtesy by bowing my head and putting my palms together in front of my chest the way I thought I knew how. The lady smiled at me.

"You must be James's friend, Janelle-san," she said, smiling.

"Yes, ma'am," I said awkwardly.

"You can call me Aunt Akari. I'm the sister of James's mom. I know your family. Very good family. I flew from New York to take care of James. Thank you for being a good friend to him. I've heard a lot of good things about you since I came here," she added.

"Auntie ..." I heard James calling his aunt from his bed.

Wooly laughed softly.

"It's okay, bro. There's nothing wrong with that. Aunt Akari's just telling the truth. Our families blend together perfectly. Brothers and sisters from different cultures ... and mothers," he teased.

Aunt Akari laughed, ruffling Wooly's hair in the process.

"So what's your plan while you're in Houston, my dear?" my aunt asked Aunt Akari. "Let me know how long you're staying so we can take you out for dinner," she added.

"I'm going to stay with James until he's well enough to travel. The doctor said he needs five more days to recuperate, and then he can fly with me to Japan. *Haha,* my mother, is really sick and we need to be there sooner. It's a blessing I didn't fly to Japan as scheduled, or James would be flying alone to Tokyo in his condition," she explained.

She motioned for me to sit on the couch, and I obliged to show respect. At the same time I was glad she told me to sit, because I was beginning to worry about overworking my right foot. I saw James frowning when he saw my cane.

"Tita Janelle, when are we giving your gifts to Tito James?" Sophia said loudly, showing me the blue and silver balloons in her hands.

"How about now?" Kenneth said, talking through his Doraemon stuffed toy like a puppeteer.

"Oh," I said, embarrassed, melting like ice as everyone's eyes were focused on me. "Sure. You may give them to him now," I said shyly.

Sophia and Kenneth ran to James's side and gave the recovering architect the balloons and stuffed toy I got for him. Wooly actually bought them for me on his way to my aunt's house after work yesterday.

He told me James loved Doraemon. Since James gave me Pikachu as a gift after my surprise party, I thought of returning the gesture by giving him balloons and a stuffed toy.

I stood up from the couch carefully so I could help Sophia untangle the balloons from her hands and put the balloons on the table next to James's bed.

"How did you know what to get for me?" James asked me, smiling, his soft hazel eyes drawing me in like magnets. "I love this guy," he said, referring to the cute blue stuffed toy in his arms.

"Trust me, I didn't have anything to do with that," Wooly said, laughing when he overheard.

Wooly's remark allowed me to break free from James's hypnotic look.

"Thanks, guys," James said, addressing me and my cousin and the kids, who had started playing their portable game devices while sitting at the foot of James's bed.

My aunt, my uncle, Wooly, and Aunt Akari started conversing while the TV in James's room provided the much-needed white noise I craved to calm my nerves down. I was still jittery upon seeing James, hoping he'd never guess I had actually developed a crush on him after spending almost four consecutive days with him.

Crush? I'm twenty-five years old. Crush shouldn't be in my vocabulary anymore, I said in my head, scolding myself.

"Janelle," James said, "Are you okay now? How's your foot?" he asked, frowning.

"It's healing well. I'm trying not to bring this cane with me on the plane when I go back home to the Philippines," I said.

James was quiet for a bit.

"How's your wound? Are you healing well? Do you think you'll be strong enough to ride on a plane with your arm like that?" I asked.

"I'm feeling better. It still hurts when my pain medicine wears off, but I can move better than yesterday. My aunt will be with me on the plane, anyway, so I'm not too worried about it. When we get to Tokyo, Patrick will be there to take care of me, so I should be good," he explained.

"That's great," I said timidly before continuing.

"James, I haven't thanked you yet for saving … For doing what you did for me. I don't remember what happened, but I'm quite sure I should've been the one that got hurt that night, not you," I said slowly.

James patted my arm before speaking, as if contemplating what to say.

"Janelle, don't say that. I'll never let anything or anyone hurt you," he said softly, looking into my eyes intently.

Please don't melt, Janelle. It doesn't mean anything. Don't flatter yourself, I told myself quietly while maintaining my composure.

Suddenly, the door in James's room opened. We both turned to look at the people streaming in.

Anthony, Camilla, and her mother came in. Camilla was holding a vase of fresh yellow tulips, while Anthony carried two boxes of donuts.

I was grateful for the interruption; it gave me an excuse not to react to what James had just told me, knowing I wouldn't know what to tell him, anyway.

Camilla set the vase with flowers next to James's bed, right next to the weight holding the blue and silver balloons I gave him. The blue, silver, and yellow hues were striking as they blended perfectly together lending a positive vibe to the room.

Camilla gave me a tight hug after ruffling James's hair and giving him a hug as well. Anthony patted me on the shoulder, smiling brightly at me to acknowledge my presence.

He and James then shook hands eagerly.

Camilla's mom mingled with my aunt and uncle, and was introduced to James's aunt. She smiled at me, sincerely I thought, when she glanced in my direction.

It looked like a scene from one of the cheesy romantic Filipino movies that I was so fond of watching back home. It was surreal because I didn't know it could actually happen in real life, and I wasn't merely watching it—I was experiencing it.

Maybe it was the happy ending of the cheesy romantic movie of my life, except I, the leading lady in the movie, didn't get to be kissed and taken away to live happily ever after by my Prince Charming.

Perhaps James—my Mr. Cutie Pie who had protected me twice even though he barely knew my story, and who was sitting there in the middle of the room among the people who genuinely cared for him, alive and well—was my happier ending.

James glanced at me, motioning me to come to the bed so he could hand me a donut from the box being passed around by Anthony. I walked over to him while everyone was busy getting their sweets, glad no one seemed to be paying attention.

"Chocolate-covered or glazed?" James asked.

"Chocolate-covered with the cream filling inside, and glazed, please," I said smiling.

James smiled, amused.

"Great choice," he said.

"Thanks. This opportunity only comes but once. Let it be known that while I was in Houston in April 2000, James Ren offered me two of the most indulgent sweets I had never given myself the chance to enjoy, just to satisfy what I'd always thought was conventionally appropriate, but after much consideration, I happily seized those wonderful, sweet and irresistible donuts," I said without pausing.

I suddenly cringed, wondering where I got my idea from and the audacity to even say it. James seemed astounded, but he quickly recovered.

"Janelle, if I were you, I'd take the whole box," he said smiling.

Chapter 57

The reflection of the moon on the water was entrancing, but it made me feel a bit melancholic.

It reminded me of that memorable night in San Antonio when James and I successfully caught the last boat tour at the River Walk; the same night my heart began beating differently for the young architect who'd spun my world around in ways I never thought possible.

I came to Houston to have a taste of my brand-new life and my brand-new world as an immigrant after my planned wedding with Anthony. I never anticipated that the dismal ending to my fairy tale relationship would usher a special opportunity to get to know a captivating person who, sadly, was fated to give me another round of heartaches.

How could I leave Houston and all the memories it had cursed and gifted me with, knowing the man I'd never forget would stay behind; knowing the man who had no intention of reciprocating whatever it was I was feeling for him, wouldn't have a chance to even know how he'd swept me off my feet?

It didn't matter if America was just a couple of plane rides away from the Philippines—the home I was hesitant to go back to at the moment. Distance had made people forget, and James and I were no different. By the time I reached Manila, James would have already moved on, forgetting he once saved the life of one silly Filipina.

It was funny how we seemed to have dragged each other into our melodramatic soap operas—my issues with Anthony and his with Daniella.

I wondered what had happened to Daniella and whether James had already reached out to her. Anthony and Camilla didn't mention anything about her when we saw each other at the hospital.

I smiled to myself, still unable to wrap my head around the fact that my own drama with Anthony and Camilla had reached such an amicable ending.

I remembered our strange farewells outside James's hospital room as Camilla and her mom gave me a tight hug, apologizing for all the pain they'd caused me, asking for my forgiveness. As strange as it seemed, I realized any trace of anger and pain I had kept inside me had already disappeared, leaving my mind, heart, and body, because none of them mattered anymore.

I recalled when Camilla had arranged for Anthony and me to talk privately in a deserted waiting area near James's hospital room so we could finally settle our issues before I left Houston. I was grateful, perhaps because I knew that it was the perfect opportunity to have our closure.

"Jan, I'd kneel down in front of you, but knowing you, I'm pretty sure you'd get mad at me for embarrassing you," Anthony said, laughing softly.

I smiled, not knowing what to say.

"Jan, I'm really sorry. I didn't know how to tell you. I was so scared, and I've beaten myself up over and over for that. I'm sorry for what I did to you back at your cousin's workplace.

"I was such a coward," Anthony's voice cracked as he burst into tears. It didn't take long before my tears began to stream from my eyes as well. I started sobbing, wiping my tears with my hands.

"Anthony ... a lot of things have happened since I came to Houston, since I barged into your apartment to surprise you. But despite all that, I want you to know that I accept your apology and I forgive you," I said quietly. "I know you love Camilla. I saw how much you cared for her when we were all held hostage by Daniella. I tried to see how I felt then—if I'd be angry or bitter—but for some reason, I felt relieved. I don't know but surprisingly, I felt glad that you showed me how much you cared for her, because at least I know you're giving me up and everything we had when we were still together for something better—for someone who makes you happier. At least, for all the hurt, spite, and disappointments we've gone through together, something good has come out of it," I added, looking fixedly at the wall behind him.

Anthony was quiet as I continued.

"I know Camilla's pregnant and I want you to know despite the hell we've been through, I've been meaning to congratulate you. But I didn't really think I'd have a chance to tell you," I said, turning to look into his eyes.

He held my hands, looking at me with sadness, his voice low and unsteady.

"Camilla came to me one night, telling me that I should go back to you so our baby would be proud of her one day for doing the right thing. She knew she wronged you, and she's been remorseful ever since she found out she's going to be a mother. She couldn't believe after everything she did to you, God would still reward her with a gift she thought she didn't deserve. When Daniella told Camilla that she wanted to hurt you, and then devised a plot to set you and James up, Camilla protested and warned her that if she continued with her scheme, Camilla would call the cops," he said. "And that's the reason why Daniella changed her plans and dragged Camilla with her instead, making her one of her hostages."

I was dumbfounded, unable to process what Anthony had just said.

"I know I've wronged you … and I've asked God why he'd bless me with two good women and a child that I don't deserve.

"Jan, I want you to know I'll never forget you. You're one of the most special people I've ever known, and even though we didn't make it as a couple, I'll always cherish what we had. I'm sorry I lied. I didn't mean to. I was caught in a bad situation and was too dumb to know how to handle it. You're an amazing person, and anyone who's privileged to spend the rest of his life with you will be very lucky.

"When I saw James the other night risking his life to shield you from Daniella, I realized there was somebody out there who deserved you more than I did. I felt small when I compared myself to him, but then again, I felt happy that I'd been replaced in your life by someone who was truly worthy of you," he said, still wiping the tears from his eyes.

I didn't have the strength to explain to Anthony how mistaken he was about James's intentions. I took in everything he said without saying a word, but I squeezed his hand in acknowledgment, hoping he'd realize that I appreciated everything he told me.

We ended our talk by giving each other a hug and saying our final goodbyes. When he walked me back to James's room in the hospital before heading out, the burden I'd been carrying around since I stepped into his apartment almost a month ago had been taken off my back.

Maybe that's what forgiveness does. It gives us our freedom back.

***

"Janelle, come on down. It's dinner time!" I heard my uncle's voice from behind. I turned around to let him know I had heard him as I quickly got up from the lounge chair and started heading in his direction.

We were at a beautiful, scenic resort at The Woodlands where we had rented a cozy cabin so we could stay overnight and not worry about the long drive back to Houston in the middle of the night.

All day long at the resort I contemplated in my lounge chair by the pool area, watching Sophia and Kenneth play in the water with the other kids.

I reminisced on my adventures in Houston, wondering how I ended up spending most of my time with James. I smiled as I thought about the charming architect who I hadn't seen for three days already, since we last talked at the hospital.

My aunt and uncle had had dinner with his aunt yesterday. Aunt Akari told them she and James had been busy preparing for their trip to Japan, and that James had already been given the green light by his doctors to travel in two days.

I'd been preparing for my trip to the Philippines as well, buying my *pasalubong*—my homecoming gifts—for my friends and family in Manila. I went with Wooly to the Hard Rock Café and other places, to get Houston-branded souvenirs like coffee mugs, shot glasses, T-shirts, and key chains.

As part of our family's tradition, I had to buy a ton of chocolates from a wholesale store called Sam's, as if we didn't have chocolates back in the Philippines. For some reason, most Filipinos equate traveling to the States with buying imported chocolates.

The Woodlands trip was our final hurrah to relax and spend quality time as a family before I left Houston. Oddly, I was also scheduled to go to the Philippines in two days, the same day James and his aunt would travel to Tokyo.

"Good evening, Janelle."

I looked at the lady who greeted me inside the resort's restaurant. She was wearing a casual outfit—a pair of shorts and an oversized T-shirt. I didn't recognize her until she was just a foot away from me.

It turned out the lady was Miss Mench, Wooly's executive assistant at the architectural firm, beaming at me. I ran towards her to give her a hug.

"Hi Miss Mench!" I said enthusiastically.

"Janelle, I'm hurt. I wonder when you're going to call me Mama Mench, *hija*," she said, smiling broadly.

"Sorry *po*, Mama Mench," I said, grinning.

"By the way, I'd like you to meet my husband. I was going to introduce him to you during your party, but *hindi ko na nagawa*. I lost track of time, so I wasn't able to do it," she explained.

In an instant, a tall, handsome older man extended his hand to me, smiling the familiar smile that I remembered distinctly.

"We've met already," the man said.

I nodded, astonished.

He was the "angel" at my surprise party—the man who told me his life story and gave me nuggets of wisdom on how to handle life in America as an immigrant, when your faith in yourself and the rest of the world gets tested.

"*Naku,* these are my herooss here in America—Menchie and Raul. Their story is inspiring. The oreeginal champions of the *polvoron* stowry," my uncle said.

I looked at Tito Boy. He still hadn't told me about the *polvoron* story that he promised me the first time I set foot in their house. I raised my brows, smiling, waiting for his explanation.

"I'll give you a clow, Janelle.

"You know what those young people say about us old-passhioned immigrants here. They say we're F.O.B.s, as in presh op da … whatchamacalldat … bowt.

"They have no idea what we all went through here in America to get to where we are now. We worked really hard. Blood, sweat, and tears *ang puhunan namin dito*—our investment to survive here—*sa* America. Now our life is so much better than bepor, because we worked hard to get to where we wanted to be.

"We should be celeybrated, not made fun of. Here in America, they should not call us F.O.B.s. They should call us *F-O-B-O-L-O-U-S*. We are *fobolous!*" Tito Boy declared, complete with jazz hands.

We all laughed heartily at my uncle's fabulous suggestion as we started to join our hands in prayer, and to say grace before having dinner together.

I peeked at the beautiful sky above us.

I hadn't realized that even though we were separated by oceans, our values and principles as a people were still intact, practiced everywhere, amidst diverse cultural settings and influences.

I gradually bowed my head, praying for the gift of family, friends, and the amazing, inspiring, and unbelievable tales behind their journey.

"God bless the *FOBOLOUS*," I whispered.

Chapter 58

I looked into his eyes.

Memorizing every detail, knowing that it would be the last time they'd look into mine with a disconcerting mix of ambiguity and affection.

"Don't look back when you leave, I won't be here," I told him, trying to hide my pain. He nodded, reading between the lines. I felt his lips on the back of my hand and then he was gone.

I opened my eyes, staring absentmindedly at the ceiling, wondering for a moment where I was. I glanced by the wall, instantly noticing my bright yellow luggage, perfectly positioned where I had left it last night after I finished packing.

I had dreamed about James again, for the fourth time since we came back from the resort yesterday. I felt tired from packing the whole afternoon and fell asleep early. Since then, I had woken up four times from the same dream—little snippets of my sad conversation with the young architect at the airport, with the same dismal ending—of him turning his back on me and then fading away in the distance.

I looked at the clock in my bedroom.

It was two in the morning.

I decided to call Jay Anne, hoping he was able to spend a few minutes with me on the phone. I knew he was at the office, busily working, but it was only a little bit past lunchtime in the Philippines, so I figured he may have time for me.

I listened to the ringing on the other end until a bored voice picked up.

"This is Jay. I'm busy. You have three seconds to state your purpose before I hang up," Jay Anne said on the other end.

"It's Janelle," I said excitedly.

"I'm sorry. I lied. I'm not busy," Jay Anne's voice progressed from bored to hyper. "Oh my gosh! I can't wait to see you, sweetie!" he continued, laughing.

I joined in the laughter, excited to hear my best friend's voice again.

"One more day, Jay, and I'll be stuck in Manila's crazy traffic again with all the cars honking and everything," I said enthusiastically.

"Awesome blossom. But before we get too excited, I want to know how your friend is—the guy I'm dying to meet so I can thank him for saving my best friend's life," Jay Anne said, referring to James, suddenly sounding serious.

It took me a minute to respond, unprepared to tackle the topic so soon after my strange dream.

"James is okay. He's out of the hospital. I talked to him the other day when we visited, and he's in good spirits. He's flying to Japan tomorrow with his aunt," I explained.

"That's good ... So how do you feel now?" Jay Anne asked, referring to my feelings about James, which I had mentioned in my e-mail to him, the day after I recuperated from our nightmare at James's apartment.

"I don't know. I guess I'm sad. It's weird. For sure I'm happy for having spent a great amount of time with James, especially during the last couple of weeks, because I got to know him better. But then again, that's just made it even harder for me to leave this place. I've gotten so used to him being around, I'm positive I'll feel miserable when I get back to the Philippines, at least in the first two weeks, because he won't be there," I said, heaving a sigh.

"Jan, I know how you feel. But you sound like you won't ever see him again. He's not getting married anytime soon or moving to another planet, is he? Houston is just a couple of plane rides away. I'm sure you'll still see each other if you both want to. You just have to keep in touch," Jay Anne said reassuringly.

"True, but even if that happens—we keep in touch and become long-distance friends—what makes me think I'll be okay when I find out one day that he's already with somebody else? James doesn't know how I feel about him, and even if he did, he doesn't feel the same way about me … There's no doubt it's just a matter of time before he falls in love with someone else. I'm sure women are lined up waiting for him to draw their number. I don't want to be another Daniella. I have to stop my stupid heart from this foolish infatuation before I get hurt again. I mean, haven't I learned enough from my experience with Anthony?" I explained, feeling depressed by the minute.

"You're right. But you're also forgetting something, sweetie," Jay Anne said softly.

"What do you mean?" I asked.

"What happened to the adventurous girl in you, my dear? What happened to the fearless Janelle I knew, who braved America by herself to satisfy her curiosity, despite the risks? You've been to places, Jan, and moving along all right, but you're forgetting your purpose," he continued.

I listened to Jay Anne, trying to see where our conversation was going.

"Jan, you're forgetting about your roses," he explained.

I was taken aback, slowly realizing what he was telling me.

"You're so concerned about how you'll get over your roller coaster journey in Houston, you skipped your main purpose as a traveler, which is to stop and smell the roses. One day you'll come back to the same place and find out the roses are gone, and you'll wish you'd enjoyed them when they were still around because you'll realize they're never coming back.

"Jan, when James talked about the cherry blossoms, he was telling you something, maybe not in reference to how he feels about you, but how both of you should feel about your friendship. He was telling you, subconsciously perhaps, to focus on the present and enjoy each other's company.

"Why are you so concerned about what will happen when you and James don't see each other anymore? Just enjoy each other while you can. Enjoy his company, his presence, his laughter, his voice, so you have memories to take home with you.

"You're too worried about James not giving you those pink cherry blossoms. So what if he didn't? You're a grown woman, Jan. You don't need James to like you back. You're in control of your emotions. Celebrate your feelings for him, and just let it be. Worry about missing him later on and deal with it. You survived your ordeal with Anthony. You'll survive life without James. And trust me, you'll move on. You can grab your own cherry blossoms and bask in your own sunshine, Janelle. Like James said, life is beautiful, but it's fleeting. Seize the moment, my dear, before it fades away," Jay Anne said.

I listened to my best friend, unable to speak, absorbing his words of wisdom like a sponge. We talked for another hour until my body begged for me to rest. We hung up and I returned to bed, closing my eyes in the dark as I prepared myself for my very last day in Houston.

***

We stood in line at the George Bush Intercontinental Airport.

James and Aunt Akari helped me check in my luggage at the departure section of the airport before heading to our respective waiting areas.

Aunt Akari decided to stay at their designated boarding area, while James walked with me to mine. We all had the same flight itinerary, except my flight was scheduled to leave an hour earlier. Tokyo was their final destination, and although I was going there as well from Detroit, it only served as my brief stopover, my connecting destination, so I could get off the plane and board another one headed for Manila.

It had only been half an hour since Wooly dropped us all off at the airport, after my aunt and my uncle and the kids had prepared a send-off lunch for the three of us.

Wooly handed me a cute little pink envelope containing photos that he had collected during my entire stay in Houston as his gift for me. I gave my cousin a big hug. He promised to visit the Philippines with Charm and the kids one summer—next year or the year after, maybe.

I hugged my aunt, uncle, Sophia, and Kenneth, promising to come back with the entire family sometime soon. I gave Sophia my Sanrio collection—the one I bought in Japan on my way to Houston—to her utter delight, while I gave Kenneth his dream Lego set, which I bought from a store called Walmart the other day. I was supposed to be their designated babysitter when I came to visit, but because of all the dramatic episodes that sprouted like mushrooms along the way, I ended up spending less time with them than I had planned.

I found it difficult to leave, but somehow the feeling brought a sense of contentment within me.

This is how every meaningful journey should end … always, I thought.

***

James and I sat next to each other, laughing softly as we looked at the photos from the envelope Wooly had given me.

The photos were mostly candid shots of everyone, particularly during my surprise party. There was one picture taken of James and me hanging out by the buffet table, smiling happily for the camera. We laughed while looking at it, because that was the time right before Daniella "accidentally" doused me with liquid chocolate.

"Have you heard from Daniella yet? How is she?" I asked James.

He paused before speaking.

"Her ex-husband called me on my cell phone while I was still at the hospital. He told me Daniella was confined in a psychiatric facility temporarily, until she got better. He said she was showing progress, and is expected to recover sooner than they originally thought. Daniella doesn't have family here, so he and her friends took turns visiting her, and Daniella was okay with that. She's planning to go back to her family in California, and her ex-husband was arranging for her travels.

"He apologized to me on behalf of Daniella, saying she'll give me a call to apologize herself when she gets better. He also told me to tell you that Daniella would like to say sorry, and wished she could have talked to you herself before you left for the Philippines. By the way, Camilla, Anthony, and I decided not to press charges against Daniella, as long as she gets psychiatric care, and hopefully, whatever happened won't happen again," James explained.

I smiled quietly, nodding my head in acknowledgment.

"So how's your foot doing?" he asked, changing the topic.

"It's great. I'm still nervous that I may twist it again, but so far it's holding up. No pain for twenty-four hours now," I said, smiling.

"That's good," he said.

"How's your shoulder and arm?" I asked.

"They're fine. Healing well, but it needs to get re-bandaged when we get to Tokyo. I can't lift or carry anything, because the stitches might come out," he explained.

"I see. Well, take care of yourself when you get to Japan, and when you get back to Houston," I said timidly.

"You do the same when you go back to the Philippines," he said.

I paused before speaking, smiling at James.

"Thank you for everything you've done for me in the last four weeks. I appreciate your time and for being there for me … More than I expected you to be," I said sincerely.

"My pleasure. I enjoyed every single moment with you," he said, looking into my eyes intently. I looked back at him, savoring the soft pools of his almond-shaped hazel eyes—every detail I wanted to mentally take a photograph of—so I didn't forget how beautiful they looked.

"Ladies and gentlemen, Flight 1065 departing for Detroit is now boarding. Please approach the gate for …" James and I looked around us as if in a daze.

I grabbed my bag and slowly stood up, straightening the creases in my soft khaki jeans absentmindedly.

James stood up as well and helped me with my luggage, making sure I had my boarding pass with me before we slowly walked to the back of the long line. He stood with me quietly until I was only a few passengers away from the boarding gate where the airline's ground crew were checking the passengers in.

"Janelle, take care. If you get bored in the Philippines, send me an e-mail and I'll call you," he said, smiling.

We'd exchanged contact information back at my aunt's house during lunch a few hours ago.

"Of course. Take care as well," I said, masking my looming depression with my smile.

"And by the way," he said, reaching for something in his back pocket. "This is for you," he added, taking my hand, putting a dainty gold ID bracelet on my wrist and securing it with its tiny clasp.

I looked at the bracelet, shocked, admiring its beauty.

The ID had what I thought were Japanese characters engraved on it. On the back was another set of characters engraved. They looked familiar, like the characters on the canvas painting on the wall in his office.

"What do they mean?" I asked, still shocked.

"The front has your name on it, and the back has mine. So you'll always remember that once upon a time in Houston, in April, 2000, James and Janelle met and had great, crazy, and memorable adventures together," he said, smiling.

"James … I don't know what to say. Thank you," I said sincerely.

"You're welcome. We'll see each other when we see each other. Take care now. Don't miss your flight," he said, laughing softly.

He patted my arm gently, smiled, and then turned around to head back to where his aunt was waiting.

I stood frozen in my spot, unable to move as the passengers behind me slowly got checked in. I felt something in my hand. I looked at the postcard-like paper I was holding, which James had handed to me along with the bracelet.

I looked at it closely.

It had a picture of pink flowers on it, with the contact information of a flower shop in New York. In the middle was a note that indicated a delivery confirmation and a date—the day we came back from San Antonio. But there was a specific section on the postcard note that caught my attention.

It read:

Delivered to: James Ren
Recipient: Janelle Marquez
Items: One Dozen Pink Cherry Blossoms

I almost dropped the note and my luggage on the floor as I stared at the truth right in front of me. I realized Daniella had been lying when she told me James was sending me roses. He wasn't. He was going to send me a dozen pink cherry blossoms instead.

What James told me in the car back in San Antonio came back to me instantly. I remembered when I asked him what he'd symbolically do for the special girl that he'd fallen in love with, and he said, "I'll give her pink cherry blossoms."

I'm dreaming. Did he really ... I thought.

I looked for James in the crowd in front of me. I could still see him walking just a few feet away. I called his name with all my might, as loud as I could, afraid he'd disappear in the distance.

"James!" I shouted, oblivious to the people around me. I did it several times, still unable to move from the spot where my feet seemed firmly planted.

I saw James from a distance, pausing, turning around to see who was calling his name, his eyes squinting. When he saw me, he smiled as if disoriented. He walked back slowly in my direction.

When he was just a few feet away from me, I heard myself saying for the people around us to hear, "James Akira Kenichi Ren." I pronounced every syllable of his full name, looking at him intently.

I could hear the entire boarding area humming, as if everyone had stopped what they were doing to listen to what I had to say.

"Will you carry me?" I asked James, not taking my eyes off him.

James stopped, standing just a couple of feet away from me, to respond to my question.

He said, "Yes I will."

Suddenly the crowd around us applauded, some whistling, others laughing heartily.

I overheard one lady saying, "Oh my gosh. How romantic. The girl proposed to the guy. I can't believe she asked the guy to marry her," she said excitedly, mishearing what I'd said—that which was significant between James and me, as our conversation in the car back in San Antonio magically materialized.

I saw James slowly walking to me. By the time he was in front of me, tears began streaming from my eyes, ruining my meticulously made-up face, but I didn't care.

James retrieved a pair of paper napkins from his travel sling bag, laughing softly, wiping the tears from my face carefully. He then held my chin as I looked up at his beaming face, his eyes brighter than ever.

"Janelle, I forgot to tell you. There's another thing I'd do to let everyone know I've already given my heart to the special girl in my life," he said, looking at me, his raspy voice sending goosebumps all over me.

"What is it?" I asked, barely finding my voice.

"This," he said, leaning towards me, putting his lips on mine gently, closing his eyes.

I held onto his arm, closing my eyes gently, savoring the moment.

My world stood still as I enjoyed the feel of his lips on mine, tasting his love for the first time, the image of the pink cherry blossoms I had always envisioned fading in my mind.

Standing there at the airport with James, seizing our special moment, I stopped worrying about our past and our future, and focused on the present, completely disconnecting from what may happen beyond what we had in front of us.

***

Once upon a time, in Houston, in the spring of 2000, my world collided with James's in the most unexpected circumstances. And in spite of the disparity in our cultures and in our lives amidst the chaos that took place in between, we fell in love.

One day, our story will fade away just like our symbolic cherry blossoms may get blown away by the harsh winds of life's uncertainties.

But that didn't matter.

What I had in my arms as we stood in the middle of the airport on my last day in America was extraordinarily special.

I held onto James for as long as I could … as if there was no tomorrow.

They say life is beautiful yet fleeting, but I, personally, believe its ephemeral nature is just a state of mind. When life wilts and fades away, love takes over, holding no dimensions or boundaries, surviving amidst the fragility of the world and the people it touches.

The cherry blossoms of this world may one day wither and wilt and fade away, but love is timeless. It's eternal. It always will be.

In Tagalog we say it differently, its meaning and implication piercing to the core, almost untranslatable.

"Ang pag-ibig ay wagas."

Another one of those Filipino phrases, James Ren, my beloved Japanese-American *kasintahan*—my lover, in Tagalog—would have to learn.

But then again, that was so much better than *"Tara let's."*

Epilogue

I waited patiently at the small table by the patio of our favorite café in Makati.

It was our usual payday dinner night, and as always, I was the first one to arrive so I could secure our spot in the secluded section of the patio, located at the back, behind everyone else's tables so we could have more privacy.

But tonight, something special was going on at the café. Our spot was occupied, as were the rest of the tables, dressed in immaculate white linen, adorned with beautiful flowers in tall vases.

Because the owner of the café knew our group, and being longtime patrons, I was allowed to have a small table that hadn't been dressed up, yet which was strangely sitting in the center. The waiter in his handsome uniform handed me a tall glass of iced tea, which I took my time to drink, hoping my friends would show up soon so we could agree on another place to have dinner.

I looked at my cell phone in frustration, knowing James wouldn't be calling me anytime soon.

It was our second-year anniversary, but he was traveling to New York to visit his family and wouldn't be available for another day. I hadn't talked to him in days, because his grandmother was in the hospital again.

James's grandmother was a sweet lady, although I had only met her through the phone. I offered a silent prayer for her, wishing she'd be well soon, hoping I could meet her in person one day.

James had met my family already and had earned a soft spot in my picky grandmother's heart. For some reason they connected—a nonexistent experience for any of my past relationships. Amazingly, since we last said goodbye in Houston at the airport, he had already visited me in the Philippines more than six times, staying for a week at the most every time.

"Excuse me, ma'am. We have to put the flowers on this table now," the waiter in a handsome uniform told me. I began to stand up, preparing myself to leave the café after I'd paid for my drink. All of a sudden, the lights in the café became brighter, enabling me to view the entire patio for the first time.

The tables looked beautiful, glowing like pink pearls, enhanced by the pink flowers in the vases, which looked quite familiar.

Cherry blossoms, I thought.

I heard the sound of violins, sweet and subdued, as if careful not to disturb the peaceful night. I looked around me, disoriented, wondering where the flowers for the table I was sitting at were coming from.

The handsome waiter placed the vase of the prettiest pink cherry blossoms on the table in front of me, motioning me to look at the tiny card that came with it.

I opened the card hesitantly, my heart beating faster, unsure what was going on.

The card read:

Dear Janelle,

These cherry blossoms may be the last ones you'll receive as my girlfriend.

James

I dropped the card on the table, shocked, yet unable to react properly, not knowing if I should cry or wither in my chair quietly.

How could he break up with me on our anniversary? What's with me and special occasions and breakups, anyway? I asked myself quietly.

I stood up, disoriented, leaving the table, forgetting my drink and the pink cherry blossoms behind me.

And then I heard my name.

"Janelle," he said in his raspy, beautiful voice.

I turned around.

James was looking at me with his pretty hazel eyes, smiling, as if amused.

I froze where I was standing.

Slowly, James knelt down in the middle of the patio, bearing something in his hand.

"Maria Janelle Marquez, the woman I promise to love and carry for the rest of my life," he paused, smiling. "Will you marry me?"

It only took a second before tears started streaming from my eyes. I walked towards James slowly, not taking my eyes off of his.

"Yes," I said as I stood in front of him.

I leaned down, touched his face, and kissed his lips tenderly.

"I hate surprises," I whispered in his ear as I drew him to his feet.

"I know," he said, laughing softly, holding my hand as he put a diamond ring on my finger, its radiance catching the light.

He kissed me lightly before the entire patio lit up. And as if on cue, the glass doors leading to the restaurant opened slowly as my festive friends and family started streaming in.

It was by far the most beautiful summer night in April in the Philippines.

Two years ago, I sat in the same café, wondering how I'd survive in America when I finally settled down with the man of my dreams and began my new life as an immigrant.

I felt James's hand holding mine.

I smiled to myself.

The next phase of my *FOBOLOUS* journey had officially begun.

From the Author

Back in October 2016, someone asked me what *FOBOLOUS* was and I got tongue-tied, not knowing how to compress a 90,000-word novel in two sentences.

My own version of the "I'm a writer, not a speaker" sentiment.

After all, I found it even harder to explain how a simple Facebook post from a friend inspired me to write my novel.

So here's what happened.

One day, in 2011, I was scrolling through my Facebook feeds when something caught my interest. It was a comic post about an immigrant Pinay grandmother looking frantically for her box crotcher.

I thought that was funny.

What the heck was a box crotcher, anyway?

Turned out she was looking for her back scratcher.

LOL, right?

But there was something nostalgic about the way the Pinay grandmother mispronounced the English words.

Her thick Filipino accent was beautiful.

And "box crotcher" was a poignant reminder of how connected yet misplaced most immigrants, myself included, had always been in the land that we've embraced as our new home.

"Box crotcher" became my silent slogan as I started collecting stories from different immigrants I've met over the years, and weaving them together into one inspirational tale that I hope would help each of us cope, as we revel in the joys and as we struggle through the sorrows, from being far away from home.

So let's go back to the question.

What is FOBOLOUS?

FOBOLOUS is the immigrant with unfathomable resolve and inner strength, who never gave up despite dealing with homesickness, exhaustion, disappointments, rejections, starting from the bottom, discrimination, freezing weather, and doing piles and piles of laundry and more house chores after a 12-hour shift at work.

FOBOLOUS are immigrants taking both the great side of being the superstar *balikbayan* back home and being a second class citizen in their new home away from home, but trying their best to make it to where they want to be despite the odds.

If you're an immigrant, I hope this story finds you.

I hope it strengthens your heart and your will to go on despite the rough roads you'll travel as you go through your journey.

I hope you'll find the time to stop and smell the roses even if time doesn't seem to be your friend.

And I hope you find your own special cherry blossoms.

Even if they say they don't bloom where you've chosen to settle.

Trust me. They do.

You just have to be ready when life hands them to you.

Acknowledgment

In 2011, I started blogging on Facebook about one adventurous girl who traveled to America. Five years later, it became my very first novel.

I would like to thank everyone who gave their time, expertise and inspiration in the creation of FOBOLOUS.

My brilliant editor, Linda Hill of Penlight Editing, who is also the award-winning author of the series, "The Magician's Curse". She polished FOBOLOUS like a skilled craftsman, providing her expert opinion and valuable insights particularly on some cultural and technical aspects of the story that have been missed or translated inaccurately. Thank you, Linda for your skills, patience, creativity, support, and heartwarming feedback.

My plot consultant and dear friend Maida Malby who spiced up this novel with her creative suggestions and critical feedback. Maida is a thriving romance novelist and the author of the book "Boracay Vows". She introduced and referred me to Linda.

My art director, creative consultant, and sister Che Mendoza who provided the beautiful dreamy sketch for the original book cover. Che is a brilliant interior designer and artist who helped with this novel's latest book cover. She is also helping in designing the book cover for the FOBOLOUS sequel.

Octagon Lab for giving life to our original book art concept.

The awesome Lucy Rhodes, designer of Render Compose, for

designing and creating this novel's beautiful new book cover.

My sister Helen Kalany for coming up with the fabulous FOBOLOUS font on the novel's website, print cover and merchandise. Helen is an amazing web designer who always captures the "cool" in the "now".

Peach and Martin Almario for the emotive, wistful back cover photo that is officially the FOBOLOUS selfie. Peach and Martin conceptualized and executed the book photo shoot in L.A.

My brother Jeff Mendoza for the creative input during the pre-publication of this book. Jeff is a successful internet creative director in global ad agencies who offered suggestions that I've rigorously incorporated while writing and marketing FOBOLOUS.

My awesome beta team especially Marylou Celespara-Lot and Nadya Buenavista who helped me set up my first FOBOLOUS book events.

Pinky Alinas and Jacqui Pastoral for meticulously editing portions of the book despite their busy schedules.

Barnes and Noble for giving me a chance to promote my book and experience my very first Author Event and book signing in the U.S. within their Sugar Land, TX bookstore.

Pinoy Houston-TV for inviting me to their TV station to talk about my novel during one of their episodes. Thank you for continuously supporting local writers like me by creating special segments in your weekly broadcast.

James Iha who probably doesn't know I exist but has unknowingly provided the inspiration for James Ren's charismatic and inspiring character.

Elaine Cedillo of Hack the Climate/Red Wizard Events for setting up my book launch at A Space Manila in the Philippines.

Everyone who came to physically and virtually support me at my Barnes and Noble book signing and book launch in Manila despite their busy schedules, having to endure horrendous rush-hour traffic, and parking frustrations.

Everyone who took the time to read FOBOLOUS and dropped a review on Amazon and the FOBOLOUS website – you have no idea what that means to me as a writer.

The people who have willingly shared their stories to me over the years and those who have inspired me to write theirs.

My parents, siblings, family, and friends for always being there to support me. Thank you for attending and helping set up the Manila book launch. And for wearing the FOBOLOUS shirts!

My husband and my kids for being the ultimate source of strength and inspiration as I go through my journey as a writer. I love you guys!

The vivacious, daring, adventurous, and inspiring Janelles of this world.

The immigrants of this world.

You who still believe in the magic of romance and the power of novels.

And most of all, God, our heavenly Father, for giving me the gift of weaving words together so I can write and share this story with you.

About the Author

Rainne Mendoza is a freelance writer with a Bachelor's degree in Communications. She worked as a Media Strategist in advertising agencies in the Philippines before migrating to the United States. She now lives with her family and their super dogs, Mochi and Appa, in Houston, Texas. This is her first novel.